The

Provoked

By

J. Edward Vance

The Roots of Creation – Provoked
By: J. Edward Vance
Edited by: Erin Engstrom and Roxane Christ
Book cover design by: Zhivko Zhelev
Interior artwork by: Zhivko Zhelev
ISBN: 978-0-9919151-0-1
Copyright 2013
All rights reserved
Published by: Angeljay Enterprises Inc.

After years of sitting to develop the story and shape the first book, I dedicate this novel to the one that has suffered most by far...

My butt.

There is a theory which states that if ever, for any reason, anyone discovers what exactly the Universe is for and why it is here, it will instantly disappear and be replaced by something even more bizarre and inexplicable. There is another that states that this has already happened.

Douglas Adams

Chapter 1

Alone

"The media knows," Albert sighed, glancing past the altar to the medieval depiction of Christ's crucifixion in the apse. "God, forgive me."

The pastor faltered and leaned heavily upon the holy table. For thirty-three years, he had given communion to his congregation from this spot. He loved doing it, along with everything else a faithful man of God did. But Albert knew he was no saint. "What have I done?" he blubbered, bowing his head before the golden cross that rose proudly from the altar's centre. His mind flashed the image of young Austin, a trusting nine-year-old boy that had been attending the church for the last six months. "And why do I hunger so to do it again? Won't you help me, Lord?"

"Help you what, Reverend?" A woman's smooth voice jolted him from the far end of the Gothic structure's shadowed belly.

Albert gasped and spun around. "Who's there?" He
wished he hadn't reacted with such panic in his voice.
"Reverend Brown finished mass over an hour ago." He
tried not to sound so guilty.

A tall dark shape swayed into the church's dimmed
lights.

"Oh...!" Albert caught his breath. "Are you lost, my
dear?" His rattled eyes focused on the woman's
curvaceous, all too alluring shape. She wore a grey,
hooded cloak that concealed her face, but little else. The
front opened beneath a high clasp, just enough to reveal
the sinuous undermost parts of her naked breasts, her
taut naval and, even more.

Excitement travelled upward through Albert's spine,
his voice splintering. "Wher..., where are your clothes?
Need I inform you that this is a house of God?"

The woman's bare feet and long legs seemed to glide
across the cracked tile floor toward him. Albert tensed,
feeling frightened and breathlessly aroused.

"Are you moralizing me?" She posed before him for a
moment and Albert couldn't help but drink in her
stunning beauty. She then lifted the edge of her cloak
away from her threadbare hips and leafless privates. "Let
he who is without sin cast the first stone, Reverend."

Her brazen message pierced his heart. Albert knew he
should have been up in arms, giving this blasphemous girl
a tough lesson in respect and humility. But then, he
couldn't help but be sidetracked and sickened by so many
of the wrongs he alone had committed within these
sacred walls.

He slowly realized something else was coming over him. The woman's voice was somehow soothing his weary, guilt-riddled mind like a cool, silk pillow against his hot cheek.

She came into the light, standing a head taller than his five-foot-ten frame and Albert looked under her cowl.

His ears and face were burning as he stared up at her exquisite, come-hither charcoal lips. Her dark complexion was flawless, her features dazzling, and she focused down at him with eyes that glistened like the northern lights.

"You..., you're not from here." Albert squeezed out the words. "I'd remember you. Are you a reporter?"

In his head, he prayed. He beseeched his Lord for help, from the shame he knew was coming and deserved, from the animosity, which slowly devoured his insides for what he had done, and from the bewitching creature that stood before him now. He couldn't help but sense the danger, as if he were a hungry fish gaping at a baited hook.

"God is testing me," he huffed. "Strength, Albert." He wiped his lips, fighting his ravenous desire to kiss her. "I'm afraid you must leave this place. I've nothing more to say!"

He tried. He honestly tried with all his will, but he could not turn away from her.

The young woman's smile grew ever more seductive. Her hands slowly went to him, gently touching. "I know what you did." Her voice rose, as if she was beginning to sing a hymn. The sound wrapped its way around his mind, gripping him, drawing him closer. "How many boys were there, Albert?"

"Please," he whined. "I..."

"Was it only a few? Perhaps dozens?" Her tune was consuming him. Somehow, Albert caught a glimpse of her hands with a numbed curiosity. They were clawed. "Did you touch them, like this?" She reached down the front of his robe, nudging his lusting groin.

"Stop!" he cried, trying again to turn away, but she moved with such swift seduction. She unclasped her cloak completely and it slipped from her smooth, bare shoulders to the cold, dull floor.

She stood beautifully before him and his entire being bristled with yearning. Her long, flowing black hair draped hypnotically over her full breasts as she pulled his stone hands up to embrace them. A sharp sting exploded from his groin and he felt his resistance shatter. He moaned, weak at first, wondering if his brittle connection with honour and righteousness had finally snapped. "God," he prayed with a heavy groan, "stay with me!"

Decency abandoned him then, and he groped the woman, thrusting himself toward her, moving to seize her as his own.

His roaming eyes focused suddenly on another peculiarity about the stranger, something he had altogether missed before, thinking absently that the light had given her odd shadows. Rising from her back were two long, bat-like wings. "No!" he exclaimed.

Her lips began to curl, revealing long, animal-like teeth.

"The Devil sent you!" Albert gasped, terror almost stopping his heart. "I have sinned! And this is my doomed result!"

Another shape rose from a darkened pew, a black form that stood menacingly and quiet.

"Not here!" Albert begged, shaking. "This is His house..., a house of God!"

The woman's hand grabbed Albert by his throat violently and squeezed it like a tightening noose. Her strength was inhuman and her carriage now beastly. She pulled him closer, until those sensuous lips nudged the edge of his ear as she spoke the last words he would ever hear, "But, Albert, surely you would know. God has left the building!"

Chapter 2

Desire

"Why must you flash that dead man's head about?" Ligeia's musical voice purred into Damianos's ears, muddling his focused enmity upon the 15th century portrayal of Christ's crucifixion in front of him.

It was a simple wood carving, stained now by the pastor's blood and festooned by gold plated images of angels awaiting the Son of God's ascension into Heaven. He envisaged the throngs of purpose-seekers who had knelt before this icon, to pray, to receive communion and to feel invigorated by the promise of the Holy Father's love.

"Do you suppose it was His love that employed this deceptive messenger of His word?" Damianos grumbled slowly. His blood-smeared lips quivered as each passing word seethed with hatred. "Sent here to rob His children of their innocence with impunity? There is no justice!"

"Bah," Ligeia scoffed.

Damianos turned from the old church's altar to see the haunting syrēne rise from an archaic pew. She moved like a fluid in her unclasped cloak, her black wings folded neatly behind her. The moon's washed out light shone through the many arched windows to reveal the spattering of fresh blood upon her rapturous face, neck and chest.

"What concern is it of yours?" she complained, staring at him scornfully. "So the moron got his jollies from exploiting young boys." She paused, growing a wide, devilish grin. "You could say that Albert, too, took energy from others to satisfy himself."

Heat swelled under Damianos's pitching ribs. "We do not cause others to suffer long. Nor do we prey upon the young. Do not compare us with the likes of him!"

"No, of course not! How could I even think it?" Ligeia was getting her hackles up. "We are perfectly respectable citizens, doing our part to keep society dignified and honourable." Her evident sarcasm abated after a few tight breaths, until at last she chuckled to herself. "Honestly, Dammie. What is going on inside that beautiful head of yours? Can you not smell?"

She drifted to the twisted, decapitated corpse upon the faded floor and took a long, unhappy whiff. "It is hard, leaden juice. I can taste the rust that flowed through his vile old body! Yet I killed him without any misgivings, for you."

She stood up again and grinned while clasping the front of her cloak to conceal her beguiling bosom with a brash swagger. "I guess he liked more than just boys."

Ligeia scrutinized Damianos a second time. "You know I hate old things! But for you, my love, I endure, although my patience with your perceived social conscience is wearing thin."

"The church was protecting him!" Damianos grunted, his hand grasping the pastor's short hair so tight he could feel the roots lifting from the dead man's scalp. "The victims would never have justice!"

"Is that really what this is about?" Ligeia chastised. "Justice? For whom, Dammie? For the dim-witted lot we feast upon? Or you?" She snarled before turning to leave, "Your eyes are darker than the paedophile's robe, as if you were still hunting for something. Murdering a damned pastor will not change anything for you, Damianos. Nothing will. Let it go."

Damianos watched, his mind suffering a tempest of hate and longing for reprisal, as Ligeia's swaying hips strode out the front gates of the church into the night.

"Syrēnes," his deep voice rolled. Damianos loved her, but the craving he felt for her was a distant second to his aches for vengeance. He stared again into Christ's suffering image behind the altar and let the smell of raw blood mix with the church's centuries old sweat.

Forever, it seemed, he and others like him had been banished to this world, driven into exile by poseurs that masqueraded themselves as friends, as intellectual superiors.

The tricksters turned as if possessed, abolishing freedoms, seizing entire families and taking away properties with brutal absolution. They killed without mercy. There was no justice.

Although only a child, Damianos remembered the horrors. "Lida..." He reached into his vision, longing still to save the sister he so cherished. To let go of her and the anger, the rage that so fuelled his every move, would likely have killed him long ago. He had a score to settle.

"God failed," he scathed. "He saves no one from the crimes of life. But I will see to it that things change." His mind flashed and his body tensed with excitement. "Do you hear me, God? If you are such a thing, then you will hear every word, see every thought and feel every twinge that comes from me. I will find a way. I will find a way back and I will sever every head from every angoros until there are none left to deceive with their twisting, lying tongues again!"

Damianos shouted furiously, and then hurled the pastor's gruesome head up at a nearby window, smashing a stained-glass image of an angel standing on the edge of a high hill. The glass shards rained down to the floor and Damianos stood in agonizing silence for minutes afterwards, letting his mind devour the deadened quiet.

That was when the voice first came to him, and changed everything.

Chapter 3

Provoked

The church had become so still that Damianos's every breath sounded like a gale. And within each blow's recess, a voice began to speak. Internally, he sensed it was not his own, though the sound of it left him at odds.

"I can give you what you want," it said.

A chill shuddered up Damianos's spine and he threw a suspicious glare at the many religiously charged symbols around him. "What?" His half-hearted reply echoed over the silence.

"The wrongs committed against you can be righted, my dear lilita," the voice continued. "The angoros have fallen from my grace. I need improved messengers. Lilitas, like yourself, can rise up from exile and restore their culture, their way of life, and reclaim their country. Freedom and justice, Damianos. Is that not what you want?"

Damianos could not ignore the lure, but still he shook his head and wondered if Ligeia's incessant warnings were coming true. "Am I mad?"

"There is a place where you must go. Into a hall, strewn with writings and stafas. I require you to translate and perform a particular galdor."

"A what?" Damianos's heart thumped loudly in his chest. Anticipation was rising, although he could make little sense of what was happening. "What are you talking about?"

"A galdor," the voice explained with benevolent calmness, "is a spell. It holds me, denying me the capacity to right the injustices laid against us both. If you can help me, Damianos, then I can help you. You must be forewarned; the way to salvation is hampered by a hidden danger. It will test the limits of your understanding and push you to madness. You see, you are to go where your delusion began, without waking up.

"It is a place buried in the darkness, beyond the shining walls of your finite universe. It goes back in time, set long before the story of men, of angoros or lilitas began. It goes beyond everything human science can tell you. You must come to a place that gave birth to what you know as The Big Bang. That is where you come from. All of you.

"It is where I started, and where I must go to finish. To find the way, it is imperative for you to locate *The Book of the Nornir*."

Damianos was confused. "The Book of the what? I know nothing of it."

"You're not supposed to. If you find the benighted child that possesses it, you will begin to know a great deal. Do not kill her. Yet. Once the way is opened, take her with you. Her presence will protect you from harm and her gift will decipher the galdor with ease. When you are done, the child is yours for the taking. The angoros, and everyone else, won't be able to stop what comes next."

The idea was fascinating. Damianos's sharp teeth chattered behind his lips, hungering. "I can't believe I'm saying this. I'll do it. Yes. Whatever it is. I'll do what you want. But I shall do no wrong to the child. It is not my way."

"Do not worry," the voice went on unmoved, "your principals will be corrected."

His breathing fast-paced and inspired, Damianos ignored the voice's foretokening, fastening his thoughts instead on its source. "Who are you?" He glanced at the cross, wondering. "God?"

"Better."

Chapter 4

Devote

"Ashes to ashes, dust to dust..."

"The sounds of a day better spent elsewhere," Gregg complained bitterly as he and his bigger, eighteen-year-old stepbrother, Dave, sat amongst a gloomy assemblage of mourners.

The rector went on with her oration in front of some thirty friends and family members who knew, felt pity for and perhaps even loved, Samantha. Her sad, thwarted existence had fallen short, leaving those left behind with a torturous sermon for her funeral while just outside the frontier church's darkly wooded walls and shining stained-glass windows teased the first sparkling warm day of spring in old Fort Langley. The whole production felt like an uncalled-for cruelty for those that still lived.

Dave looked agonized. "How much longer?" His quiet outburst was met swiftly by a surprising swat across the back of his head. "Ow!"

"Stifle it, David. Would it kill you to take a few minutes to think of someone else for a change?" his stepmother, Gregg's mom, scolded from the pew behind, while Dave's dad, whom she married when the boys were still infants, gnashed his teeth.

Dave's awkwardly strapping form slumped next to Gregg's lean build. "Jeez, Laura's givin' me that glare again."

"She's right, you know," Gregg struggled not to fuss over his mom's name. "You can go and play with your band of donkeys later."

"My what?"

"You know, those twits that know how egocentric you are, but are still willing to be seen in public with you." Gregg still wasn't sure if the message reached the mailbox or not. "Your friends?"

Dave scoffed and then buried his head into his clenching hands, grumbling.

"Shh!" Gregg's mom was at it again. "Show more respect for Auntie Sam."

Sighing, Dave whispered, "For as long as I knew her, I did. But she's dead now, isn't she? Lucky woman that. After all, it must have been something she really wanted." He chuckled, making an obvious reference to the fact that Auntie Samantha committed suicide at the ripe old age of thirty-five. Then, quite suddenly, he shuddered. "Christ, she gave me the creeps!"

Gregg had to agree. She was as odd a woman as any he'd known. Her face was so haggard; her whole body seemed ready to leap at the slightest noise.

All Gregg could remember now was the look Auntie Sam would give him every time they were together. It scared him, as if she knew something, something that she wanted to tell, but never did. Often Gregg would be left practically breathless. Kind of like he was now.

"Jesus Christ, I have to get out of here!" Gregg took to his feet and crouched down the aisle, avoiding his mother's reaching grasp and growling voice, casting his eyes straight ahead for the beaming sunlight that broke through the spacious gaps in the shut exit doors.

He escaped and walked alone behind the white church house, solemnly traversing the tired old lane that passed by there. The rector's voice carried through the building, floating softly by Gregg's ears between the sweet sounds of song birds perched joyously in the jungly mishmash of bordering trees and overgrown shrubberies. He found it all most unlikeable though, for his mind was in need of unbothered peace in order to sort through its mixed bag of thoughts.

She had shot herself in the head with a rifle. He tried not to envision the scene that his mother was the first to discover. The concept of death and afterlife and the conditions for its success pressed heavily. "Condemned on Earth, what does she face now?"

His eyes wandered distractedly from the gravelly, broken pavement at his feet to the leaf-littered blue sky above his head where the tall trees leaned mightily over him. His mother had said Auntie Sam was beautiful and trusting once. She was betrayed and her deepest scars never healed.

His head swayed. "Praying didn't help at all."

Images of Heaven teased him amongst the trees' creaking boughs and he envisioned a rapturous place of breathtaking purpose. "Seems a little cruel, to dangle a carrot like that then flog the poor girl and expect her to take it in good grace. Are you a masochist, God? Gettin' your fun taunting us peasants, are you? Then throwing us in Hell when we can't take it anymore..."

He bent over, despairing. "God, what is the point to life when all you have to look forward to is misery. Help me understand. Why are we here?"

He sighed, eyes rising again until his sights were strangely captivated by the white wings of a gliding gull, spread wide, and he fantasized that they were the wings of a more blessed creature. "Send her an angel, God," Gregg solicited rather distrustfully. "If you really exist and if there's really more to this whole... parade to the inevitable, send her an angel. She could have used one here. It's only fair."

After he said the words, he quietly snickered, demeaning himself. "And when you're done that, would you send me one, too?"

A stirring at the end of the lane drew his attention. To his surprise and embarrassment, his great-grandmother was hobbling toward him. Despite the refreshing warmth in the air, she wore a thick wool coat that made her look like a runaway church bell. "Come to seek answers, have you?" she queried in a way that made it sound like she already knew exactly what Gregg was doing.

He didn't want to admit to anything incriminating. "I just needed to get out of there. It was hot."

His great-grandmother looked him over, like only a gazillion-year-old woman could. "Ah," she nodded. She gently patted his shoulder, then turned away. "Alright then, cool off." Before she got too far, she glanced up at the ruffling trees and said, "She loved you, you know. Very much."

The revelation hit Gregg like a hot iron rod digging into his brain.

"She wanted to keep you hidden and safe."

Gregg didn't know how to react to that at first. It didn't matter, because his face seemed to sneer all on its own. "What?" he scorned. "Keep me hidden? Grammy, I hardly knew the woman. She was psychotic! And to be perfectly honest, every time she was around I wanted to sneak away and hide."

Great-Grandma stared him down and Gregg cringed. The old woman had blue eyes made of steel and when angered, he thought those peepers could gouge a hole through a bomb-shelter door. "My granddaughter was many things, Greggory. But don't you ever talk so flippantly about her again! She endured more than you can imagine, and refused to lose the one thing she held most dear."

"What, by killing herself?" Gregg argued. "What more is there to lose?" His emotions were taking over. Death was such a terrifying enigma. Thank goodness his great-grandmother must have realized it and turned her heat-ray vision off.

"She didn't think there was more she could do here."

Gregg's brows wrestled over his nose. "You knew she was going to do this." It was not a question.

His great-grandmother just watched him for a breath, as if turning something over in her mind, until she finally responded, "She was living a waking nightmare, Greggory, terrified that you were in danger."

Gregg's response was a tad fuddled, "Me?"

"Yes," she said with a strange, ominous undertone. "She only spoke of you, and the best way to keep you safe. Until you're ready to perform your role."

Nothing could have made Gregg more confused. "I don't get it."

"She seemed to think you will someday."

Chapter 5

Connections

Gregg, his legs folded before him, opened his back seat window, craving space. His step-dad, Patrick, looked like he was doing much of the same behind his son, while Dave revved the family Honda's tiny engine to Gregg's mother's obvious chagrin. The funeral was at last done and soon they'd be home. Praise God.

He listened, humiliated, as the car's annoying whine, made more embarrassing by the piercing squeal of the loose fan belt, heralded their approach up their normally quiet, suburban road, lined mostly by dull, out-of-date homes and high-reaching trees. As soon as the beater lost consciousness in the driveway, Gregg threw open the door and took off.

He meandered through the back yard where it was peaceful, slowly making his way around a number of unfolding shade trees toward the ravine that bordered the rear. Having time to let his mind wander, he kept going over thoughts of Auntie Sam and his great-grandmother.

"Why did that nutty woman want to keep me safe? And from what?"

He was suddenly knocked out of his reverie when an unseen assailant grabbed him and thrust him into a hidden opening in the hedge that bordered the eastern length of the yard.

"Whoa, hey," Gregg shouted on wobbly legs.

"God, I was starting to think you'd forgotten," came the feminine voice of his attacker.

Gregg knew instantly who it was and, after tumbling into a concealing cavity between two trees, he gazed up and happily took her in. A shapely girl of sixteen blessed with long, white-blonde hair and sparkling blue eyes, she was the neighbours' adopted daughter and since early childhood, Gregg's best bud. "Jesus, Jody! A simple hello not good enough for you, you have to tackle me and drag me in here?"

She grinned impishly as he struggled to avert his eyes from her delicious curves, making his thoughts and loins leap to dizzying, un-buddy like places.

"Admit it, Greggo, you love it when I rough you up," she teased.

He grunted wishfully, "I'd love it more if you'd take your shirt off before you did."

"Pardon me?"

"Nothing," Gregg shied away.

Her glorious smile returned. "Whatever. Now, nous allons..." As Jody obviously struggled to find the words and pucker her lips in just the right way to pronounce

24

them, Gregg remembered the French test he'd promised to help her study for. "...apprendre le français. There, did I get that right?"

Having fixed himself, Gregg gave her a cynical look. "Oui. How long have you been practicing that one sentence, you lynx?"

"Since I got out of the shower this morning." Her chuckle was hypnotic. "I Googled it. Too bad I can't use it in class. You said you would help me, Greggo. Sooo, teach me some friggin' French!"

The next three hours were nothing short of bliss for Gregg. Jody, with her butchered French, managed to shake him of his cheerless mood. They were at times kneeling on opposite sides of his bed, books strewn across the mattress, and he found himself staring in wonder while her tongue twisted and lips kinked around the words.

He also couldn't help but gawk, as inoffensively as he could, at Jo's breasts that from time to time practically gushed out of her shirt's generous neckline. On one such occasion though, the pendant from her gold necklace slipped out and dangled like a clock's counterbalance.

"What are you looking at?" Jody wondered. "Did I spill something?"

"No." Gregg rattled his head, thinking fast. "I was just, uh, looking at your necklace again."

Jody seemed pleased. She took it and placed it so Gregg could have a better view of its finer details, even though he'd seen it at least a thousand times before. "It's symbolic of creation, you know." She always said that, pointing out the various representations for this or that. It was probably the one thing her parents left her in this whole world and so far as Gregg knew, she treasured that piece of jewellery like nothing else.

"You see here, this is the shape of a hill, as if rising up from a sea, like the Primordial Hill. And atop this hill is a tree, like the Tree of Life." The metal at the centre of the tree's stem seemed to have a few faults to it. Either that or the middle of the thing was hollowed out for some reason. He and Jo never could figure it out for sure. "And this ring that surrounds the whole thing looks like a shield, a barrier to safeguard it all."

She smiled at it, sighed, then pulled the neck of her shirt and let the weighty little talisman sink back to its yummy hiding place. She also made sure to stay more upright after that.

Late afternoon drifted into evening and they nuzzled shoulder to shoulder, leaning on Gregg's headboard together, reciting, "Où sont les toilettes?" and chuckling afterwards.

Dave walked into the boys' shared bedroom griping loudly, "Christ! Dad's playin' Meatloaf again downstairs!" Shaking his head, he emptied the contents of his jeans' pockets onto the nightstand that separated his bed from Gregg's while humming the tune to 'I would do anything for love'. "I hate that song! I hate any dopey love song that my Dad will sing along to." He stopped himself, grumbling.

Jody chuckled, and it was like music to Gregg's ears. "What's wrong with that? I love that song! God, I haven't heard it in like, forever." She got up and began fixing her clothes and collecting her things. "You just don't know what love is. God, it's everything to me. If I didn't have love in my life, then I'd probably end it. It's not worth living anymore without love."

"You wouldn't kill yourself," Dave chided. "Silly girls, always being over-dramatic."

"Shut your flytrap!" Jody warned. "You don't know what I'd do! You don't know me! You don't know what it's like to...!" She pressed her lips tightly and growled, "I bet you don't know what you'd do for love, Daveyboy, except pause and turn the page... or click the mouse."

"Shya, good one Dr. Scorn. I know exactly what I'd do for love," he scoffed. "I'd do everything right..., and make her shout, 'Yes, David. Give it to me, give it to me'!"

Jody rolled her eyes with a huff and poked her index finger down her throat. She looked sheepishly at Gregg as she leaned over to pluck another book from the floor, unwittingly showcasing her mouth-watering cleavage to him again. "What about you, Greggo?"

"What?" He shook himself from his stupor. "What about me?"

"What would you do for love?"

He lurched. *If only she knew... after all this time, how could she not? Tell her. Say it*, he told himself. *Tell her how you feel.* But his tongue kept agonizingly still in his mouth as she stared at him, waiting. "I... I... I'd run right into Hell and back."

The smile that spread across her wonderful lips told him it was a good answer.

"Lucky bastard," Dave blasted Gregg and then turned his attention to Jo. "It's from like, the first bloody verse of the song. You can't tell me that you're going to buy that crap?"

Jody chuckled, her smile a little less electrified while musing. She suddenly exclaimed, "Well, I'd like to stay and keep… learning. But it's getting late and I should get ready for tonight."

"Tonight?" Gregg's voice broke.

"Oui, monsieur." Jody grinned. "Sean will be picking me up at 8:30 for our date."

"Wha…?" Gregg's heart cramped. "On a Sunday? But, you have that test!"

Jody laughed. "It's okay, Daddy!" She nudged him playfully and gave him a peck on the forehead, "I won't be late and I promise I'll do well on the test." Then, with books in hand, she blew him another kiss and made for the door. "Merci, mon amour! Good night!"

Dave gave Gregg a shove and then went to the computer on the cluttered desk at the far wall. "Sean. I wonder what that jock does for love? Maybe you should ask him?"

Gregg sat on his bed, alone, looking forlornly at the empty space Jody had filled just a minute before. "Amour?" he said to himself, doing his best to ignore his stepbrother and wondering if Jody used Google to translate that one too. "Mon amour," he repeated, feeling his lips creep up into a ruffled grin. "My love?"

"Like a woman loves a pet," Dave teased, eyes focused on his Facebook page. "That's kinda what you are to her, you know. Just to be clear."

"Please, shut up," Gregg groaned.

"Awe, c'mon. Don't get Jo's panties in a tangle."

"Are you implying that I'm wearing Jody's undergarments now?" Gregg shook his head, unimpressed.

"No. I'm implying that you're kind of a girl."

Gregg shot out of bed and pulled down his pants for Dave to see. "Does this look like a girl's?"

Dave flinched, "My eyes! You damned hermaphrodites! Is there no end to your surprises?"

"Shut-up!" Gregg threw a pillow at him.

Dave took it upside his head and a strange look overcame him. "You know, I miss this."

Gregg was confused into silence.

"We used to banter on for hours like this, about nothing in particular," Dave reminisced. "I'm referring to your sexuality, of course." Gregg reached for another pillow and Dave laughed. "I miss it! I do! I remember so many times thinking how much I liked having you as my brother, before you started taking life so seriously. What happened?"

Gregg locked eyes with him for a stretch, thinking. He glanced at the nightstand and noticed the name printed at the top of a loosely folded receipt, Riders Liquor Store, and he knew Dave and his goof friends had been stocking up on booze again. "There were good times," he admitted. "Maybe I grew up too soon. And maybe I got tired of waiting for you to catch up."

Chapter 6

Discovered

Four months Damianos had hunted, rustling past shrubberies, low-lying branches and parked cars like a swift breeze. *He told me where the path begins. He can feel it.* Damianos hunkered down within the skirting of a tall cedar tree, situated in the front yard of a characterless home in a sedated neighbourhood and he glared earnestly across a dark street to another dull house where the scuffed front door and porch were barely illuminated by a single incandescent light.

He said the entrance to this hidden place is shut. Sometimes, the voice echoed seemingly without end, becoming most irritating. Yet Damianos still found it compelling. And after suffering frustration after frustration trying to find the orphan child he was told held the answers, he prayed that finally success was near. *She is the one. She must be.*

The sky whooshed behind him followed by heavy footfalls. He turned in time to see Ligeia fold her wings and crouch with him in the darkness. "She's coming!" she warned.

The moment was intoxicating when he heard the whine of an approaching motorcycle. He stepped to the edge of the shadows to catch a clearer look. The bike's headlight swayed left and right as it came near and Damianos heard a girl's voice complaining, "Would you stop that? It's not funny!"

"She is with a boy," Ligeia said. "His handling of that vehicle is much worse now than it was before."

"Drunk?" Damianos suspected.

Ligeia nodded then griped, "We have been hunting here long enough. When will we go back to warmer climates?" She rubbed the goose bumps on her bare legs.

"Let the rousing of the chase warm you," Damianos replied, resolute. "Everyday that passes brings us closer to reparation, and more."

He turned in time to see Ligeia purse her soft lips, the flaring anger in her eyes reflecting in the dim-lit night. "Sometimes I wonder, my love"—she sounded wary—"if it had been me who heard voices in my head, telling me to cross sea and country in search of some parentless bitch with a gift to decipher a spell for which I had no explanation or direction, would you have followed me?"

Without freeing him from her fixed look, she stood up, grabbed Damianos's long black coat and yanked him back into the cedar tree's shelter. He could hear the motorcycle's engine rev time and again as it pulled into the driveway across the street. As much as he yearned to focus his attention on the driver and passenger, his better judgement told him that, at this moment, he had to answer his syrēne. He still needed her.

"Of course, my love," Damianos answered as believably as he could. "For I love you like no one else in this lonely, deplorable world." He took hold of her. "How could I ever let such beauty slip away?"

Her scowl lightened and he knew he had her. That was his strength. His magic. Damianos leaned closer and kissed her softly, letting his heat drip into her body until she wilted such as a black rose in his hands.

All the while, he was listening to the commotion brewing across the street. When he felt satisfied that Ligeia was sufficiently subdued, he left her leaning against the sturdy tree trunk and peered out into the faint distance where the dim porch light glowed.

There appeared to be a brief struggle. The girl, on whom he placed such high hopes, slipped away from the motorcycle while the boy sat proudly upon his cushioned seat, lifting his showy helmet as he belched.

Damianos scrutinized the girl. "She's wearing very little."

He heard the girl say, "I told you, Sean. I'm not ready for that."

Sean's voice carried, slurred with dopey sarcasm as he dismounted his ride, "What? What are you talking about?" He reached and grappled her, clinging to her as if playing until he pulled her shirt's thin straps over her bare shoulders.

"Sean!" the girl argued. "You said you wouldn't pressure me."

"C'mon... you just might like it."

Not appearing the least bit reassured, she twisted more feverishly and broke free from the boy's hold. As she turned away, Sean must have snagged a finger on her top, pulling the fabric down farther.

Damianos grinned. "This is interesting."

"Are you sure?" Ligeia suspicious voice whispered in his ear. "What about your insatiable devotion to justice? Seems a bit unfair at the moment."

Damianos didn't respond. He was waiting. *What will you do now, my little orphan girl?*

"Come on, Jo," Sean wheedled. "You're teasing me again."

Jo retreated, keeping out of the boy's reach as she pulled her shirt back into place. But Sean lunged and grabbed her again. He tugged so violently that the fabric ripped.

The girl yelped and fell away onto the dewy lawn, her flimsy knit top ruined. Rolling to her knees while her shirt slipped down to her elbows, she made frantic attempts to cover her unrestrained breasts by folding her arms.

Strangely, insofar as Damianos could tell, this Sean boy's aggression didn't continue. He seemed to be stuck gawking at the girl's uncovered back.

"It's true then... the stories about your back." Sean shook his head, cringing, as if wanting to blot the image from his mind.

What about her back? Damianos wondered. But his speculating was cut short.

"Hey!" another boy's voice yelled.

Damianos glanced at the house next to Jo's and caught a glimpse of a figure, leaning from a dark second-storey window, before it swiftly vanished into blackness.

The surprise must have diverted Sean's attention as well because the next thing Damianos noticed was the half-naked girl beating the boy from behind with a heavy stick. Sean barely managed to mount his bike and spin the engine to life while fending off the girl's attack.

The rear wheel screeched and Sean made his fast escape, the red taillight sinking into the distance.

A brief moment of quiet passed until Damianos couldn't keep a hearty grin from spreading across his face. *This is it. She's alone. Now is the time!*

He moved with supple ease through the darkness while Ligeia let loose with musical laughter behind him, no doubt entertained by Sean's hasty retreat. He quietly lured the syrēne from hiding and together, with their usual stealth, they closed in on his target.

Jo was alone and sobbing, apparently heedless of the danger lurking in the shadows. But before they could reach her, a door suddenly burst open. Damianos froze and spotted a boy bounding toward the girl from the house next door. It was the same dwelling that he hearkened the cry from only a minute earlier

A tall, thin figure leaped into the bleary light as if charging to a fight and Jo shifted herself swiftly, covering her breasts with one arm and waving the stick with the other. "Go home, Gregg! I don't want to see you now."

This is unexpected, Damianos thought.

"Who is this?" Ligeia ruffled. "I want to get this done! I'm cold!"

"Where'd he go? Did he hurt you?" The lanky boy sounded menacing. At least, he seemed to be trying.

Jo dropped the stick, and her shoulders, and began sobbing again. "What do you think?" she snapped.

"She's angry at him?" Damianos whispered, confused.

The young slender fellow stepped toward Jo with arms bent in a hesitant, reaching gesture.

"Don't come near me!" she shouted. "I've told you a thousand times, Gregg, I don't need you to protect me anymore. I'm not a little girl."

Gregg appeared unsure, his tall stature angling this way and that.

"I'm not a little girl!" she bellowed with renewed vigor.

"But, Jo…" Gregg muttered to her naked back. She was already racing for her front door. She was frantic as she fumbled with her jean's pocket until she found a key to open the way in. Jo dove behind the walls of her home and sealed it shut.

Gregg stood there, motionless, long after the porch light was turned off.

Damianos watched him silently, or so he thought, because the boy turned suddenly and peered into the night. *That's strange*, Damianos observed.

"What's he doing?" Ligeia spoke softly.

"Shh," Damianos grumbled. "He's hunting." He cautioned himself to keep still. *Humans have dulled senses. He won't see.*

Gregg's squinting eyes, as expected, ran right by Damianos. Even Ligeia did not seem to attract the boy's attention and, feeling perhaps a tad smug, Damianos let a wisp of pent up breath blow past his pearly whites.

Gregg must have somehow sensed Damianos's miniscule breath and zeroed in on it. It was the only explanation. For unbelievably the boy was staring through the black night directly at him, and the only thing to break their implausible eyeball-to-eyeball connection was Ligeia's wondering voice.

"Can he see us?"

Damianos replied, shaking his head, "My love, we have found the benighted child."

"How can you be so sure?" Ligeia probed. "Is it because of her confusing mood swings?"

"No," Damianos growled, meeting Gregg's stare a second time, watching the boy's pupils become flushed with awareness and then pigmented with a confusing stew of alarm and, could it be, indomitability? "It is because of the company she keeps."

Chapter 7

Examining

Gregg stood peering out his bedroom window, flashing his teeth at the moon when fits of yawning demanded it. He glanced at his shared clock-radio. It read 3:41am. *This is stupid*, he thought. *I need to get some sleep.*

But spotting two weirdoes crouched in the darkness just across the street had a way of filling an imagination with a whole wagonload of heebie-jeebies. Gregg couldn't close his eyes without being awash in nightmarish images of spooky freak show characters trying to do all sorts of nasty things to Jody. It made no sense.

Something stirred behind him, grumbling, "What are you doing?"

Gregg glanced back to see Dave's messed up noggin poking up from under his comforter. "Nothing," he answered. "Go back to sleep."

"Are you still waiting for her to come home?" Dave's voice was disparaging. "You suck. There are laws for people like you. Let her be and get your white-boy butt in bed so I can go back to my naughty escapades with Katy Perry."

"She's already home," Gregg replied, about ready to collapse.

"Katy? Get out of my fantasy!"

"Jody, you widget."

"Then what are you looking at?" Dave muttered.

Gregg shook his weary head, but at the moment he wasn't even sure anymore if what he'd seen was real, if it had actually happened. "There was this guy standing in the dark, just staring at me. At least, I think there was. I can't explain it. Maybe it's just adrenaline, I guess. It was like…"

"A freakin' dream? Putz," Dave blurted. "Get to bed before I level you with a flying elbow."

Gregg huffed and then glanced out the window a few more times. Sleep was dragging him to his pillow. *It felt so real*, he mulled.

Chapter 8

Taken

Every morning since she was old enough to ride her bike alone, Jody ventured into the unknown, vehemently refusing to have anyone join her. Gregg stood many times, baffled, at the end of her driveway while Jo pedalled into the distance and around the bend, solo. She kept her experiences secret.

But not this morning.

Gregg cycled hard behind her, doing his best to leave enough distance between them so as not to be noticed, and hid amid the trees when it looked like they had arrived.

The cemetery?

He had no idea this was where she went, but he had little time to think about it. A tall dark figure was watching Jo kneel in front of a grave and the sight sent chills up Gregg's spine. *It's the same guy I saw last night, I know it.*

His heart raced and his hair stood on end. That odd adrenaline-like feeling came back. His vision seemed to pick up more colours, his nose caught scents he couldn't comprehend and his ears dished on Jody's stressed voice from a ridiculous distance. All the while a single certainty throbbed in his head; *this is going to get bad!*

His body felt as if it was no longer his own, as if he had somehow hijacked a predator's physique. He moved through the brush like a stalking cougar, disbelieving his own intentions. Into the open he crept, eyeing the stranger's every action. Jody's safety was at risk, Gregg was sure of it, but the wild will that pressed him ever closer was confusing.

I'm not a fighter, he kept telling himself. *That guy must be a hundred and fifty pounds heavier than me!*

"I can help you, Jody." The stranger was obviously lying. His black eyes were as virtuous as those of the witch's that gave Snow White the poison apple. "Where is the book?"

Jody sobbed, her back bending as she sat upon the cold grass.

Gregg could bear it no longer. Although his limbs practically ached to lunge at the dark man and tear him apart, his mind faltered. Instead he managed only to let out a timid breath, "Jody?"

She spun around and he took in her reddened, desperate eyes. The cretin grabbed Jody's chin and rotated her head toward him again, as if doing his best to ignore Gregg's presence altogether. "The book! Where is *The Book of the Nornir?*"

Heat swelled behind Gregg's eyes, his muscles tightened and he moved forward with hands spread, ready to claw and rip.

But a black shape swooped down before him and hammered him hard in his chest. He fell back to the wet earth gasping for breath as his assailant came into view.

"It's you again!" She snarled in a musical fashion. It was a dark-skinned woman; a practically naked Amazon that had, of all things, bat-like wings and a lung-crushing punch. She stared at him for a time with an expectant smirk lighting up her wildcat face. But her expression soon changed to one of confusion. "Why aren't you dying?"

Gregg balked. He followed her befuddled look to his chest and belly and nearly fell backward a second time. "Jesus!" He choked on his own breath. His grey shirt was drenched in blood and shredded in two places. He wanted to scream, but the woman fanned her wings before he could do anything, the sight robbing him of his breath.

"How did you get by me?" she demanded.

She flung her curtain-like coat to the ground and Gregg gawked at her voluptuous figure, distracting him from his gruesome wounds. Though she snarled and gnashed her surprisingly pointy teeth, threatening, Gregg was enfeebled by the flaming hot sting pulsing from his groin. What blood was left flowing in his body seemed to all be heading to the same place. He'd never seen those parts of a real woman before.

She went to him and wrapped her long hand across his face, holding him for her inspection. Her touch was thrilling and the way her smooth skin varied with her

41

every move, every breath, seemed to be pulling Gregg deeper into a trance. She was so close, so tantalizingly close. His hands yearned to reach up and brush against her ebony breasts, so mouth-wateringly near. But sadly, she forced his gaze up to meet hers.

She looked angry as she examined him. "No one sneaks by me. How did you do it? How are you staying alive?"

She leaned over his head and sniffed his thick, sandy blonde hair, leaving Gregg to gape lustfully at her chest. He'd clean forgotten about his injuries, feeling nothing from them. If not for the sudden sound of Jody's whimpering voice, he'd likely have forgotten about her too. "Jo!" he called to her. But the hypnotizing creature on top of him held him motionless.

Her smelling continued downward until her thick wet lips came close enough to kiss Gregg's cheek. Terrified and flustered by the hormonal deluge lighting the fireworks in his pants, Gregg remained as perfectly still as he could, wondering if she was going to take a bite with those fangs of hers or begin some awe-inspiring orgy that he'd fantasized about since he was thirteen.

But time and again, she only breathed him in. She looked baffled and reluctantly let him go. "Why can't I smell you?"

"Uh, soap?" Gregg offered.

She scowled, then sniffed the hand she'd used to hold him. She let out her long red tongue and licked it.

Gregg almost fainted. "Wha..., whatchya doin?" He tried to sound cool, but watching her licking her hand and fingers with that tongue? Man, this winged woman was something else.

She scowled again, "That's strange." She eyed him with a demand. "Come here."

Gregg heard Jody's voice intensifying and from the corner of his eye, he noticed her tussling with the man in black. Gregg hated himself for not averting his eyes from the winged chick long enough to think things through, but she was just so damned captivating. He didn't get up and hurry to Jo's side. Instead, he leaned closer to the naked woman with a yearning forcing him to obey.

She pulled him the rest of the way and he tumbled, until his messed-up chest touched hers. He instinctively feared the hammering pain that was sure to come. But it was insignificant. He snuck a look down to see that his blood had sloshed onto the woman's silky smooth skin and he squeaked awkwardly at the feel of her yielding flesh against him.

A sly smile lit the woman's face. She cupped his jaw again, forcing his attention up and holding it. "I don't like you. And I never like to be snuck up on."

"Gregg!" Jody cried. "Gregg!"

Jesus, Gregg, he told himself. *Snap out of it, man. Jo needs you.*

The winged woman's lips twitched and then opened slowly. Gregg felt like a melting cube of ice floating in a warm glass of water when he saw that wet tongue move so thirstily. Although he shuddered at the sight of her lengthy front teeth, he couldn't turn away.

Her face filled the gap between them, and her nose gently nudged his. She drew in another tender breath, and then grinned. She had him. There was no arguing it. The vixen could do anything she wanted and he'd be friggin' okay with it. He felt as stiff as an iron rod and as malleable as Play-Doh at the same ruddy time. *Stupid puberty*, he groaned to himself.

Then, slow and sure, came her tongue. And when it finally wet his bone-dry lips and reached to fondle his stuck dumb tongue, Gregg thought he could feel himself passing through to her, like rainwater into an open drain. His heat, his anxiety, his soul seemed to be pouring through his mouth into hers. His body became limp and his thoughts sank.

This coercive arousal sent a hint of terror, though, from somewhere in the lowest dwellings of his consciousness and if things had continued, it might have been the last mental tremor he ever experienced.

But something ended their connection and the split was quite a jolt. They both shot back from each other and after a few blurry moments, Gregg opened his eyes, feeling his senses quickly return.

The tall man in the trench coat was dragging Jody across the wet lawn and grave markers toward a huge, stretched SUV. "Jody!" Gregg shouted.

The naked winged woman seemed to be recovering from the separation herself when she finally grumbled, "What are you?"

Flustered at first by the woman's odd query, Gregg was far too concerned for Jody to allow himself any further distraction. His fascination with the naked chick died away, replaced once again by a fierce desire to get Jo.

But the stubborn harpy kept getting in the way. "You're clearly not what you make yourself out to be," she apparently decided. Gregg noticed the woman's widening eyes and expectant smile. That sight unnerved him more than when she was snarling like an animal.

"What?" Gregg asked.

"I shall have to find another way to kill you," she purred. Her look became more playful, almost smitten. She ran her hand lightly over her blood smeared front, then eagerly extended her red-stained fingers into her mouth and sucked them dry. "If I must," she added with a pout.

In that moment, Gregg's head swirled, wishing that he could remember all the warnings his stepfather had given him over the years about women. "You know, I have my own hormonal stuff to deal with right now, but I don't use it as an excuse to abuse perfect strangers!"

"Lie!" the man dressed in black hollered over his shoulder and the demonic winged woman spun around. The stranger was struggling to fold Jody into the back of the huge, black vehicle when he barked, "For pity's sake, you bat-winged Eros, kill him!"

Lie curled her lips and muttered, "Of course, you I have to kill, while he gets to be as sadistic as he wants with her. It's such an unfair world, don't you think?"

Gregg's head hurt enough before he came to this place, now he wondered if it was about to implode.

The man in black slammed the door and turned to meet Gregg's eyes. "Killing men is your specialty, Ligeia." He was coming closer, his black-orbed eyes growing wider with every step. "Are you unbalanced?"

"Really, Damianos?" Ligeia's voice flowed placidly into the air. "I am no more mad than you." She grinned at Gregg and sent him a flirtatious wink. "He is only a child, Dammie. It makes me anxious to see how obsessive you've become, to have me slaughter a mere boy."

Damianos moved like an advancing thundercloud, darkening the earth with every step. His face, ridiculously flawless, appeared to be scowling. "You know as well as I that this is no mere boy." He towered over Gregg's tall frame, blocking out the sun's warmth, and with a swipe that felt like a sudden gust of wind, Damianos ripped Gregg's shirt clean off him.

Gregg stumbled back, seeing his chest and belly for the first time. There were no wounds, no scars, nothing.

Damianos took the stained shirt and held it to his face, licking the blood from the tattered fabric before casting a devilish glare at Gregg. "Jivita," he declared with apparent dismay.

"He's not pure," Ligeia added. Her look had plainly softened toward Gregg, even becoming defensive when Damianos raised his hand a second time. "There's at least some human in him. Anything you do will be energy wasted. You must have expected this when you first saw him last night."

Gregg spoke up, though with hesitation, "Let Jody go."

Damianos grinned, but only a little and Ligeia appeared disappointed. Before Gregg could utter another sound, the man in black lunged. Gregg felt the tearing next, as if there were still layers of clothes upon his thin frame being ripped away, but he knew there were none. Pain seared across his body from every slash, again and again, as if Damianos was pulling him over a deli meat-slicer. His flesh wrenched away as he stood there immobile, bearing the digging and gouging, while pieces of skin and meat flopped to the ground.

Gregg heard the screams. But they weren't his. Jody must have been watching from the car. *Don't look at me! Run away! Run* away, his thoughts cried.

Gregg fell back from the tossing and stripping, the wind cold and biting over him, until he lay limp and blind. He discerned wetness and knew it was his butchered meat. His nose filled up with the stink of his blood and his ears burned. Jody was bawling, her whimpers only worsening the utter pain running through what was left of Gregg's body.

"No!" he heard Ligeia warn. "You mustn't eat a jivita's flesh! Too much will consume you in the end!"

Damianos grumbled, then a moment slipped by before Gregg heard his attacker's voice. "It's sad. Should the sins of the father be allowed to pass down to his offspring without remorse? Without justice?" It sounded as if he was mocking him. "You see, my love? The voice that guided us here was not imaginary at all. We have found a haven for miscreants of an awful sort. Corrections must be made here. Things must be righted."

Jody's cries continued as Damianos instructed Ligeia, "Go, but do not trifle with the girl. She must know where *The Book of the Nornir* is."

"What will you do with him?"

"Whatever pleases me, my love." His voice was a warning.

47

Another moment passed and Gregg heard the man come closer. There was the sound of a short leap before the beast's pressuring tone forced its way into Gregg's raw ears. "Does it hurt? What you're feeling now? I can tell you, it looks horrible. Quite ghastly, to be honest. I've been told that jivitas have a flaw. Pain. It can be intense. Is it not? There is a part of me, however small it is becoming, that makes me want to apologize. It's not like me to be so wasteful. But you brought it out of me, you monster."

The emotion behind the voice increased. "If you'll excuse me, I have a book to find and your pretty little girlfriend is going to help me."

Gregg heard Damianos grunt, as if exerting himself before trotting away. Shortly afterward, Jody's bawling exploded and it sent great jolts of angst through Gregg's still breathing corpse. He then noticed something even more unhinging. Light was disappearing from his perception.

No! Jody! I can't die! Oh, God. Don't let me die!

The physical pain was numbing and the sounds of commotion started falling from his thoughts like rain from a cloud, until there was nothing.

Nothing, except an unsettling awareness of the nothing.

Chapter 9

Revealed

Iris stretched awkwardly on her couch, breathing in the pungent smell of generations past. The last few weeks had been hard, culminating with her granddaughter's funeral the previous day.

She sat her weary old body up from her mid-morning nap, brooding over the fact that she had lived so long, only to see an awful many of those she loved pass away before her. The pain in her heart seemed only outdone at times by the pain in her abdomen, sapping her of energy far too often these days.

Get up, she kept telling herself. She needed more wood in the fireplace. It was like the beating heart of the house. As long as she kept it burning, the home's pulse ran warm and soothing. When it was cold, there were mysterious eddies of air that abounded within these old walls, chilling her bones and making her skin bump.

Iris glanced beyond her opened red velvet drapes through the sliding glass door and sprawling meadow to where the woods towered high above. Known simply as such, *The Woods* took up at least 70 acres of her land. Iris's forefather, John Hayman, was granted the title in the late 1800s from his former employer, The Hudson's Bay Company. He fought away all attempts to harvest those woods and clear the entire place for farming, believing there was greater value in leaving them to grow while the race to strip the land around them heated up.

John cut enough to build the house and outbuildings and to open adequate space for crops and livestock. The rest he left, making The Woods a towering forest island amidst a sea of sprawling development, grass and roads.

At least, that was the 'official' story she and community historians were told. Iris's father had said something very different in private. "Those damned woods are haunted," he had told her when she was a child. "People go in and never come out. People come out that never went in. Not even the Indians dared hunt in those trees."

Iris shuddered, trying to focus her thoughts on other things. It looked like it should have been a warm spring day, but once she stoked the fire alive again she slumped back onto her couch and clung onto her blanket, smothering herself with it. For over a hundred and fifty years, this homestead had been filling itself with memories, memorabilia and, to Iris's utter bedevilment, those inexplicable cold drafts.

From her spot on the couch, made cosy by her impromptu napping, she eyed one precious beam of sunshine gleaming in from those southern windows. The dark wooded room never seemed to be blessed with much more than that come the summer months. Ironic that better teasings of radiance came only in the bitter cold of winter when the sun never reached high enough to climb over the roof. It often looked like a pale balloon hovering precariously above The Woods' piked tips of stretching firs, hemlocks and cedars.

The old artefacts inside watched starvingly as the brightness made its daily peek in at them. Shelves lined the wall facing the great stone fireplace. Stuffed in organized glory with books from every age and genre that her grandfather had collected during his travels, they were never in any danger of becoming washed out by invading daylight. And in the centre of the room, surrounded like a queen by her courtiers, sat a dark, opulently crafted antique table. Homely, unadorned armchairs and a doughy couch were clustered around it and upon the latter, Iris was resting.

"Damn," she complained. "I suppose I should do something today." The prevailing feeling was to clean up. "Damn, damn."

She looked about, wondering where to begin. *The floors?* No, she decided the vacuum was too loud and heavy. *What about the windows?* "Bah, it'll only rain and make things spotty again." This really wasn't going well.

Finally, she settled the issue by trudging into the kitchen and picking up a rag. Dusting seemed the easiest thing to do. "I'll break myself in slowly. No sense in overdoing it on the first day."

As she got busy on the bookshelf, she became more interested. She made up her mind that not a speck of dust was getting by her this spring. "Gaw." She curled the end of her nose when she reached the upper shelves of old tomes, all blanketed in powdered filth. "Suppose it's been a while," she muttered while inspecting a particular dark, leather-bound book.

Her father had discovered it while exploring the property when he was a child. Its pages were dressed in beautiful handwriting that was unfortunately untranslatable. It was presumed to be Russian, but later accepted as nothing more than some obscure gibberish. Still, the book was pleasing to Iris. She glided her finger over its edge, thinking of her old dad before going to fetch a stool from the closet and setting to work.

She had to stop more than once to escape the tiny particles she'd upset into the air. "Suppose it's been a very long while."

She choked while in a precarious position and pulled several books down trying to regain her balance. "Damn!" she burst, glaring down at the smut spreading across the wooden floor. Left unheeded, she knew they'd rise up one day as killer dust bunnies. Iris breathed a heavy sigh. "Now I'll have to clean that too."

Shaking her head in aversion, her eyes caught on something leaning against the back of the shelf where the books had been. "What's this?" she wondered as she reached for an old, tattered-looking envelope. "Well I'll be. How long have you been hiding here?"

It had a wax seal that looked hazily familiar. It was of a hill, with a tree growing from its peak, all held within a fine silhouette. It irritated her that she couldn't recall where she had seen this image before.

She felt something lumpy inside and came down from the stool. The mess on the floor forgotten, she quickly switched on the lamp under which she carefully opened the envelope and pulled the pocket wide.

"My key!" she gasped. She tipped the singular content onto the table and stared in amazement. It was an old, pitted, worn out little skeleton key that Iris had been missing since she didn't know when. Attached to it by a string was a white tag that read simply, *Cellar.*

"I thought I lost you. I actually forgot all about you after a while." As far as she knew the little cellar, hidden in a nook of the basement, was empty and the door locked. She was probably the only one left alive who could recall its existence.

"Who would lock it, put the key in this envelope and hide it in a place where no one would look?" she wondered.

Energized by her discovery, Iris moved like a grey-haired shot to her basement, sinking deeper into old, neglected places. She opened the lock on the small wooden door at the end of a stoned, subterranean hall she had to crawl to get to, poking around the narrow passage with a broom stick first to clear away the spiders' webs layered over bygone years.

"What fun!" she said to herself, for the distraction was doing her wondrous good. Iris, well aware of her mind's tendencies to do the opposite, was seeing past her pain.

She managed to ignore even the discomfort of the rough stone floor gouging into her knees as she forced her head inside. "Aha!" She tensed excitedly. She reached in and grabbed two old, wooden orange crates, one much smaller and lighter than the other, along with a weighty leather sheathe. Iris pulled them out one at a time as a strange twinge began pricking at her thoughts.

She had seen these three things before, in a brief, fleeting crack of time when life was strenuous and unforgettably emotional. Iris remembered the exquisite young woman who had held them. She had been intensely secretive on occasion, but Iris knew that the last few days before her death she'd spent collecting things and keeping them from her troubled husband. "She must have hidden them from him," Iris mused aloud.

She began the journey back up the corridor to the open basement, grunting with each laboured tug, thinking these newly found items rightly belonged to the woman's next of kin, Iris's goddaughter.

Jody Fraser.

Though a proud, honest woman, Iris couldn't help but feel a smattering of curiosity. Her desire for excitement was being delightfully rekindled. "But, no..." She slowly ascended with the last item between two rows of bottled wine. "Fight it, Iris. You're a bloody old woman. I should want nothing to do with this."

As she paused, sitting in the cool quiet of her home's substructure to recover from her exertions, she simply could not resist having at least a quick peek inside one of the crates. "Damn," she muttered. "I suppose I could do with a little more excitement, to keep my mind off things. At least, a wee bit couldn't hurt and who knows if anything better will come along before my bag of bones becomes next year's fertilizer?"

She picked the heavier of the two crates since it was closest to her and heaved it onto her lap. She opened the lid with eager fingers. Inside was a thick wrapping of dark cloth. Iris felt a surge of guilt pull her hands back. "What am I doing? No. I mustn't intrude any further than this. It doesn't belong to me!"

She slapped the lid shut.

But she couldn't put the crate down. The attraction was incredible. "I could die just dragging this stuff upstairs. One look," she argued with herself. "One look and then I'll wrap it up and pay my respects at their little memorial. There's no harm in that. I've had a lifetime of refraining from depravity, for the most part at least. Surely this slip won't condemn me in God's eyes."

Just to make sure, she flew her right hand before her in the sign of the cross and looked guiltily up to the ceiling. Then, feeling satisfied in general, she lifted the lid a second time.

She reached for the black, featherlike cloth and peeled it away. An icy breeze blew across the back of her neck and she lurched, thinking someone was behind her.

"Hello?" But there was no answer. "Damnation!" she cursed. "Bloody drafts are everywhere."

Her fingertips started tingling, as if going numb. Iris became increasingly annoyed. *Oh, these silly hands!* she swore to herself, thinking the feeling was rooted in her carpal tunnel. All was forgotten however, when Iris first beheld the book. "Oh, my goodness," she exclaimed softly.

It filled the crate almost to its edges, its surface a strangely dulled blue-grey as if made more of metal than board covered with paper or leather. There were no words, only remarkably detailed artistry. Raised leaves vined the corners and the three bindings, while the front cover was flushed with complicated, embossed shapes.

Her memories flicked back to an argument she had once overheard Jody's mother and father having on the porch. Their voices were heated, at times fierce. Jody's father wanted to avoid something, to keep something from happening again. He said he had to destroy a book. "What was it?" Iris puzzled. "The Book of Near? ...Fear? ...Beer? Damn again!"

Obviously, Jody's mother had disagreed and must have somehow snatched it away in this crate she'd likely found in the barn. There were tonnes of old things in there.

"What's so important about this book?" Iris' eyes scanned the design from tail to head without pausing for any true appreciation. She couldn't help but notice above the centre, though, where there was a rather unremarkable circular depression a little smaller than the palm of her hand. Within it, to one side, was a small, raised version of a pentagram: a star enclosed in an even border.

Toward the bottom edge, or tail of the cover, was a design that looked curiously like a nest of loosely tangled yarn, twisting and winding in a messy, chaotic fashion.

Snarled in amongst it were three globes, and a dragon. Iris gazed at it, awed at how life-like and creepy it was. The more she looked the more supernatural it appeared to be. She even shuddered and blinked trying to focus. "Did you just... move?"

Even though there was much more to see and absorb, Iris pulled back, as if dragging herself from a trance. *What is this?* Just then, she remembered Jody's mother mention something to her husband in a short peace between them before the accident took both their lives.

"Don't let his voice rule your thoughts and ruin your soul! Stop trying to dodge what must come, what has already come to pass. Your daughter needs this book. It is the veiled story of us all."

Chapter 10

Reminiscence

He's dead!

Jody's thoughts clashed, battling to squeeze out truth and logic from her traumatized, imaginative mind. Flashes of hope and rescue had devolved into panic and terror, as she had watched the man in black, that wildly handsome animal, attack Gregg. The beast had practically shredded poor Gregg to his bones before tossing him into an empty grave.

My God! Gregg!

After what happened with Sean the previous night, Jody had felt both angered and defenceless. She didn't like it and decided to borrow her adoptive father's pocketknife to keep with her just in case that prick tried to attack her again. Lloyd wouldn't miss it until the fall when he went on hunting trips to the interior.

Then, a pilgrimage of sorts to the cemetery seemed in order. When the tensions of real life got to be too much, Jody often went there to seek out her parents' marker. Although only her dad's body was ever found and buried, her mother and father shared the same plaque, and Jody still felt a link with the both of them there, however hopeful it was.

Solace came easier when she imagined being closer to them. Loneliness and a washed-out memory of the only two people she was ever sure had really loved her left her resigned and vulnerable. There seemed few things in this world that could break through that. One of them was coming to this plaque and laying a flower next to the inscription, R & A Fraser - 1995.

The other was Gregg.

Why did you follow me? I told you to leave me alone! She imagined things would have been better if she'd had the knife with her the previous night and frightened Sean off with it. She wouldn't have cut the horny bastard, though. She didn't think she had the gall to do such a thing, but at least Gregg might not have been the wiser and let his over-protectiveness get the better of him. He could be so stubborn about things like that.

When she and Gregg were still kids, maybe five, maybe six, her back was acting up, as it often did, sending waves of searing pain up and down her spine and across her shoulders. She didn't let anyone get close to her wounds, fearing doctors like the plague. But as vehemently as she had argued, Gregg had always refused to go away.

She cried in her room, unable to hide the burning despite keeping herself face down on her pillow, while Gregg knelt on the floor beside her. Then, with movements so slow and sympathetic for a young boy, he put his hand on her shoulder.

Jody knew she had overreacted to his touch by arching her back and squealing the way she did, but up to that point, no one other than her adoptive parents had laid a finger so close to her scars.

Gregg never flinched and never showed signs of repulsion. He held onto her, gently, but with surprising strength and warmth.

Jody relaxed in the end, feeling, of all things, better. She breathed many times before she was sure, and she looked at him.

His dear blue eyes were sparkling like diamonds. He was crying.

Jody didn't understand back then. She was the one who was suffering, not him. Not knowing what else to do or say, she tried smiling.

Gregg smiled back, snurked, then asked, "Are you happy now?"

Jody nodded, but she could be stubborn too. "Why did you do that? I told you to leave me alone."

Gregg looked single-minded. "I'm not going to leave you."

Jody remembered feeling comforted in that moment and how she placed her hand over his, still on her shoulder. "Do you promise?"

"Forever and ever," was his emphatic reply.

I forgot, she admitted, barely registering her current situation. The stretched SUV came to a stop and the engine was silenced.

Trees and brush surrounded them. Behind was a long, narrow path and in front was a worn, dilapidated old house. Ivy consumed the single story home, including the crumbling chimney and the sagging roof.

Her chauffeur stepped out and moved toward the passenger door and Jody. His tall, dark figure sparked an explosion of terror in her. After all, it was he that so brutally murdered Gregg. The way he moved, the ease with which he had sliced Gregg into pieces with his bare hands.

He's not human. The realization was bizarre.

While she waited, breathless, for the stranger to come, something stirred in the long passenger area. Jody jumped in panicked fright. A woman practically slithered from the darkened corner. She had been so still, Jody had somehow forgotten all about her.

But she remembered the wings.

Chapter 11

Illusions

Gregg fathomed the cold and confusion. There was no sense of the passing of time or space, only a perceived notion that it still existed, somehow.

In the consuming darkness, he noticed a tiny glob of heat emerge, swelling, throbbing, seeing it like a hovering droplet of molten metal. He had heard about people having near death experiences and seeing a comforting white light, thinking, believing it was Heaven or God hearkening them to the great beyond.

So what's this?

Gregg could feel it growing, like a splitting headache from his worrying mind. The more he puzzled over it the hotter it got, and suddenly the black nothingness around him oozed into lurid, redder, unnerving things.

And he couldn't stop it.

He tried to fight, though he had no legs to kick, no hands to punch, and no head to turn. He would scream but for the lack of lungs to breathe. Then somehow, by a means he couldn't explain, he felt a heavy strike knock him hard, and the gates of Hell seemed to shut in around him.

Blackness and quiet returned. Slowly a befuddling haze washed over his sights. Shapes began to appear. He had the ability to move again, feeling his hands and arms and legs return.

Something in the mist advanced. He wasn't alone.

Gregg looked up from where he lay. Someone was above him, breathing, skin pressing against his.

His sights cleared and his misgivings turned to excitement as he gazed into Jody's shimmering blue eyes lighting before him. Heat radiated from every part of her glorious body and her lithe skin gleamed. He stayed there, looking up in awe, drinking her in as she leaned over his naked body.

Jody's long silken hair cascaded over her perfect face, burning like fire each time she tickled his bare features with it.

Oh God, how he wanted to kiss those lips! But whenever he moved toward her, she reached out and push him back down, giggling. Her eyes, as deep and as sweeping as a clear sky before dawn, made him a willing hostage, although his hands wanted desperately to grasp her and pull back the meagre clothing that concealed her magnificent body. Her breasts pushed against the sheer fabric before them, leaving little of their sinuous virtue to the imagination.

"How did you get here? Where are we?" The questions pressed their way from his open mouth, but they fell to the side time and again whenever Jody laid her finger upon his lips, her head kinking just a little and her playful smile looking down at him.

It didn't matter. Nothing did, because somehow, at last, in this most precious moment, here she was, here, with him. She pulled herself closer, raising one of her unclad, faultless legs and wrapping it tighter around him, gathering herself fully on top of his hankering flesh. His body tensed, feeling her skin coming together with his, unable to stop the urge to press his body against hers.

She chuckled, nibbling her lip as she looked at him with those bewitching eyes. "Not so fast," she teased softly.

She lowered herself over him, her hair draping around his face and tunnelling his vision until all he could see were her beautiful eyes, adorable nose and those divine red lips. Gregg froze, Jody's hips straddling him firmly, sensing the gentlest touch of her sheathed breasts suspended just above his disrobed chest. She stayed there, grinning, as if waiting.

His head motioned, jerking ever so little toward her. She didn't hold him back this time. Her lips opened and he saw her moistened tongue preparing to receive his. His neck tightened, lifting his head up as he wet his lips.

But something unexpected happened.

His face couldn't reach hers. And before he thought to open his eyes and see again, he felt suddenly alone, and very cold. He gasped, looking about, hearing her voice fret behind him. Gregg turned, leaping up to stand.

He noticed a long, shining rope linked straight into his belly at one end, while the other seemed to skim high and away to some unseen place. He touched it, even pulled on the fibrous line, but it had no effect.

Jody was looking back at him with a pained expression. The sight stung him and he felt his young, eager manhood shrivel. *What is it? What's wrong?* he wondered.

The white expanse around them closed in, becoming shaded, hardening into a long, stone corridor. "Don't leave me!" Jody cried, stepping back toward a bend in the damp, mildew-stained hallway. "You promised me!"

"Jody?"

"Gregg!" She reached, but behind her suddenly stood the man in black, his hands clenching her slight clothing while he flashed an insanely polished smile. With movements that were smooth yet screaming fast, the man ripped away Jody's apparel, spun her around to show her mangled back and dug under her skin with gouging fingers.

Jody's blood gushed as he peeled her open like an orange. Under the gore, Gregg thought he spotted blotched, pale looking clumps and strands of things that simply shouldn't be.

The sound of her screams sent waves of horror up every part of him and he desperately wanted to go to her. But as the man in black took Jody into the hallway, her screams boring deeper into unknown chasms, a cloud emerged above Gregg and from it a reaching hand clamped onto his shoulder, keeping him from storming after her.

"No!" Gregg spat. "I have to find Jody! I have to go to her!"

A crazy woman's familiar tone rang out and Gregg glanced into the centre of the cloud. "Chasing the illusion is what It wants! It's luring you to frigid darkness!"

Auntie Samantha! Her face looked much more assertive than he remembered.

"It's a trap! The Darkness will do anything to ravage the light! Jody doesn't exist here! She must never exist here!"

Gregg stood transfixed in the hallway, confused.

"The Darkness has a shell and Its pull is strong. Its concern begins on the mind, because it is there that confusion reigns so easily, in a thinking tool caught between realities that can process only one. I knew the time was approaching. I knew the Darkness was looking for you. No one would listen. They thought I was insane. So I came here, where the mind is not so hampered, should you be inclined to blow the fog from your thoughts."

Gregg was reeling and he said the first thing that came to him, "But you're dead."

"So are you," she glared impatiently, "unless your body has gained your father's habit of pulling the spirit back."

Bewildered, Gregg felt a tugging and noticed the gleaming cord tighten and stretch.

"My grandmother must help," Sam said. "She has something for you. The key is on the bookshelf! Tell her. Tell her that I forgive her!"

A powerful, sturdy yank pulled him hard and lifted him up and away as an irrefutable awareness overcame him.

Provoked

Life, he realized, would never be the same.

Chapter 12

Consternation

"Damn principles," Iris grunted while turning her Volkswagen into the cemetery. Her conscience, it seemed, had won the best of her and she'd decided to visit the plaque left in memory of Jody's parents and bring a blossom from her treasured garden as a peace-offering for peeking at things she more than likely shouldn't have.

Fascinated by her discovery of the book, she'd continued unwrapping the other two items. The second crate was an utterly foul and disappointing mystery, for inside she found a bloodstained mess: a pair of ghastly old bird wings cached in a black, velvet-like material and nothing more. Rather sickened by it, she put that crate to the side and undid the leather sheathe before she could talk herself out of it. There she found a dark, enigmatic sword. Seeing it again made her skin crawl while thoughts from the past bombarded her.

It was a weapon Jody's father had once brandished, likely taken by his wife without his consent. What put the chill in her veins, though, was remembering an almost identical sword flashed at her front door by a drenched, bedraggled stranger reeking of alcohol the night Jody's parents died. There was one difference in particular, she remembered. The stranger's sword was aglow; practically throbbing with... dare she even think it, life?

The drunk had been looking for Jody's mom and dad, but Iris made it clear they weren't at her house. Oddly, he'd asked for the date and, when told, became incensed, more with himself than Iris it seemed.

He paused, considering something before bouncing back with an anxious, uptight demand. "Should you see this sword again, I pray you, give it to Gregg! The moment it comes into your grasp, you must do it! I've come so far, so very close!"

He turned to leave, appearing defeated, paused, and looked back at her wanting to know the exact time. His eyes flashed with anticipation. Then he grabbed Iris and hugged her like a sentimental child before muttering something bizarre, "Sometimes, to find all the answers we must be mindless."

After that, he ran to his car and peeled out of sight. Iris never saw him, Jody's parents or the sword again. Until this morning.

Now she was eager to put her conscience at rest and return home. "Right, let's get this over with."

To add to her anxiety, Iris didn't like driving much anymore. Her reflexes had become far too slow and her mind tended to wander behind the wheel, especially today.

Iris's head whirred as she parked and reluctantly scanned the area. As far as she could tell, the place was dead quiet. She chuckled. "Everyone must be sleeping."

Towards the front of the sprawling grounds were several tall coniferous trees shadowing a few small monuments into which people laid to rest the cremated remains of their loved ones. The lawns beyond were rather flat and unhindered, the graves marked by plaques rather than headstones. Iris thought the view was at least a little less dreary this way.

Her first attempt to step out was quickly aborted when her right leg got pinned under the steering wheel. "Lord Almighty, you know life has lost its lustre when the only one unwilling to let go of your once greatest asset is a damned cheeky Passat."

She finally got out and hobbled a few yards over the grass, letting the garden's sweet smells and soothing stillness calm her. When she reached the memorial she was searching for, she laid down the flower.

"Hello," she whispered, perhaps to their ghosts if they were listening. "I found your things, at last. I suppose they must be for Jody, except for the sword, so I've been told. Although I can't think for the life of me why Gregg would need one so badly. And what's this book all about, and the bird wings? I must say, you've left your poor girl with a real puzzle."

She quietly admitted that behaving in bewildering ways was pretty much the norm for Jody's parents. They were a downright peculiar pair from the first time she'd laid eyes on them, trudging across her blanketed field during a heavy snowstorm. Really, it was hard enough to forget that winter without their sudden arrival into it.

The cold and snow belonged more to an ice age than the Fraser Valley in the 1990s. Iris worried more than once that her roof would cave-in from all the white stuff piling up on it. And the drifts at the base of the house were so high they reached near the top of her first floor windows on the west and north sides. The roads were bad too, and Iris's driveway was unquestionably impassable.

So when she glanced through her sliding glass doors at the sound of a strange man's distressed calls, she nearly fell over backward by what she saw. He was tall and broad, his dark hair long, his beard thick. Upon his back, Iris caught sight of the teed end of a sword and he held a striking young woman in his solid arms, her golden hair long and twining down the front of them both, the loose ends blowing in the wind.

They wore clothes that belonged more on people from a different time, in a different climate, very far from Fort Langley. The woman's skimpy-looking gown fluttered about her body over what few parts of skin it covered, the fine airy cloth as white as the buffeting snow. His attire was much more threatening. Dark, thick leather covered his torso and a kilt-like skirt wrapped around his waist and draped over his legs to his knees. His thick neck was harnessed by a heavily clad ornament that spread over his shoulders and his muscular arms were bare.

The trespassers wanted in, badly, but Iris was hesitant. The man pleaded, and she could see the woman was in agony. He said she was pregnant.

Finally, Iris's sense of compassion won the day. Besides, if that great big man with the damn sword really wanted to, he could have just smashed his way in and killed Iris in a heartbeat. No one would have known what had happened to her for days in that storm.

Life just kept getting weirder after that, she mused.

She realized the peace and fresh air at the cemetery was doing her some good. Perhaps it hadn't been such a bad idea to go for a drive after all.

At least, that's what she thought until she started hearing some very unnerving groans.

"Mmm, no."

The voice was so inexcusably familiar it made Iris's ears stand up and quiver. Her eyes, scanning at first, started dashing this way and that.

"I have to find Jody! Jody!"

"Please don't be Gregg," Iris beseeched the blue sky above her. She glanced over and noticed a hole in the ground. A fresh grave. "Please, please, please."

Suddenly, with a demonic sounding grunt, a pair of hands grasped the edge of the pit, quickly followed by her rattled-looking great-grandson. Gregg's eyes looked like they were swimming as he tried to climb up. He lost his balance and slipped back into the earth.

Iris, already numbed by the day she was having, looked down crossly at the plaque by her knees, curled her lips and took the flower back. She unravelled herself slowly into an upright, standing position. Well, mostly upright, and she limped towards the hole in the ground.

Gregg must have gotten his wits about him by then because his second attempt to get free was much more successful. He leapt up and cleared the edge completely, landing square on the wet green grass. He stood much straighter than Iris, but there was something Iris had much more of than he did at the moment.

"Where the devil are your clothes?"

Gregg nearly fell back into the grave when she spoke. He caught his breath, looked at her with an absolutely baffled expression, then glanced down at himself and gasped, "Aah!"

"Your hands are hardly a wise choice for daytime apparel, boy, especially when you're going out for a walk," Iris lectured at his ineffective attempt to be decent. "What happened to you? What are you doing here?"

"I..." These were clearly more complicated questions to answer than Iris must have realized. "I... uhh..."

"Is there someone else in that hole with you?" Iris queried. Maybe it was some morbid fad with young people to execute perverted labours in other people's final resting spots.

Gregg's odd facial contortion gave her the answer she needed much faster than his ability to speak did.

"Right," she said in all seriousness, wiping her brow, relieved. "So it's no then, is it? Good. That makes things a bit better. Or, maybe it doesn't? Come along then, get your doodle into my Passat before you become some sort of unhealthy sensation on YoungTube."

"YouTube," Gregg corrected.

Iris waved her hand. "We'll talk in the car."

Chapter 13

Meaning

Gregg counted each agonizing second before his great-grandma finally pulled her car into his driveway. He bounded hurriedly for the house sporting one of his Grammy's shawls around his waist. "No one's looking! No one's looking!" he kept telling himself as he rooted under a hibiscus plant in the garden where the family kept a virtually submerged clay pot in the dirt. Inside was a spare key and as soon as Gregg had it, he started fumbling with the door lock.

"Gaw," he heard Grammy declare. "It really has been a long time since I've come here. Laura's doing a smashing job on the garden. And did Patrick reseal the driveway? I remember when you were just learning to ride your bicycle on this. It all looks much better now."

Gregg didn't say anything; he wanted to get through that damned door so bad he was shaking.

When at last it opened, he hurried up the steps and raced to his room to put on some clothes. He couldn't remember the last time it felt so good to slide blue denim over his bare legs. He heard his great-grandma enter and call up to him, "The air's still a little stale in here though! No drafts, I guess. Did you need a hand with any... *ooh*. Have you added more steps since I last visited?" For the first time, she sounded apprehensive.

Gregg came out and peered curiously at her from the top stair. Her face seemed to light up a little. "You look taller from down here."

His head tilted to one side. Grammy was such an odd old woman. He wondered if it was some natural quirk in the bloodline. In all the craziness of his day thus far, she was making it all appear trite.

But that was wrong. Nothing about today was trivial. He clawed the grooved skin on his forehead, focusing his thoughts and emotions. "They took Jo, Grammy," he said as resolutely as he could. "I need to find her!"

Grammy did so well at keeping her cool, it was tough to read if she was bothered or not. "I know, dear. You told me in the car." She turned and sat on the step.

"Well, shouldn't we call the cops or something?" Gregg asked, coming down to meet her.

"What would you like to tell them, dear?" Her voice was dry. "That a naked woman with leather wings and pointy teeth hit you so hard that you bled through your clothes, yet you have no marks on your skin to prove it? Nor do you have any clothes! Or that a tall, handsome man dressed all in black with fingernails like knives cut you up into tiny pieces and left you for dead in an open grave?

Inexplicably however, you got up without any sign of detriment that could be used as evidence, not even a beastly zit?"

Gregg's head started whirring again. "How did I not die?"

Great-grandma appeared disappointed. "It's called hallucinating, Greggory. Poor Laura will be devastated to find out you've been doing Lord-knows-what."

"I don't use drugs!" Gregg shouted angrily. "And it was not a hallucination!"

Grammy raised her hands submissively. "Alright then, it wasn't drugs. That being the case, what else can you remember?" He couldn't tell if she was actually interested or not.

"Jody..." Gregg summoned the memory as best he could. "After I blacked out, things kind of morphed into a dream. At least, I think that's what it was. Jo was there. It was white. No walls. At some point, though, things changed. It got dark and cold. We were in a cave, small, a wintry feel to the place. The man in black took Jody from me into some passage." Then he lit on something else. "I wanted to follow, but someone held me back. It was Auntie Sam."

Saying her name sent Gregg's thoughts back to her funeral when he had escaped to the old lane only to be found by his great-grandma. "You told me she wanted to keep me safe, that she was terrified and that I was in danger. What did that mean, Grammy?"

The old woman's expression went wide. "What are you saying, that you saw Sam in the afterlife?" Her eyes turned sharp in a second flat. She was definitely not kidding around now. "I don't like the direction this is going, Greggory. It's unkind to mock the dead."

"Does this look like the face of a prankster?"

Grammy's stature seemed to decay. "This is getting unhinged," she said, perturbed. "Alright, I'll tell you. But I swear, boy, if you so much as snicker at any of it..."

"There's not a snicker in me, Grams. Not a single one."

His great-grandma let out a heavy breath. "Samantha had an unusual perspective about life, and death. She believed, like some, that we are all one - united, not like members of the same family, but like elements of a much grander coalesced entity. Like a candle in the sun, each of us, everyone.

"But there is a darkness rising that threatens to snuff out that sun, one flame at a time. It is that darkness that had Sam worried. It's not something that is changeless or simple, but is alive, dizzyingly astute and resourceful. It preys on us in our minds. And when we die, the darkness takes us, keeping us from the sun, until that heat and light are lost in an eternal nothingness, forever.

"You must understand that Sam never really got over her attack, Gregg. She scarcely slept or ate. She was delusional."

"I don't care," Gregg said. "What else can you tell me?"

"Well...," Grammy shrugged, "She believed that there was a way to stop this 'darkness', as she called it. That there would be candles born with divine attributes that, given time to grow, could outwit and engage the darkness, shining their light where none exists. Samantha was convinced this calling was yours, and Jody's."

Gregg wasn't sure if he was listening anymore. His mind was moving too fast, unable to absorb anything. "This is too much." He was getting lightheaded. "When I saw Auntie Sam in my dream, she put her hand on me and told me something. What was it? Something about the darkness having a shell? Its pull is strong?"

Grammy looked like she had seen a ghost. "How, how did you know that? Did Laura tell you? I know I haven't, and Laura's the only other one who would know..."

"No, Grammy. I told you. I saw Auntie Sam. But I didn't have much time. What is this shell?"

"A beast," she stammered. "A colossal monster whose insides are complete, eternal darkness. Sam said it was hidden, but its gravity is always on us, drawing us to it like a black hole in space." Grammy could hardly speak now; her typical stranglehold on her emotions was failing. "I can hardly feel my toes right now. If this is all true, what can it mean?"

Something sprang to Gregg's mind. "She said you must help me. That you're supposed to give me something."

"Me?" She had an odd, sheepish expression on her face. "What?"

"I don't know, but the key is in the bookcase. Does that help?"

Grammy's facade was getting markedly worse. "This isn't happening."

"And Auntie Sam wanted me to tell you that she forgives you."

Great-grandma's face crumbled. "Oh, my dear Sam! She worked, no, obsessed for years. We never gave her the benefit of the doubt. I stopped listening to my precious granddaughter. What an awful person I was to be so cruel, to think so lowly of her. And she did it. To think that she's put herself in a place to keep you safe, in death!"

"Grammy, what are you supposed to give me?"

She seemed at odds still. "Well, it's hard to explain really. It's so impossible to make sense out of it. How did she know that I would find...? Oh, dear Sam." Grammy looked painfully apologetic. "We thought she had gone mad. I tried. I did my very best to be supportive, but she just made no sense." Great-gran rolled her head, huffing, "This can't be happening. I must be a silly old coot! This whole course of events cannot possibly be happening!"

She got to her feet, escaping the confines of the house's small entranceway and stepped into the sun, her dark blue eyes glaring fiercely into his mom's cultivated plants.

Gregg followed. "Grams, what am I supposed to do?"

She huffed a few more times, as if the words were too heavy to blow past her wrinkled lips.

"What?"

"Damn it, Gregg! Save our souls!"

Gregg's mouth gaped for a minute. "'kay, what?"

"I don't know where she got it from, or why," Grammy conceded, "but she utterly believed it." Her head must have been getting heavy on her old neck, because she couldn't seem to raise her gaze high enough to meet his. "She kept repeating it, over and over."

Gregg lost his breath and leaned upon the open doorframe. His brain felt—as odd as it was—empty. It was as if he was falling again, except this time his eyes were open and he knew he was still standing. "From what?" the words tripped over his tongue.

Grammy shrugged. "How should I know?" She moved away from him, this time heading toward her car. "You didn't know how traumatized she was, Greggory. I should have been better to her. We all should have been better. I didn't believe. It's the very same reaction I had with you today. Honestly, when I drove the car out of that cemetery, I had all sorts of lurid explanations running through my head about what really happened to you. I kind of hoped one of them would be true."

Gregg didn't feel like he'd hit the bottom yet. His feet were light, unbalanced. All the while he kept wondering about who this man in black was and what he wanted with Jody.

He went over what happened in the cemetery as his great-grandma kept running on about something in regards to faith and doubt.

When Gregg had first approached Jody at the cemetery this morning, the man in black was growling at her, "The book! Where is *The Book of the Nornir*?"

"Grams?" Gregg jostled her, interrupting her train of thought. "The man in black kept bugging Jo about a book."

The lines on her face jumped. "Book?"

"*The Book of the Nornir*?" He hoped he remembered it properly. For some reason, old myths and characters he'd learned about in school, called Norns, came to mind.

Strange and bizarre did not begin to describe the range of Great-gran's facial twists. "Nornir?" she gasped. "My God, that sounds familiar. Could it be? Yes. Yes, I think it is. *The Book of the Nornir*. I still can't believe this is happening. At least, it's not easy to accept. I mean, who can blame me? I'm just an old woman."

She grabbed Gregg from the doorway and pulled him to the car. "I need a priest. I need a guru. I need to get back to the house and I need to show you something. And then, I will need a very big glass of wine!"

Chapter 14

David

For Dave, school began that day as it most often did: with a discomforting ambition to get the hell out of that jail.

The drudgeries of a dutiful life bent on accountability and trained accomplishment were never that attractive to him. Whooping it up with his mates was all he really thought about and this singular conviction made him naturally accepted among a certain uncomplicated league of characters.

Dave was smart enough to see it. He appreciated the shallowness of his behaviour, and the potential for immediate and long-term disaster, but he believed forever and a day that he would steer clear of any real problems.

Lately though, his actions were becoming more reckless, and he noticed a deepening pit in him wanting to be filled with something greater. *But what?*

He never seemed to have the time to focus on it much. His hectic life didn't allow for it and his brooding faded as he cheerlessly prepared himself for the day's more scholarly lessons.

"The sword of Damocles…" Dave sat at his desk, while the teacher bellowed theatrically before the class. "Legend or myth, it is a Greek anecdote that does well to illuminate the human experience of… what?" He scanned the room, no doubt looking for the daftest expression amongst his pupils' faces. "David?"

"Damn it." Why couldn't he just be allowed to stare out the bloody window and think about Kirk's upcoming party Friday night?

The teacher glared. "Pardon?"

"Nothing." Reluctantly, Dave straightened himself up in his seat. He glanced around the class. Most everyone appeared neutral to his situation, but the two girls across the room had their eyes on him. They were almost certainly impressed with the way his favourite striped shirt made his muscles bulge when he flexed.

Leah, the drop-dead-gorgeous red-haired girl, looked particularly moved and Dave couldn't help but angle his back and arms for another drawn-out tightening. She smiled at him and he threw her a cool, controlled acknowledgement.

"David!" the teacher barked and Dave sat bolt upright.

"Hmm? Oh, yeah. Right." He almost lost his composure there, but remembered the importance of looking impertinent and quickly put on a facade of aloofness. "Uhm, I don't know. The experience of life sucking?"

The teacher pondered the answer, rolling his eyes, considering, until he finally wrinkled his nose and grunted, "Explain."

Dave, of course, hadn't a clue. *Eff-off will yuh? What do I care what the stupid story is about?* He sat dumbly, letting his vapid expression do the talking, hoping that his persona of cool stuck to its guns.

"Now, I can see where you're coming from David," the teacher said, breaking the silence. "I'm not saying that you're wrong. You could be right actually... I suppose. A lot of Greek philosophical writings seem to cling to a similar theme. No one is truly happy with their life until faced with the perils of death. Suddenly, life doesn't 'suck' so much. I'm glad to see that you read it, David. I'm impressed."

Dave's eyebrows climbed up his forehead. "Thanks."

It was during the lunch break that Dave noticed something was amiss. He was in the mood for gloating, but Gregg wasn't sitting at his usual spot in the corner of the cafeteria. *Hmm, he's always here.* Gregg had taken off early that morning; Dave had a fuzzy memory of it. It was something about smothering Jody, he figured. Dave didn't know why he bothered thinking about it. He couldn't care less.

But the fact that he caught himself scanning the room for Jody too, made him suppose otherwise. *Gregg's never missed a day of school.* Dave wondered if his brother had finally managed to get nearer to the girl he so adored. The pious momma's boy. What would make him skip out today?

He nearly dropped his tray of food as his mind tripped over nightmarish images of Gregg actually getting it on with Jody. Super-hot Jody. "No way!" he grumbled. But he didn't dwell on it for long, because the second Leah walked into the place his attention was fully distracted.

"Grr, I'd like to nuzzle up to that." He lusted at her curvy figure. Moving like a leopard through low-lying brush, Dave crossed the busy lunchroom, sneaking up behind Leah to pat her on the bottom. "Hello, my lovely. What are you doing this Friday night?"

By lunch's end Dave had secured a date for the party, and wanting to gloat, he parked his butt near Gregg's locker to wait him out. *We'll see who has the bragging rights now.*

The bell rang and the hordes around him dispersed into their many classes, but Dave remained. *He's not coming,* he realized. *He's really not here.*

Two of Dave's comrades came strolling up the hall. Michael was a rather tall, mid-sized fellow who always wore a black leather jacket with tassels, even in the dog days of summer. He had straight, long, blonde hair and a patchy layer of peach fuzz across his face, while Kirk sported shorter, darker hair with a dinky rattail at the back. At 17, Kirk already had a bulge growing under his shirt that everyone was sure evidenced his habit of drinking more beer than water. All three of them were missing the same Metalwork class.

Michael threw out a disarming smile. "And how is Daveyboy today?"

J. Edward Vance

Dave wasn't sure how he felt at the moment. Gregg's life was built on routine and it bothered him that something might have knocked his stepbrother from it. But once more, he couldn't aim his attention at it for long.

Kirk leaned into him with an inquisitive look. "Gaw, you look terrible man. Doesn't he look terrible, Mike?"

"Yes, Kirk, I believe he does. Absolutely terrible. Horrid, you might say," he carried on animatedly. "What do you make of it?"

"I'm not sure, to be quite honest. But I think I know how to break him of his dazed state," Kirk snickered. "Or is it that I know how to help make his daze more enjoyable? I forget."

Michael wrapped his arm around Dave's thick, unmoving neck. "Brilliant! I like your thinking. What's up, Daveyboy? Steroids no good this week?"

"I don't use steroids, you dorktard," Dave retorted firmly.

"He speaks!" Kirk quipped.

Michael hastily gripped Dave's shoulders. "Quickly now, before we lose you, what's your next class my good man?"

"Uhm..." Dave's face wrenched. His friends could be such idiots.

Michael chuckled. "Oh yeah, it's Metal, right? I forgot. You're in our class."

Kirk rolled his eyes, exaggerating it with a theatrical sigh. "Egad, man! He's fading faster than I feared! We need to do something, Dr. Mike."

"Good grades, Dr. Kirk! You couldn't be more right. This fellow needs attention, stat! We'll need at least 333

86

millilitres of Canadian lager, fast!" Moving with haste, they both guided Dave toward the school exit.

Resistant at first, Dave's efforts soon wavered. "But, it's not even 1:00."

Michael scoffed, "Yes, yes, your concern regarding the importance of attending our local house of learning is most admirable, my boy. But there are some life-lessons that can't be taught in a bloody classroom."

As they entered the parking lot and approached Michael's pimped grey 1979 Camaro, it became obvious that Dave no longer needed to be dragged along. *It's only Metalwork.*

Michael opened the passenger door, letting Kirk pull the front seat forward and hop into the back. He then ducked to the other side and out of sight in the driver's seat.

"Here." Kirk handed Dave a cold can of beer, pulling into view a small cooler filled nicely with a six-pack. "Take one of these now, followed by another right after. If you're feeling any better, keep drinking. If not, we'll have to bring in the hard stuff. How are you with vodka?"

Bewildered and surprised, Dave wondered how he'd managed to get himself into such a weird situation. But rather than analyze his predicament further, he simply gave in, too pleased to refuse, and practically inhaled it.

"Can I have another one?" he asked. Michael and Kirk laughed while Dave quickly set to work on his second drink. "So, is everything still on for Friday?"

Mike and Kirk exchanged a glance, bummed. "Sorry, Daveyboy," Kirk said annoyed. "We can have the party, if you still want, but our source of booze has dried up."

"But your cousin always gets what we need from the liquor store," Dave fussed.

Mike's cousin was twenty-three and had been working behind the counter for the last six months. For a moderately inflated price, he'd get Mike all the beer he wanted.

"He got canned last Friday," Mike admitted sadly. "Turns out he had been buying sauce for other minors too, and he finally got caught. The guy's busted and we're drinking our last cans as we speak."

"Crap!" Dave kicked under the dash. "This Friday was going to be so awesome."

"We can still have the party, Dave. Mike and I finished getting rid of the scraps of hay and horse crap in the barn yesterday. Now, if I can just get rid of Mum and Dad," Kirk joked.

"Well, you still in?" Michael asked.

"Are you kidding?" Dave scoffed. "It's not the same without the boozathon. Damn it. There has got to be another way. I gotta date this Friday and there's a hankerin' in me to see some liquor-flavoured boobs."

"Listen to you. Hoping to turn Kirk's barn into some animal breeding ground, eh? Who's the girl?" Michael probed.

"Leah Nasstics." Dave couldn't believe his good luck.

"Leah Nasty?" Kirk looked so jealous. "Gaw, I love redheads! You bastard! I dream of doing all sorts of objectionable things with her in my sleep."

"I don't wait till I'm sleeping," Michael added. "And I prefer guys. She's a game-changer. Man, Dave. You must drink Holy Water out of the tap at home or something.

That old, bewhiskered, robed guy in the sky really loves you."

"Yeah," Kirk agreed, but his eyes were distant suddenly. "But you know, notwithstanding the old image of the Divine One, do you think God should look more like Chuck Norris or Pink?"

Michael massaged his brows and sighed. "We've talked about this a thousand times, Kirk. I'm supposed to be the gay one."

"Look, either way, God would kick some serious ass. What do you think,"—Kirk patted Dave on the shoulder—"God's lovechild?"

Dave chugged the last of his second can of beer and groaned, wondering just how the conversation had veered off in this direction. "I think you guys are cracked. I don't have time for your God-babble. I am my own God. This body is my temple and this brain is my minister. With them, I create my own heaven here on Earth. And I'm going to make Leah a part of that."

Dave licked his chops, envisioning how things would go with her, especially after a few drinks. "There is no divinity, boys. Only tangibility. I'll keep making my own way and God can keep minding his own business."

Michael and Kirk glanced curiously at each other before they both looked at him, bewildered.

Dave glared back. "What?"

"What's it like? Being you?"

"I don't know," Dave snarled. "Refreshing?"

Michael gave him a nudge. "C'mon, Stephen Hawking. Open your eyes. Life is the definition of magic. You have plenty to be thankful for. It can't just be an accident that, well, you're not a bad looking guy. Athletic, fashionable..."

"Dude," Kirk cautioned, covering his ears. "Can't you just sext him?"

"I said he's not bad looking, not do-me gorgeous, you friggin' homophobe. Jeez, what do you have against my people? Remember, Trish and Monica are gay and you can't stop begging them to let you watch. And I don't mean ogling as they chat over lunch. God help you if you live long enough to get your prostate checked."

"Bah! One day they'll say yes, I can feel it." Kirk patted Dave on the shoulder again. "It's okay, man. You can blame your parents, if you want."

"Why?" Dave asked. "I don't need to blame anybody. My dad is more interested in his own life than mine and my mom pissed off when I was like two, or something."

"What do you mean?" Michael asked.

"She decided she loved drugs more than me," Dave recalled, crushing the empty can in his hand. "That bitch and the God that made her can go straight to Hell for all I care. Now, are you guys gonna prattle on like a coop full of hens, or are we gonna figure out how we're going to find some booze?"

Chapter 15

Worm

Ligeia folded her wings awkwardly, doing what she could to move along the winding trail without snagging them on low, broken branches that always tried to scratch her. "I hate this place!" she groaned, longing for warmer locales.

Earlier, Damianos had hauled the screaming girl out of the SUV and dragged her behind the house. Enveloped in perpetual shade, it sat on the fringes of a long forgotten, overgrown wood. A horse they'd stolen from a nearby hobby farm was tied up there, waiting for their return and Damianos had thrown the girl across its back.

"I hate how he looks at her," Ligeia grumbled under her breath.

She was forced to take up the rear as they followed the narrow path going deeper into the green shelter.

To make the experience even more indignant, the horse's long, wispy tail kept darting ahead of her, as if the stupid beast was parading his huge horse ass in her face. Ligeia glared at the girl's tiny, wobbling body, wondering, *what makes her so special?*

The jivita was ridiculously concerned for this snippy girl. It rattled Ligeia's mind why a creature so rare— practically mythical to her until this morning—would bind itself to a pathetic human girl sandbagged by imperfections on her back and in her demeanour.

She does smell good though, Ligeia considered. But Jivitas did not indulge themselves upon a living body's flesh. At least, she didn't think so.

The girl hugged herself, as if to smooth the goose bumps across her skin, and kept glancing nervously in all directions. "What are you people? Where are we going?"

At the sound of her shivery voice, Ligeia wanted to slit the girl's throat. "Quiet!" she warned, and the moment the space around them opened enough, Ligeia flapped her wings and pushed herself on top of the horse's back.

The girl shrieked as Ligeia grasped onto her, hissing, "Why? Why does your Gregg try to shelter you so?"

"What?" Jody's body cringed and dodged, but Ligeia was not about to let her fall away.

"Do you satisfy him well?" Ligeia was wary. "How does someone like you please a jivita?"

From the front of the horse's head, Damianos came into view. "Now, now, my love..." he started, "Do not assume the girl is the jivita's whore. There is more than one way to win someone's heart and devotion."

"But no other way is as effective, my love," Ligeia responded coolly. "Would you not agree?"

Damianos tightened his lips before turning his attention toward the girl and smiling. He laid his powerful hand upon her leg.

"Seduction, Lie. An allure that is more instinctive, almost accidental. It is the worm on the hook, creating high hopes where before there were none. It is the most potent source of attraction."

Ligeia stiffened, seeing Damianos's flagrant move to show who the superior predator was. But the girl rejected his touch outright, flinching back with a pitiful, petulant noise. It made Ligeia grin.

Damianos's face remained composed, inviting even, and Ligeia felt her body tense. *Damn, he's good.*

Her thoughts reflected back, as they often did, to the way he used to look at her. Damianos was so handsome, fit, ruthless. He was everything Ligeia had ever wanted in a partner. The way he beheld her with those haunting eyes, she could tell he lusted for her, hungering for her like nothing else. She couldn't help but fall madly in love.

They used to hunt together, each one trying to outdo the other. She would ensnare the man-quarry: filling their ears with her song, teasing their eyes with her body, until they came so close they could reach out and touch her rapturous flesh. How she savoured the sudden moment when those men awoke from her spell only to realize it was too late.

She never admitted it openly, but what she enjoyed most was watching Damianos do the same with the woman-quarry. To her, he was the epitome of erotic attraction. To women, he was a god. From behind a door, around a corner, under a shadow, he would appear as if from a misted dream. His smouldering eyes trapped his prey willingly and his deep, suave voice almost blew them off their feet. He would beguile them with his confident smile and sweep them to their doom in his powerful arms.

More often than not, their gorging would energize them, creating physical surges of desire that coursed through their bodies. She'd long for him to take her like he did his victims and he'd tease her, baiting her with his charm until she could bear it no longer., Then his natural cruelty would take over.

Their love was violent. Scraping, clawing, screaming. He always seemed to know just what to do to make her peak with bliss, something no man had ever done before. He was the only one she'd known that could control her so... energetically. He was her drug, and the high was far too wondrous to be discouraged by the harrowing lows that followed. Recovering from their lovemaking could take days. When it was really good, it took much longer.

Now, since that voice filled his head with rubbish about justice and whatnot, there was not much left of that carnal passion in his dark eyes. What excitement remained seemed to be locked onto that dim little girl. *I bet the jivita looks at her the same way.*

A small sunken patch of land sheltered by the looming forest was before them. The perpetual gloom of moss-laden tree trunks and branches here made an adequate clearing beneath for two sizeable wall tents.

Ligeia skipped off the horse's back and stretched, detesting the constant chill. Damianos took the girl into his arms and opened the nearest tent flap. That was when she started revolting.

"What are you doing? Let me go!"

He manoeuvred her around just so and placed her, belly down, in the middle of a cot, pinning her there with his knee. Ignoring her outbursts and struggles, he ordered Ligeia to bind the girl's limbs and secure them to the four corners of the bed with the bungee cords he had stored with other useful things in a box left on the dirt ground.

"Oh my God!" Her voice was frantic with terror. "Jesus, what are you doing?" She cried and squealed like a live pig about to be skewered for the fire.

Ligeia took pleasure in wrapping the cords tight around her wrists and ankles. The girl could scarcely move, but that didn't stop her from trying.

With a grunt, Damianos's poise vanished and he flashed his clawed hands behind her head, slowly grasping onto her clothing before ripping her shirt and bra away, wrenching the fabric hard from under her and throwing it to the side.

The girl's body tensed and arched, stressing to its limits. Her voice panicked. The sight made Ligeia's heart race, strengthening the urge to pounce and attack that slight, tempting neck. After all her fussing, her naked skin glistened with sweat, releasing an almighty fragrance into the musky tent that practically dragged Ligeia nearer.

"No one will hear you, my child." Damianos leaned close, almost frothing at the mouth. "And if you do not calm yourself post haste, my syrēne and I might not be able to keep ourselves from..."

He pulled back the long white-blonde hair and let out his tongue like a thirsty dog, licking her slowly from her shoulder to the back of her ear.

"Oh God! Please stop! No!"

Damianos breathed deeply. "You are such a good worm."

Chapter 16

Separation

Damianos went over the voice's commands in his mind as he stood alone next to a tall, moss-laden hemlock. Those mysterious instructions throbbed in his head. Their influence was near constant now, like a never-ending drone.

"To find the way, it is imperative for you to locate *The Book of the Nornir*. You must come to a place that gave birth to what you know as The Big Bang. That is where you come from. All of you."

"But where is it?" He shook in frustration. For the last hour he had asked the girl pointed questions about the book and she seemed to know nothing.

Damianos had been a hunter for a long time. He prided himself on his observant style, learning how humans behave, what their strengths and weaknesses were. He thought himself well capable of discerning their shifty undertones as truth or fabrications.

"She doesn't know." He believed her.

"What now, my love?" Ligeia approached, impatient as usual.

"Search her home," Damianos concluded. "Tear it apart, if you must. Find that book."

Ligeia's eyes narrowed. "And what will you do?"

"Someone must stay here with the girl."

"Indeed!" The syrēne had that look again. Her shoulders spread apart some, standoffish. "I'm sure you'll treat her well."

"At least when you return with the book we can be certain the child will still be alive." Damianos was not about to leave Ligeia with her.

"You don't trust me?"

"I know what makes you tick, my love." Damianos grinned. "Only a brief risk analysis was needed. I think it best that you go and I remain."

A sly smirk spread across Ligeia's coaxing face. "Tell me, my love, what does this book look like?"

He swallowed his annoyance. The voice had never explained how to identify the book.

"Is it big? Is it small?" Ligeia was teasing. "Does it look in any way similar to this one?"

She pulled out her pocket-sized text and fanned the yellowed, weathered pages. It was sadly worn, its covers and binding made of animal hide, while the inside pages were a tight gathering of delicately shaven tree bark.

Ligeia treasured it, most often keeping it secret and hidden. It was the syrēnes book of spells and magic; a gift passed down from her mother. Even Damianos was not allowed to hold it.

"Is it thin? Is it thick?" she went on.

Damianos huffed. "You are more trouble than I care to deal with."

"But you do." She hid the book under her cloak again and spread her arms around him before whispering into his ear with a sultry voice, "For good reason."

Damianos struggled, but managed to hold off the sudden urge to take her into his grasp and ravage her. *Not now*, he told himself. He pulled his head back and looked into her broiling eyes. "Very well," he relented. "I will go to the girl's home. But I swear to you, if any harm befalls her I shall cut off your pretty head."

Ligeia appeared disappointed, but her composure soon returned. "I promise." She backed away, hauntingly crossing her left breast with her finger.

Damianos paused, still unsure if he could trust her or not. He started down the trail that would take him to the edge of the wood, then turned back to Ligeia. She stood there, again with that bewildering smirk; it unsettled him.

"Spend the time distracting yourself," Damianos suggested. "See what is written in your book about the jivita. We've not seen the last of him."

The expression on Ligeia's face changed, igniting more misgivings in Damianos's mind. "Be careful, Lie. Your features give you away. They might lead to suspicions of your faithfulness."

"Bite your gorgeously long tongue," Ligeia bristled.

"He is not one of us."

Ligeia rejected the argument, but then her eyes gleamed. "He can be much worse."

Chapter 17

Murder

Damianos walked cautiously to the roadway, knowing how much the whale-of-an-SUV would stand out on Langley's rural streets. Ligeia wasn't coming with him this time, so he didn't need the extra space.

Instead, he waited until a perfect stranger stopped to pick him up, something Damianos was used to.

"Where are you headed?" the rather attractive brunette in the driver's seat asked, eying him appreciatively. It was obvious his charm was having its usual effect.

Damianos leaned toward the open window and smiled. "It's not safe to pick up hitchhikers," he warned as the woman opened the passenger door.

Thirty minutes later, Damianos left the car down a dead-end road and lured the woman into a long, winding ravine with the promise of wild, decadent passion. *I did try to dissuade her*, he mused as he deposited what was left of her under the stretching fingers of a blackberry bush.

He cleaned himself in the lapping stream that flowed there and followed it until he recognized where he was. Making his way swiftly now, he found the yard he was looking for, walked across the lawn to an open sliding glass door, and let himself in.

"Who are you?" a female voice surprised him. Damianos looked beyond the kitchen entrance to a short round woman, wearing nothing but a towel.

"My apologies, miss," Damianos bowed his head. "I was hoping for some assistance."

"To do what?" She was unusually abrupt with him and started moving for the phone next to the fridge.

Damianos ramped up his bewitchery. "I am a friend of Jody's, you're adopted daughter." This sort of thing always seemed to happen after a good feeding. His magnetism waned, demanding more effort.

The woman paused. "I know who she is. What are you doing befriending a sixteen-year old girl? Are you a paedophile? Can't you find anyone your own damned age?"

This was going to be harder than he expected. "You have a sharp tongue." He wielded his typically inviting smile. It always worked wonders with women. "Tell me, how old are you?"

It was a stretch, but he kept his voice and features controlled, *Come on, you ugly bat. Look at me. Look at me.*

She scrutinized him alright, shaking her head as if to break the start of his trance. "I'm a happily married woman." Her eyes jetted to the fridge door. There was a picture of her, Jody, and a big bear of a man who was most likely her husband.

"A wonderful family portrait," Damianos said admiringly. "Jody's lucky to have you both."

He moved closer, enticement in every step. *She's cracking.* Her face showed more hesitation, her feet seemed stuck to the floor.

"That, that's close enough," she warned, but it was indecisive.

Damianos put his hands on her bare shoulders and felt the last of her resolution peel away. She shuddered, then let go of her towel and put her arms around his waist in a noose-like embrace. It was a jolt strong enough to make Damianos wheeze.

"Jody's at school for a while yet and Lloyd won't be home until 5:30." Her voice was excited now. "Come on, handsome. Let's see what little old Lois can assist you with."

In the bedroom, the minutes that followed were among the most unproductive Damianos could remember. *This woman is relentless.* He was tempted to kill her, if for no other reason than to stop her mauling him, but he kept up his suave act. He gently prodded Lois about stashes of old books in the house. Perhaps there were items of sentimental value for Jody. Something. Maybe Lois would let him have a quick look around the place.

"Why all the talking?" She kept complaining, yanking on Damianos's black coat while kneeling on her king-sized bed. "We can do that later, if you have any strength left."

This is ridiculous. Damianos was not prepared to let this stout, middle-aged woman rough him up. Killing her should not have been an option; you couldn't ask questions of a dead person. Still, he pondered the matter more than once. *I won't leave too much blood*, he told himself. *I'll be quick!*

Lois growled like a rabid dog then jumped clean off the bed into Damianos's arms. "Whee!"

He finally had enough and threw Lois flat onto the bed, but she only appeared more delighted.

"Oh, I like it rough!" she screamed. "I can't believe I'm doing this, but I want you so bad."

"Do you?" Damianos challenged. "How bad?" He removed his coat and unbuttoned his black shirt, showing off his powerful torso to Lois's obvious enjoyment. He spread her legs and set his knees between them, moving his hand very slowly up the length of her inner thigh.

"Oh, God!" she panted. "Very bad. Very, very bad!"

"Then tell me what I want to know and I will bring you a sense of bliss you'd never dreamed possible," he whispered, skimming his face low over her body, letting his warm breath enchant the surface of her naked skin from below her navel to the length of her neck.

Finally, he murmured into her ear in the most seductive manner he could, "Jody possesses a book, perhaps handed down from her parents. It is of great interest to me. I want it, more than you want... this." He gently stroked between her legs and her back arched in eager response.

"Don't stop, please," she moaned.

"Tell me where it is."

"I don't know."

"Tell me." Damianos stopped being gentle. "I need to know, now!" He pinched her.

She gasped at first, then gritted her teeth in evident pain. "I don't know!"

"That's not good enough, Lois," he growled, clamping down harder. She tried to squirm, but he wouldn't let her. "She has the book, and I want it!"

"Okay! Okay!" Lois cried. "I'm telling you the truth. I don't know about any book of hers." Her facial features appeared to race for a better reply. Finally, she pleaded, "Why don't you check with her Godmother?"

Damianos let go. "Godmother?"

"Yes. Jody's parents gave her a godmother," Lois blubbered, her hands cupping between her legs. "But she was too old to take care of an infant and decided to let us have Jo instead. She keeps in touch. Maybe she has it."

"Where might I find this godmother?"

Lois rolled onto her side in a fetal position. "She lives in the village somewhere. I don't know exactly. I don't visit. She and her family are all a bit strange for me. We put up with them, that's all."

Damianos flared his hands, ready to inflict more suffering. "You don't seem to know very much, Lois. I already have an idea what kind of wife you are; now I'm learning more about your capacity as a mother."

"No!" she wailed. "Please, don't hurt me." She made a meek attempt to point with her finger at the wall behind the bed's headboard. "Over there," she said. "Check over there."

Damianos was confused.

"The Brogans, Patrick and Laura..." she added between pathetic breaths. "They live next door."

Again, Damianos was puzzled, but knowing the jivita lived there, his hopes for a simple progression of things were quickly vanishing.

"What does Jody's godmother have to do with them?" He considered killing Lois in a very untidy way now, so as to send a clear, compelling message to the monster next door. Damianos's visit to Jody's house had not gone nearly as well as he hoped and as soon as he plied all the answers he could from Lois, he planned to silence her irritating voice for good.

"Please," Lois snivelled. "Jody's godmother is Laura's grandmother!"

Chapter 18

Revelation

"Do you know the way home? I'm sure it's around here, but I can't seem to find it."

Jody's head bumped up. "Who said that?"

It was like her mind kept playing cruel, unpitying tricks on her. She heard a voice, sometimes many. Perhaps it was the trauma. How could a simple, unexciting school day stray so far from normal?

She didn't know how long she had been lying on this lumpy camp bed, but at least those monsters had cleared out. For the love of God, she wished she could get warm. Her bound limbs ached like crazy, but still her body struggled to contract, to conserve heat in a tight ball.

She thought she was going mad. The voices were most often confusing, muddled by layers of chatter. But once in a while she could pick something out from them all.

Despite this perceived abundance of company, she saw no one and felt unbearably alone.

"Gregg," she groaned. "I can't believe it." His horrific murder kept playing behind her closed lids.

Fearing what those bizarre animals might do to her, she wished like crazy she could reach the knife she kept hidden in her back jeans pocket. It was hopeless though, and she whimpered and pressed herself deeper into the dank, smelly mattress. "Please God, help me."

Every time she thought about Gregg, her belly felt emptier. "Damn it, Gregg." Now it seemed God was her only prospect for deliverance. "Please. I can't do this alone."

"Tsk, tsk," someone chimed as if in song, "Heart-breaking." This voice was real.

Something rustled outside, making Jody hold her breath. It was coming closer to the edge of the tent's yellowed, musty wall. The countless voices in her head all seemed to be calling out some sort of warning before falling away into silence.

The flap opened and the winged woman, called Ligeia, stepped in, her sleek silhouette moving smoothly to a nearby table. She lit a kerosene lamp and the golden, dancing light reflected ominously off her dark, haunting face.

"Do you know how many of my prey screamed for God before my embrace?" Her smile had a wicked twitch to it. She slowly ran her fingers over Jody's long hair before calmly sitting down next to her on the bed.

"It's confusing to me that people put so much faith into such an obvious fantasy. Think of it logically, child. If

God really existed, can you imagine the thought processes he must have gone through along his many advances in creation?

"The mystery of the cosmos, 'Incomparable'. The perplexing grandeur of this earth and the web of life that fills it, 'Sensational'. The dominant species of animal put here to rule over this extraordinary world forever and ever, 'Oops'. Perhaps it is God's way of punishing everything else truly significant."

She paused. "Clever. At any rate, your big, angry fairy in the sky is not coming. He never does. That's why after two centuries, I'm still here."

"Two centuries?" Jody's body tensed up again, pulling hard on her restraints as Ligeia fixated on her naked back.

"I know." Ligeia shrugged her shoulders in a flattered manner. "It's criminal. The way I look. It's because I absorb my victim's vitality, you know. I like twenty-somethings best, it gives me that full-bodied presence. But I've been known to picnic on teens." She gave Jody's bum a solid squeeze. "Mhmm, you'd do me just fine."

Ligeia inspected Jody's half naked body, perhaps comparing it with her own. Jody's heart froze, suddenly remembering her dad's knife.

Ligeia paused and then traced her fingers toward Jo's right back pocket, "What's this?"

Oh no!

Ligeia wormed her fingers in and dug out Lloyd's blade. "Ooh…" She unfolded the sharp cutting surface and admired its edge. "What's a little girl like you doing with a big tooth like this? You could hurt yourself." She folded it again and put it in her cloak pocket. "I'll hold onto it for you."

Jody sank, while Ligeia's eyes drifted off someplace else, clearly thinking about sinful things. A moment later she seemed to come back to the present.

"It's so disappointing when Dammie feasts on some old thing." She shuddered suddenly. "How can it be so much colder in here than it is out there?"

Jody watched her. "What are you going to do to me?" She tried to sound strong.

Ligeia's thick, charcoal lips curled up and she placed her hand upon Jody's spine, delicately tracing her features with unhurried fingers. The stunning beast looked as if she wanted something and was searching for the right way to get it.

"Your true hero is dead now. Obviously," she added with a curious flutter in her dark eyes, "he must have loved you to do what he did." Ligeia's hand slid further down Jody's back to the rise of her buttocks at the edge of her pants. "Did you know that?"

Jody barked louder than she meant, "You killed him! You and that other monster killed him!" Her jaw clenched so tight she could hardly speak. "Why? What did we ever do to you?"

Ligeia's smile widened, her hand reaching just under Jody's jeans. "You really don't know." It was as if she was talking to herself.

"What are you going to do to me?" Jody asked again, her breaths short.

Ligeia's fingers pulled away and began stroking Jody's neck. "You smell wonderful."

Jody didn't know how to respond to that and an awkward moment dragged on.

"Promises..." Ligeia turned her eyes away, focussing on the lantern's languid flame. "You're a stupid girl."

She got up, reached under her scant cloak and pulled out a ratty looking book. "I've learned jivitas can feel a person's uncommon characteristics. They become fascinated. It's their nature." She sounded resentful.

Jody was lost. In more ways than one. But maybe she could buy time and keep more pain and humiliation away by keeping this bitch talking. "What are you talking about? What is that book?"

Ligeia's expression turned mischievous. "This?" She started flipping the pages, licking her lips. "This is a collection of writings that I find sacred. It is my bible, and I always keep it close. It's from my mother who added to it what wisdom she gained over her years, as her mother did before her, and so on. And whenever I am faced with perplexing questions in life, invariably the answers are in here."

"For example?"

Jody realized she probably shouldn't have asked that question because it elicited a clear look of sinister delight from Ligeia's centrefold-like face.

"For example,"—that grin was definitely not good news—"Damianos has been on this perverse hunt for you without giving me any clear reason for it, other than a voice in his head told him to."

Jody's mind kicked. "A voice in his head?"

Ligeia must not have heard her. "I know he has a vendetta with the angoros, but humans are just food. No one really hates their food. Do you feel more fulfilled kicking a cow in her udders before you drink her milk? I think not. I, for one, do not hate humans. Mosquitoes, yes. I despise the competition."

She found the page she'd evidently been looking for and was searching the right passage with a probing finger. "So, I had been wondering what possible connection can a cow have with the angoros? And as much as I'd love to taste your unpasteurized cream and find out, I was forced to make a promise not to do so. But still I wonder..." She eyed Jody's bare skin again. "Could it be any more obvious? You are not a cow."

"Is that a good thing?"

Ligeia flashed her long fangs, snarling, "No. There are no angoros left on Earth. Our peoples did away with them long before I was born. Glorified by half-witted humans for eons, angoros are in fact a contemptuous scourge. If, as impossible as it sounds, you are one of them, this creates a very disturbing state of affairs for peaceful, human-hunting citizens like Damianos and me. And it presents another layer of questions that need answers. One in particular knocks against my skull as if Dammie was drumming me into a headboard." Ligeia's voice rose, becoming more powerful and determined. "Like, where, my child, did you come from?"

Jody's skin was crawling, anxiety itching everywhere. "Please, I don't know what you're talking about. I don't even know what an angoros is! I'm just a girl!"

"We shall see," Ligeia said, her eyes grazing over the page in front of her. "This spell was written in the time of the human's Roman Empire. The angoros hid themselves amongst the cows, so to speak, and this spell would weed them out. It rouses the angoros' hearing until they leap out screaming, clutching their ears, writhing."

Ligeia took a breath, labouring first with the individual words. After several failed attempts, she managed to string them all together. "Serpens est scriptor condemnationem vestram!"

Suddenly, Jody's head rang with a single white noise. *Oh no!* She was beside herself. *What's happening?*

Ligeia kept repeating the spell, each time making the scratching, scraping sound in Jody's ears sharper. It came to her as more than just a boom or buzz. It was tangible, hard and violent, like dozens of tiny gremlins digging into parts of her inner ears, gouging and peeling things away.

Battling against the growing urge to rattle her head and scream, Jody pressed her teeth down on her tongue and did her best to keep breathing. She tried to conceal the torture, not giving away the streaming tears she rubbed onto her pillow time and again.

Clearly disappointed, Ligeia eventually stopped. She stared at Jody for what felt like an eternity, just watching. Grumbling something to herself, she closed the book and yanked Jody's head up by her hair.

"Why aren't your ears bleeding? It says you should be screeching and thrashing like a baby in boiling water. Your ears are supposed to bleed!"

Jody was crying, though her hair being pulled was actually an improvement to how she was feeling a moment earlier. None of it seemed to satisfy Ligeia.

"This is very confusing!" She fluttered her wings and huffed out of the tent.

Jody remained frozen on the bed, her hearing slowly recovering. She ached to reach her ears, but her hands couldn't escape the restraints.

"She's gone now. It's okay." The voices started coming back. "Do you know the way home? I must be lost."

Jody started crying again, opening her mouth for the first time since Ligeia read the spell. She had tasted the blood earlier, but didn't realize how badly she had bit her tongue until she noticed the red stuff slobbering past her lips onto the tear-soaked pillow.

She swallowed as much of it as she could. Then, she manoeuvred her head and face, flipping the pillow over to its dry side, all the while wondering, *what's happening to me?*

Chapter 19

Pressed

Gregg sat agitated in the passenger seat as his great-grandma finally hastened the car up her driveway towards her old, weathered homestead.

The way was long and winding, bordered by mature cherry trees in fluttering bloom. They sped along the front twenty acres of rolling, grassy fields until they reached the crest of a soft knoll where the house ultimately came into view.

"God, I hope Jo's alright. How is this going to help me find her?" He lurched, helplessness driving him crazy.

His Grammy jeered, "You must think me a much wiser old woman than I am. I'm just taking this one step at a time, Greggory. It's the best way to keep from falling down."

She brought the car to an abrupt stop near the huge rhododendron bush in her front garden, killed the engine and sat with her hands gripped rigidly on the steering wheel. Gregg could tell the gears in that woman's head were grinding something fierce.

"What?" He couldn't take the stillness.

Grammy turned those hardened eyes at him. "Come with me."

She wiggled out of the car and walked into the house. Gregg followed her straight into the sunken living room where she pointed to a wooden crate placed upon the coffee table. "Have a look," Grammy instructed while she fed the glowing embers in the fireplace with more wood.

Inside, Gregg beheld a uniquely emblazoned book. "Wow!" He'd never seen one quite like this before. He placed his fingers over the design and traced the amazing images.

"Jody's parents fought over that thing. I made every effort to butt-out of their business, so I don't really know why they were so engaged by it. I seem to think that her father wanted to destroy it.

"You see, he tried to control everything, and he stressed about the most ridiculous details." Grammy paused and scratched her chin.

"Why did it take me until now to see the parallel with Sam? The efforts he made, he alleged, were to keep those he cared about safe. And the connection goes even deeper. He was the one that came to Sam's rescue the night she was attacked."

The news managed to jerk Gregg's fascination from the book. "You're kidding. I never knew that. Jody's dad?"

Grammy nodded. "He saved her life. It was he that fought off that monster. A short while after that, Jody's father really went off the deep end. He blamed himself for

Samantha's anguish, her downfall, and his failure to keep it from happening in the first place."

His great-gran appeared at a loss. "He persisted on punishing himself and those around him with the most bizarre notion that he had to stop the suffering from happening all over again."

Grammy drew her anxious gaze to the growing fire, its flames flickering in her deep eyes. "He did something," she said with a shudder. "Something terrible, to Jody. And the babe was never the same bubbly little girl after that. Her mother was devastated; such a comely rose, wilted, ruined. She bawled over Jo for days. He did something to her," she flared angrily. "And things got worse."

Gregg couldn't believe what he was hearing. Before this, he knew nothing about Jody's parents. "Her back." He thought about Jo's ugly scars, the wounds that hurt her both physically and mentally. "Her dad did that to her? But why?" He was appalled. "You kept all this secret? Even from Jo?"

Grammy looked ashamed. "It's not a very nice secret to keep, Greggory. Would it be better to add to Jody's upset? It's best that she doesn't know." She kneaded her wrinkled face. "The whole situation was awful. There's nothing to be done about what's been done. Jody's mother told me she was going to do whatever she could to keep her berserk husband at bay. One of those things, I've learned, was hiding this book with the dragon on the front."

Gregg traced the outline of the dragon image again, absorbed. It felt as cold as his mom's granite countertops, ominously so, and he pulled back.

"There is something very odd about it," Grammy said.

"I'll say," Gregg agreed. Above the eerily real-looking dragon and its immediate surroundings came a turning point in the cover's fineness. The messy noodles that twisted and turned around the beast rose into a blank depression where everything went sort of plain, save for a thin projection of a five point star inside a circle. "What's this for? Is it Jewish?"

Grammy peered from her spot by the fireplace. "It's a pentagram, Greggory. The Jews' symbol is the Star of David. Plenty of people have used the pentagram's design for their own purposes, but to see it circumscribed like this makes me think of something more pagan-like. To my understanding, the five points of the star are supposed to represent the four classical elements of earth, fire, air and water, bound together with the Spirit."

"Do you think this is it?" Gregg wondered. "That this is *The Book of the Nornir*? What the man in black is looking for? What's it about?"

"I don't know." Grammy wiggled her earlobe. "I haven't pulled it from the crate and looked inside it yet."

In no mood to waste time, Gregg heaved the old tome from its coffin, plunked himself down onto the couch and placed it on his lap. "It's heavy," he gasped. "How'd you get it up here?"

"It wasn't easy."

Gregg took hold of the top right corner and tried to pull back the cover, but it didn't budge and there was a sharp sting that surged up his arm to his elbow. "Ouch! What gives?"

He flipped the book onto its side and realized it was clasped shut with a fearsome looking lock. "Darn it."

Gregg's eyes flashed over the clasp. It seemed to be created out of the same metallic material as the rest of the book, but was shaped into a formidable-looking dragon's head. In its gaping mouth, as if daring any hand to draw near, was a dark and mysterious hole that gave the book's overall artistry a look of dread and foreboding.

Great-gran looked closer. "Do we need another blasted key?"

"I don't know," Gregg answered, inspecting the orifice. "It doesn't look like there's any place to put one." His face approached the dragon's head, hunting for clues, when the beast seemed to come alive, shaking and glaring with ominous eyes. A biting chill pressed against Gregg's chest, blasting through his shirt, and a shivery dread flooded into his heart.

He jerked back and threw the book from his lap onto the tabletop. "Jesus!"

"What happened?" Grammy glared. "Why did you do that?"

Gregg caught his breath. "The lock! It... it's like this thing is alive! Didn't you see?"

"It's possessed?"

Hearing his great-grandma say it suddenly sent a load of doubt to the forefront of his mind. "This is crazy. There must be some other explanation."

He got up and paced the room, agonizing over the two abductors in the cemetery, the death experience, Auntie Sam and now this unbelievable book. "What the stink is going on today? Why is everything so weird?"

Great-gran slowly stepped away from the fire toward the hall. "There's something else I need you to see. It once belonged to Jody's father, but now I wonder if it isn't better handled by you."

Gregg, more interested in the book than his grammy's talk at the moment, inspected the lock from a safe distance. He peered nervously into its gaping mouth, seeing nothing but the dark end of its throat surrounded by sharp, threatening teeth.

He heard his great-grandma open the door to the basement when the phone rang.

"Dash it! Always when I'm busy!" She came shuffling back into the living room and answered, "Hello? Oh, hello dear..."

Gregg thought it odd that the old girl always found it so vitally important to answer the stupid phone. An idea came to Gregg suddenly and he nervously stuck out his index finger, aiming for the dragon's mouth.

"Maybe it doesn't need a key."

As he got closer, the beast's jaw moved. Gregg pulled back in an instant, his lungs stiff. If he hadn't just seen it, he would never have believed it.

He glanced across the room. Grammy was absorbed with the phone and had that impatient look on her face.

"Yes. Greggory is here. Yes, I'm aware of that, Laura, and I meant to call..."

Crap, Gregg cringed. *It's Mom. She'll ruin everything.*

His mom was the least likely to talk about Samantha or anything remotely out of the norm. In all these years, his mom had told Gregg almost nothing about Auntie Sam and absolutely zilch about Jody's parents. *Why?* Gregg suddenly realized there was a lot he didn't know.

His mom was such a stick in the mud. Gregg moved away from the book, petting his finger, and went to pout at the front window, knowing full well that his mom was likely wanting him home to explain why he missed school today.

God, I just want to find Jody! I have to call the cops, he decided. *But what if Grammy was right? What do I tell them? Explain that Jody has been abducted and demand they find her, that's what!*

His eyes flashed on something down the driveway. *A car? Is someone coming?*

"What?" Great-grandma sounded alarmed as she spoke loudly into the phone. "That's horrible! When did this happen?"

Whatever his mom was telling her, it was bad. Grammy's voice was fractured, sometimes weak, sometimes excessive.

"Are the police there now? Oh, my God."

"The police? Why? Did they find Jo? Is she alright?" Gregg wanted to know, but Grammy hushed him with a nasty scowl.

"Yes, I can bring Gregg home…, pardon? Alright, goodbye."

Grammy lowered the phone and looked at Gregg intently. "This is dreadful." She motioned for the hall again. "I need to give it to you. I shouldn't delay another second."

"Why?" Gregg's heart was running scared in his chest. "What happened to Jo? Where is she?"

Before his great-grandma could answer, or make another move, Gregg's attention was drawn to the driveway again. He joggled his head more than once to make sure he was seeing things right.

"Hey, how did she know we were here?" He recognized the vehicle.

"Who?" Grammy's voice was bothered.

"I know that car. It's Jody's mom's. Hey! Maybe she found Jo!"

"Get away from that window!" Great-gran's shrill cry sent an icy spike through Gregg's heart. The look of terror on her face was something he'd never forget. "Lois has been murdered!"

"Murdered?" Gregg nearly tumbled into an end table.

He stared petrified as a tall, dark figure advanced from Lois's Ford and, as the man in black came near, Gregg heard his Grammy's shaky voice lament, "Am I too late?"

Chapter 20

Composure

Bent upon his success, Damianos announced to the voice in his head, "It's inside."

"Take it! Take it!"

Damianos saw through the window's glare a large, unique-looking book almost within his reach, sitting in the open on an old coffee table next to a wooden crate. *That must be it!* What a joy it was to be so close, so wonderfully near to the book that would show him the way. *Justice for all!*

However, as he peered more carefully through the glass, he spotted an old stout woman stooping at the far end of the room and a tall lean presence standing beside a couch. This virtually extinguished his earlier hope of a quick in and out.

"He's here," Damianos groaned. Very little was going smoothly today.

"Who?"

"The jivita."

The voice sounded unbothered. "Kill him this time."

Damianos watched irritated as the boy hastily swept thick red curtains across the window. "By all accounts, cutting him up into little bits should have already done that. Yet, here he stands in a single piece, alive."

It annoyed him to no end that he, an accomplished slayer to say the least, was perplexed and perhaps even a little nervous about this adolescent half-breed.

"Fear will not hinder you, Damianos. I will not allow it."

Damianos stopped his want to gripe, feeling a surge of cool inflate his stature as he moved toward the front door, and the book.

"How did you do that?" He was sure the voice was the reason for his sudden swelling of poise.

"Temperament is my speciality."

Chapter 21

Showdown

Damianos stood outside the house, staring at the front door for a long time, letting his intuition tell him what awaited within. "He knows I'm here," he told himself. "What will he do?"

Gregg had seemed unaware of his capabilities in the graveyard this morning. If he had been, Damianos might not be standing here presently. "I must be smarter this time."

Damianos hurried to the back of the house.

His nose caught the conspicuous smell of burning cedar emanating from the chimney above and his eyes briefly glanced at the trail of smoke ascending to the clear blue sky. As he did, he also noticed the high peaks of the treetops in the distance.

"That's interesting." Those woods looked familiar.

He heard a commotion and rounded the corner in time to see Gregg creep out an open glass door with a wooden crate held under his arm. *That must be it. He's hiding the book.* His jaw quivered, so beguiled by the game was he.

"Give it to me, boy," Damianos grumbled. "There is nowhere you can run that I cannot find you."

Gregg jumped as if from his own skin. "No!"

Damianos walked closer, steadiness in his every stride, while the half-breed winced and tumbled back into the house. Damianos followed and scanned his surroundings.

The place was old, seasoned, rich with the flavours of time and alive with a hungry snapping fire in the hearth. The old woman was gone and he wondered if she snuck out before he had come to the rear of the place. Gregg appeared to be alone, bumbling toward the middle of the sitting room still clutching the crate.

"Where is Jody? What have you done to her?"

"Give me the book," Damianos commanded, reaching out his hand.

Gregg's movements were jerky, but his resolve seemed sure enough. "Jody! Where is she?"

His snarling made Damianos wary, but he knew not to show it. "Give me that book or I shall cut you again!" Damianos surged forward and Gregg fell next to the coffee table onto the Persian rug. "Did I not suffer you enough pain already?"

"Obviously not, 'cuz I'm still here, you big arse!"

The jivita's body language seemed at odds with his threatening tone and Damianos found himself leaning on the self-composure the voice had inspired in him. Gregg's confusing manner was making it difficult to tell whether Damianos should attack or be more cautious.

"Your juvenile hormones are betraying you, aren't they, eliciting this deranged attachment to the girl? You think you know her, don't you? But she is a deceiver, boy. Her entire life is a lie."

This would be so much easier if Ligeia was here. Getting into a male's head was her thing, not his.

"She is a wicked breed, not worth your engrossment. Find someone else, jivita. The sinner is mine!"

"No!"

Then Gregg did the unthinkable. He threw the latch that held the fireplace insert's glass door and swung it open. The flames inside heaved from the additional oxygen, their hot fingers reaching and stretching while Gregg held the crate with a single-mindedness lighting his face.

"Give Jody back," the little bugger warned. His eyes were suddenly inhuman, as if set ablaze. "Or I'll burn it!"

No! The voice howled in Damianos's head.

Damianos held back, dubious. "You are a stupid mutt!"

"Stupid and crazy!" The boy spoke sharply, twitching the crate closer. The animal in him was turning on. "Give Jody back and I'll give you the damned book!"

Damianos's head was spinning, swearing over the frustration this ignorant monster kept presenting.

"Bah, why?" he bellowed. "Why do you want her back? Is it love? She will break your stubborn little heart! She cannot love you," Damianos lowered his voice. "She is a liar, an impostor that has done and always will do what she must to get what she wants and she doesn't even

127

realize it. She doesn't love you. She can't love anyone. Because she is afraid."

Gregg's aggressiveness shifted back and forth. "Afraid? Of what?"

Damianos couldn't help but grin, just a little. "Surely you must have realized it. Unless your immature age hasn't given you the insight into a woman's mind yet."

He knew he had struck a chord that now gave him the advantage. "How do you think I penetrated her wall so easily at the cemetery this morning? She swept grass clippings from her parents' tiny plaque and kissed their names. She told them she missed them, then asked if they missed her, if they still remembered her."

Damianos had found it effortless to worm his way into Jody's head after that, to infringe upon her vulnerability and exert control with bribes of affection and companionship.

"She doesn't understand why her parents had to die. Sure, her mind makes sense of it. Her heart, however, focuses on the nonsense. Was it me? Did I do something wrong? Did they not love me? And, of course, if they didn't, then why?"

Damianos noticed Gregg pull the crate back from the flickering firebox and continued, "Jody, like most girls her age, can come up with countless reasons not to be loved. The wounds on her back give her imagination even more rations upon which to feed."

"But..." Gregg faltered. "I told her..."

"Nothing you told her can fix things, boy," Damianos cut in. "Because you can never give her what she requires.

Has your family not made mention of it before? What you are?"

"Jivita?" Gregg mouthed softly.

"You don't know what that is, do you?" Damianos was practically teasing now. "Have you ever lost your temper before? Have you not felt the tension inside giving rise to a boiling heat and menacing designs on violence? Have you never succumbed to it? Perhaps throwing something in a fit of rage and been surprised by how far or hard you've cast it? Maybe you've hit something, or kicked, when the need is too great to stifle, and been amazed at the damage you've inflicted."

Gregg lowered the crate, his eyes briefly staring at the fire's dancing flames. "I put my fist through the wall before. It was at school when this boy kept bugging Jo, teasing her about her back. I wanted to kill that guy. I wanted to rip his fat, smart-ass head from his neck. Instead I broke cinder blocks with my bare knuckles. I heard later that they thought someone had vandalized the building with a sledgehammer. I just thought the blocks were rotten or something."

"It can be a powerful force, no?" Damianos continued. "Losing control of your emotions is key. Relinquishing yourself to pure, crazed excitement is what frees the colossus inside every jivita. Imagine what could happen if you let your guard down, say in that blissful stage where romance gives birth to passion? The animal in you will do much worse to your lover than breaking a hole through concrete. If nothing else, know this. Love is something jivitas can never have with someone unlike themselves.

Forget the girl. Give me the book and I will give you something better in return."

Gregg's eyes flashed on him, though he said not a word with his tight-lipped mouth.

"I can show you what you are, teach you your limits and find you your perfect mate. Only I can do this for you. Growing older here with your family is fruitless. It will only lead you to bitter disappointment. You do not belong with the humans. Sooner or later they will discover you and they will chastise you and cast you out forever. You will kill someone, Gregg. Someone you love. It's not your fault. It's just your nature."

Damianos paused, curious what Gregg was thinking. The half-breed seemed to be looking inward for answers, perhaps considering his future as a beast for the first time.

Lamentably, Gregg's carriage stiffened and he said, "What are you planning to do with Jo?"

Damianos sighed, disappointment clenching his jaws. "What does it matter?"

"What's it matter?" Gregg baited, holding the crate angrily. "Maybe she means nothing to you, and maybe this stupid book means nothing to me!"

He approached the fireplace door again and before Damianos could utter a word, Gregg cast the book into the hungry flames and sealed the hatch shut.

"Fool!" Damianos screamed. "What have you done?"

The voice roared in Damianos's head, compelling him to leap and attack the jivita where he stood. They struggled together until at last Damianos ripped at the boy's flesh and managed to throw him down.

Damianos swung the door open and reached into the searing hot box with his bare hands. Flaming tongues tasted his flesh and hot ash blew across his skin, yet the voice's cries pressured him on to grasp the burning crate and heave it to safety.

The prize freed, he straightened up just long enough to realize that not only was the crate on fire, but so were the sleeves on his black coat. His hands suddenly felt the shocking agony, fast and heavy. Damianos's body shook from the sting, yet his mind kept his hands shackled to the crate. He couldn't let it go.

"Put it down!" he told himself more than once. "Put it down!"

An abrupt stirring to his right reminded him he wasn't alone. Gregg flew over the couch and tackled Damianos to the floor. The crate went flying, crashing at the foot of an armchair.

"You better not have killed her!"

Gregg started swinging, but his motions were unpolished, awkward.

Damianos had much greater concerns, for the searing pain was worsening and the flames were spreading up his arms. He flung himself away from the boy, thrashing and crashing into anything and everything, trying to get the coat off. He scarcely heard the old woman's scream.

"Oh, my God! Greggory, the house is on fire!"

Damianos flung off his coat and skipped and bounced, looking for anything to cool his tortured skin. Only then did he notice the woman and Gregg surrounded by growing hedges of flames. He eyed the crate, fully ablaze, and felt that tugging again to fetch it from harms way.

This time, however, he held himself back, fighting the alien urges.

But the voice had other ideas. "Get that book!"

Damianos's movements twisted like a puppet on wrenched strings.

"No! My hands! My hands!" He banged his way down a hall and found a washroom, dashed into the bathtub and started the shower, letting its cool rain soothe his cooking flesh.

Through the water's sprinkling and streaming noise, Damianos heard strange sounds. They were like bursts of air echoing through wide spouts. His mind rushed to find the answer. *Fire extinguishers!*

The pain subsided and the voice in his head returned. "Get that book!"

Chapter 22

Mothers

The fumes were thick and hanging, choking Gregg as he snuffed out each remaining pocket of flames. "Jesus! I'm so sorry, Grammy!"

He stopped the crate from burning, then the armchair next to it. Bits of the wooden container flaked away with light tendrils of smoke swimming up as it smouldered.

His great-grandma, meanwhile, showed surprisingly little concern for the only house she'd ever lived in. "It's only stuff. When everything is said and done, you can't take it with you. Ashes to ashes... and all that." Her voice sounded as if she didn't entirely believe what she was saying.

She opened the windows and the front door to let the air move. "Now, let's have those drafts really show their worth." She went to the sliding glass door at the back and then looked around, panicked. "Where did that nasty man in black get to?"

Gregg wiped his brow with the extinguisher still in his hand and looked over his shoulder. "Crap!" When Grammy had peeled out of her hiding place in the other room earlier, Gregg had plain forgotten about him.

Bumping heads with the creature that had before handled him with such ease had gone much better this time. Gregg found himself playing with the idea that with a little more luck he might have actually won.

"He was on fire, wasn't he?"

His black coat was still breathing smoke on the floor. Gregg kicked it, annoyed that the schnard had buggered off. He was also indecently curious about what Damianos knew about jivitas.

"Would you look at this!" Grammy objected. She held an old, burned up portrait of her posing with Gregg's mom and Samantha when they were kids. "Damn." She pulled the picture from the broken frame and stared at it, letting loose a rueful sigh.

Perhaps the moment was grossly mistimed, but Gregg had a lot of things to contend with right then and he couldn't help but dwell on the idea that he was not all human. It required an entirely new mindset.

"Grammy, what am I?"

She responded with an odd expression, but must have realized pretty darn quickly her scam-of-a-lifetime had been irreversibly disclosed. "Sit down."

Grammy proceeded, be it cautiously, to the couch with the never-ending yield. It was bespeckled now with ash, but she didn't let it bother her. There she sat and waited until eventually Gregg got the idea and hunkered down beside her. It was a struggle not to droop into each other.

"Greggory," she began with obvious angst, "sixteen years ago, your mother was romanced by someone. A stranger. Lucy was his name. He seemed nice, kind, fun, helpful, sheltering, all that. Coo, and did he look like a young Cary Grant," she added with a curious snicker. She paused. "Where was I?

"Right, Lucy. Let's see, he had short, sandy brown hair and brilliant eyes. Oh, dear me, those eyes. They were a twilight blue, deep and haunting. Yet that wasn't the most peculiar thing about him. There was always something more that was so bafflingly different.

"He avoided all talk of his past, where he came from, what he did and who his family was. Whenever asked, he said mostly the same thing, 'I came out of a hole in the earth and for too long I wandered.' When he saw your mother he said it was as if he could breathe again and finally shed his age-old hurt.

"It didn't take long to pick up on the fact that Lucy and Jody's father did not like each other much." She chuckled. "Who am I kidding, they absolutely hated each other."

Grammy looked to be considering things. "Jody's father also showed affection for your mother, though to what degree I cannot say. I know he confided things to her. Perhaps many things. Stresses escalated between the three, as expected. And one night, everything reached a head. I fully anticipated some sort of trouble, but never once did I think Lucy would attack your mother so violently."

"Violently? What happened?"

"I don't think anyone knows why he did it," Grammy went on, as if for her own consideration. "To the very end, she defended him despite everything. Maybe he just lost control as your mother believed, or it might have been something more malicious. It's a stumper, no doubt about it. He almost killed her."

Gregg did his best to fathom the story. He had never heard of his mother almost getting killed before and she certainly said nothing about his father, ever. She always seemed to avoid such talks by any means. He knew his dad had been a no-show during his entire life and, as a boy, had learned to get over it and look up to Dave's dad for that kind of guidance.

And what was with Jody's father sticking his nose into everybody's business? If things were going well between Lucy and his mom, why did he have to mess it up? As much as Gregg tried to fill in the dark spaces, he couldn't make all the pieces fit.

"I don't get it. My mom was attacked too? And no one thought to tell me this before?"

Then Gregg remembered the man in black telling him that love is something jivitas could never have with someone unlike themselves.

"Poor mom," he groaned. *Poor me*, he thought, reflecting on the perfect moment he'd dreamed of for years, being with Jody, loving her. Now he feared it could never happen.

His mind recoiled from that thought and he reached for anything positive to hang on to. At least Gregg could be glad that his mom wasn't so abused that she'd never recovered. He'd seen her in a swimsuit enough times in his life to know that there weren't any scars to speak of.

"Jeez, the girls in this clan really know how to pick 'em."

Grammy just looked at him, sliding her head from side to side. "I'm so sorry, Gregg. Laura's going to chew me up for telling you this, but she's not your real mother. Samantha was."

Gregg felt as if he had just been smacked upside the head with a slab of granite, knocking his tongue right out of his mouth. He sat there for a time, numb.

He'd always thought his life was so boring, so normal. Often, he'd complained that his life wasn't more exciting. Now, years of memories, mundane and uninteresting, flew across his mind in a whole new light. Birthdays, holidays, camping trips and the like; it all corresponded now to someone else's childhood. It was a lie. His previous life was a dream all along and today was the day he had to wake up. Except this moment was like being somehow trapped between sleep and awake, unsure of what to believe as truth or fantasy.

Questions whirred: *who am I? What happened? Where is my family? ...dead?*

Did he just lose his mother and not even realize it? He'd walked out on her funeral! "I'm an orphan?" Gregg shuddered.

Great-grandma reached around his shoulders to hold and comfort him.

"Just like Jo? That's why Auntie Sam"—it felt too awkward to acknowledge her as anything else right then—"kept looking at me so strangely, isn't it?" From his earliest memories, she'd treated him differently from everyone else. Now he understood why.

"It was her idea," Grammy clarified. "She wrestled with the option to abort the pregnancy. It was well within her right to do so, but that instinct that builds in a woman to nurture and protect her child saved you. Despite what your father did to her, she was determined to accept the result and love you always. But before she came to term, her recovery from the rape seemed to plateau. Nightmares plagued her dreams and anxiety haunted her days, all the time worrying for your safety. She feared that not terminating the pregnancy might have been a curse upon you, rather than a blessing."

"But, how can it be?" Gregg stopped her, catching on to something that should have been obvious from the start. "There are pictures in our photo albums, even a blown up portrait on our wall, where Mom"—again, he stumbled, unsure of what to call the woman he'd only ever known as such—"was pregnant. There are some where you can see her belly, Grams. She was really carrying something in there, and if it wasn't me then I'd sure like to know what the hell that was."

Grammy let out a heavy breath. "You're right. Laura was with child, something that her and her husband, Trevor, had long dreamed of. She went into labour three months prematurely and the baby didn't survive."

Grammy's stalwart eyes wept and she covered her mouth with a trembling hand.

"There was so much pain in the family. So much pain, everywhere. The loss devastated her and Trevor. Samantha was swift to hatch the plan that would give you to them, to raise as their own, with the promise that no one else in the world would be the wiser. You were practically due any day. Everyone seemed on board. Laura and Trevor would get the child they so wanted and Samantha's heart would be more at ease knowing you would grow up safe and hidden."

"But things didn't get better for Samantha, did they?" Gregg said and Grammy agreed with a remorseful nod.

"The tension never went away. She told me her thoughts kept wanting to betray her. And as for Trevor, well, he couldn't take you. He had his reasons. After months of living with a crying, pooping, never-sleeping baby that wasn't his, he decided that loving you the way he would his own son was impossible. So he made Laura choose. It was either him or you."

Gregg thought of how his life might have gone if his mom—er, Laura—preferred Trevor over him. "I'm glad she picked me."

"Me too."

Gregg paused, absorbing as he gazed into the gradually fading fire in the hearth. He wasn't all human. On the flip-side, he wasn't all jivita, whatever that was. But he was all orphan. He kept telling himself, over and over, letting it sink in. What a rotten day to suddenly find out your mother passed away, committing suicide no less, in an unusual attempt to keep you safe from someone or something you never thought existed.

"I never said 'I love you'. All these years, I never told her. She spent every Mother's Day of my life alone." He felt sick. "All for what? And I still don't know who my father is. Or what he is, or was. Or why he did what he did. I guess I shouldn't hold my breath that will ever change."

He slapped the couch cushion, raising a brume of ash. "How can I ever know the truth about who and what I am?"

Someone stepped into the room behind him. "Forgotten about me so soon?"

Chapter 23

Plunder

Damianos coped with the pain in his hands and lower arms, using the throbbing agony to nourish his determination. "The offer still stands, half-breed."

Gregg quickly got up to face him, but was creeping farther away. The old woman meanwhile looked to be having an odd bit of bother getting off the couch, heaving and groaning.

"Why do I still have this damned thing?"

From the corner of his eye, Damianos spotted the remnants of the crate. With relief, he noticed through charred bits that the book was still inside. Perhaps it was still in tolerable condition. If he could just get it back to camp, he might find the pages intact.

"Take it! Take it!" cried the voice.

Damianos sprang toward it, but was immediately tackled. He and Gregg clashed, thumping and slamming about the place.

It was after Damianos found himself half embedded into a wall that he realized the jivita's power and skill, though still raw, were growing. Add to that, Damianos's damaged hands seared with every strike against the jivita. Clearly, taking the book was going to require a different approach.

Damianos shoved Gregg to the floor and trampled over him to get to the old woman.

"No!" The jivita clambered to get up while Damianos took the old droopy bag of skin by the throat.

"I could kill her!" he warned.

Gregg stepped back, his hands up and opened, while his head skidded left and right. "No! No, don't!"

"It's... all... right," the old woman groaned, choking on every word. Damianos glared into her eyes and saw no fear. She was ready to die. "There's... something... in the cellar... for you!"

"Maybe death is an acceptable outcome for you, my dear old purse. But watching you die will be a most damaging experience for your young freak!"

Damianos lifted the woman off her feet and Gregg let loose with a high-pitched scream.

"I'll kill you! I'll kill you, goddamn it!"

Damianos slid him an unimpressed glance, and then smiled as he squeezed the woman's neck shut. "Try, you crass, loud-mouthed little bastard!"

Gregg's whole body shook and to Damianos's dismay, the hard lines of the jivita's shape began to haze. In a frantic attempt to keep him from turning into a confusing fog, Damianos lunged and swung the old woman like a club at Gregg, knocking the boy flat on his back.

The woman crashed into the bookshelf and fell into a mangled heap on the floor. The heavy piece of furniture, still laden with texts, wobbled above her.

"No!" Gregg was getting up again just as Damianos had hoped.

Damianos stepped to the bookshelf and pushed it over, crushing the old woman underneath. Published works spilled all around, including a very large volume seemingly made of a tin-like alloy.

As Gregg rushed to the woman's side, Damianos scooped up the scorched crate and hurried out the open sliding glass door to freedom.

"I have it! It's mine!" he cheered, his teeth clenching as his aching hands held the wooden container.

"It's mine," the sobering voice reminded him.

Chapter 24

Destroyer

Pissed that her spell had failed to reveal anything about the girl, Ligeia's hot breath fogged into the dank gloom around her. She could stand the bloody cold of this place no longer. Nor should she have to.

She entered her tent and lit a propane heater, fanning the inadequate warmth with her wings.

"Screw him!" She knew Damianos wouldn't be happy. He didn't want to give anyone a chance to find them. Releasing streaks of heat up through a patch of uninhabited trees when authorities might be out with helicopters using temperature-sensing technology to search for a missing teenage girl was definitely a risk. At this point, Ligeia couldn't care less.

She laid her book and the little bitch's knife to the side, unclasped her meagre cloak and tossed it to the corner before digging through a wooden chest that held clothes she'd tailored especially for herself. Thankful she

144

brought it to this awful place, she pulled out a grey sweater-dress.

"I can't believe it." She shook her head, freeing the back of the sexy frock so it could fit around her wings. She'd loved that outfit the minute she first conceived it, both longing for and dreading the day she'd actually need to wear it. "I finally get to try you on."

Ligeia hated covering her physique, but adored how this body-hugging, long sleeved mini dress left her legs unclad, her torso warm and her shape spine-tingling to anyone who cast eyes on her. She also appreciated the hood and quickly pulled it over her head, adding the matching boots for her chilled feet.

She paid little attention to Jody's whimpering in the tent next to hers. "Urchin."

Ligeia leaned back on her cot and began flipping through the pages of her book, attempting once again to find out what was so special about this girl and how to stop the jivita she was sure would come back. She thumbed past the section where her ancestors had written mostly of their interactions with humans and how best to taunt them.

She felt sufficiently accomplished in that field nowadays, thanks to her studies of the book and her natural physical endowments, but the spells always intrigued her. Lamentably, most of them were woven into long, verbose tales of trials and affliction and Ligeia really hated to read. Inspiring unbridled fear in the eyes of a strapping man in the prime of his life was fun. Looking at stale words on a page was an exhausting bore.

She turned page after page, running her finger over the text, hoping to reveal any obscure content, occasionally coming across mildly curious scraps like 'Enchanting a man's delight,' 'Enchanting a man's fervour,' and 'Enchanting a man's love'. At that last spell, something in her chest pinched.

Hmm.

She read it, fancying the potential of its usefulness on fascinating jivita half-breeds. Like most of the enchantments, it was written in Latin and required a hypnotic lock with the target. Ligeia wrestled with her tongue just to speak the words properly, never mind singing them.

"Tribuo mihi vestri pectus pectoris." She churned on the cot and grumbled. "Stupid language."

She flipped the pages in a huff. It seemed much of the rudimentary wisdom written in the book evolved from the time before Christ. As a child, Ligeia remembered her mother telling her of when their kind and others routinely battled in the open, appearing to the primitive humans as wars between divine beings. They believed syrēnes and the like were Gods, or tormentors sent by the Gods, to be worshiped and feared.

Ligeia's mother, when asked, said that her ancestors, like the others, had come to this world through some mystical gateway. A bridge that carried them from unhappiness by way of flashing light and blue fire to a new home of freedom and promise. Once here, however, a purge of sorts was needed to do away with the last of the vile holdouts from the old world. The angoros were the greatest scourge, and they manipulated the humans into thinking they were messengers of divinity and spiritual understanding.

At the time, Ligeia had little interest in such stories. She was much more aroused by things that affected her life in the now. And, as was second nature for every syrēne emerging from childhood to maturity, Ligeia did what was expected and killed her mother. Only it was before her forbearer had finished teaching about the old days. Ligeia's weakness, she often chafed inwardly, was her impatience.

As long as they ate well, syrēnes never grew old and died. It was up to the next generation to do away with them, so that the young could inherit their foremothers' qualities and harvest the human tribes of the earth unimpeded. Ligeia didn't hate her mother. She had just done what she was supposed to do, fully aware that one day she might raise a child of her own and look forward to the same end.

For a species that never liked to share, this surprising willingness of the parent to sacrifice herself for her young was deemed quite a magnanimous custom, even amongst other races.

Lilitas too lived on and on, however, they eventually reached a stage where they no longer believed there was anything more to learn or experience with their being. Finished with existence, they would stop eating and do something lilitas called 'tyah jatti', which was their way of leaving the body and freeing the spirit.

Damianos had come across the flaming bridge and, upon his arrival, was filled with an inexhaustible sense of purpose. To go back and let loose an apocalyptic revenge, he'd told her.

He'll never die, Ligeia accepted.

"I wonder what it must be like," she pondered, "to live so long."

Part of her was glad she and Damianos had not produced a child. Half-breeds were rare, a biological scarcity that well-born people most often feared as unrefined and fickle. She couldn't be sure what a hybrid syrēne would look like, or how it would behave. She shuddered to think what would happen if she had a boy, instead of a praiseworthy girl.

Male syrēnes existed, but they lacked wings and the true superiority of the females. It was hard to find them in a world saturated by humans because they looked so much alike.

"Hold it..."

As the delicate weathered sheets slipped between her fingers, Ligeia spotted something rather menacing. She flipped back to find a crude drawing of a monster. The pages there were stuck together. That must have been why she couldn't remember ever seeing this depiction before.

She tried to free the yellowed leafs and, in so doing, discovered reddish blotches hindering her efforts. When she accidentally ripped a page, she almost screamed at the indignity. Upon closer inspection, it was clear the smudges were blood. *But whose?*

They looked and smelled old, very old, and the handwriting was difficult to read. It was a language Ligeia had practically forgotten. 'Ellagio', the syrēnes' natural vernacular. These few pages must have been written by descendants who had crossed the bridge, before they had adopted human speech.

At first the text looked mostly like scribble, but then Ligeia started recognizing letters and characters. The drawings were crude and unsettling, of beasts seemingly made of cloud. Finally, satisfying Ligeia's sudden excitement and fuelling even greater enthusiasm, she found a word that was repeated throughout the body of the paragraphs. It was likely the descriptor for the illustrated creatures and what early syrēnes had called them. Their original names from the other side of the bridge.

It confused Ligeia, but the connection was clear. What she knew as jivita, her ancestors labelled 'Alal.' She said it softly with a nervous breath for now she understood the meaning.

"Destroyer."

Chapter 25

Alals

Ligeia almost leapt right off the cot, clambering to her knees atop the mattress and resting the book on the blanket in front of her. She hovered above it reading frantically, identifying words and translating them as fast as she could.

"They fought with the rising," she discovered, "these godly beasts. They conquered the dominant, opposing armies, destroyed their cities, and put their giants to death."

A war. Ligeia tried to imagine it. Her ancestors' homeland, a place filled with syrēnes and other magnificent pedigrees fighting side-by-side and against each other, absorbed in an environment of strife and enmity. The idea felt so human.

"I never knew." Truthfully, she'd never had an interest in knowing before. But that was changing.

Plowing on, she found her ancestors were refugees, like Damianos. They'd fled the old world. Sarion was its name. And they hadn't been alone in doing so. She also learned that syrēnes and lilitas had fought on the same side as the alals, but their affiliations ended soon afterward.

"Getting too close will leave one consumed by the tempest that rages always inside an alal..." she pieced out, bit by bit. "They are without a true rival. When outwardly peaceful, they take the shape of those around them. When excited, alals become more mighty than the mountains, more unpredictable than a storm."

Then the tone and nature of the descriptions changed.

"She was cast out from the rest. And when I found her in the chasms of Kulleet, I killed her and the baby."

She apparently was a syrēne named Latt and by the sounds of things, she fell in love with a jivita: a cardinal sin. She had survived intercourse with him, but could not hide her pregnancy from other syrēnes for long. Though many tried, no one could kill Latt.

Latt had bragged that she and her unborn child would live forever—going against syrēne practice—because she possessed the jivita's ability to heal. It was unclear in the text how she had acquired this amazing talent.

Understanding the danger of letting a jivita half-breed live, the author of the story, Ligeia's ancestor, went in search of Latt,. According to her, it had been a jivita, mixed with some obscure race, who started the war on the old world. A war that led ultimately to Sarion's ruin.

Ligeia's ancestor evidently discovered a way around Latt's healing abilities. Using a little-known spell, she broke Latt's power and murdered her with the child still latched to her womb.

Ligeia sat, totally absorbed. This was it. This was what she was looking for. Slowly, she said the words and imagined singing them into Gregg's captivated ears, "Racksana asta. Prazamana vyapaya."

Minutes ticked by as Ligeia took in the story. She was happy to have found the answer she needed, but the discovery that her curious attraction to Gregg was deemed such a bad thing by her kind was a disappointment. There was something about him that appealed to her.

She closed the book and lay back on the cot, thinking. She had learned two spells now that she could use on the jivita. One would leave him vulnerable, while the other could make him her lover forever.

What to do?

Chapter 26

Frustrated

Damianos hurried to his stolen car and hesitantly grasped the door's latch. His hands were hurting something fierce now; just having the wind pass over them as he charged around the house smarted. He placed the crate on the passenger side and sank into the driver's seat.

He grimaced at the key he left in the ignition, grinding his teeth to near powder as he gathered the perseverance to twist the damned thing. What a delightful sound it was when the engine caught.

He sat back and breathed deeply, glancing over to the high trees behind the house. There was one fir in particular that was towering above all others; it had a bend in it near the top. It looked so familiar.

"Hurry!" the voice in his head demanded. "Get to the girl!"

Again Damianos pinched his lips together, focused his eyes and readied himself to stomach the pain. He shifted the car into gear and gingerly gripped the wheel, grunting as he drove down the driveway.

"This had better be worth it," he grumbled.

Speeding toward the modest rural street at the end of the property, he cut the corner hard. His hands twitched as if they were being raked through hot coals, forcing him to let go of the steering wheel. The vehicle crashed into a ditch and the exploding airbag smacked him in the chest and face, while the crate rocketed off the passenger seat and broke apart.

Damianos groaned. What a rotten day!

Straightening up, his sights landed on the book, now visible amid the remnants of the burned and battered crate. He adjusted his head and fastened his eyes on the unexpected title. *National Geographic Atlas of the World - Seventh Edition.*

His head slipped back against the seat, dizzy, his insides plunging into a bottomless abyss.

"That little shite!"

Chapter 27

Helpless

Gregg had never seen someone die before. Being a teenager, he'd never really thought about it.

Sure, he'd caught fish with Dave and his dad in the past and thought little of his catch as he walloped the shifty things with a bonker. He'd seen road-kill countless times and it never bothered him. This was different. This was affecting him like no TV, movie or XBox game ever did.

His Grammy had been old as long as he'd known her, but there was always so much life in her eyes. Now, in this entirely unanticipated moment, Gregg saw nothing but the emptiness that lessens a person to a mere shell.

What do I tell mom? That well-dressed prick, I'll kill him! Jesus, I have to find Jo!

At least Damianos hadn't taken the book with him. He must not have known what it looked like because it more or less fell at his feet when he brought down the bookshelf.

He'll be back, Gregg realized, focussing on how still his great-grandma was. How wrong it was to see a heavy bookcase on top of her fragile back and legs and how painfully quiet the world around him suddenly seemed.

"Grammy?" His voice was soft, almost childishly so. "What do I do?"

A tiny murmur pricked his ears.

Gregg poked his head up and peered around the room, then looked back at his great-grandmother. He came closer, reaching with his hand. "Grammy?"

He thought he saw her brows twitch, then noticed a virtually imperceptible movement under her skin, below her chin. Her heart was still beating. "You're alive? Holy crap, you're alive!"

Gregg leapt to his feet, gripped the bookshelf and heaved it up so hard and fast it rutted the wall. He paid no mind to the physics. Instead he stood rattled over his Grammy.

"Are you alright?" He knew it was a stupid question, but he couldn't think of anything better at the moment.

Great-gran's chest started stretching outward again now that the weighty shelf was gone and her curled fingers twitched. But she couldn't do more than groan pitifully. Long seconds dragged by before her eyes finally opened to Gregg's utter delight.

"Grammy!" He took her hand, but let it go again almost immediately at her agonized cry and the expression on her face.

"911," Gregg suddenly got it through his head. "You need an ambulance!"

He rushed to the phone and did his best not to sound like a blubbering child to the operator. After lurching through the questions the woman on the other end of the line asked, he was told an ambulance would be on its way as quickly as possible. However, the operator warned, calls in the area right then were high and it might take longer than usual for paramedics to arrive. She told Gregg that his Grammy may have suffered a spinal injury, and gave him suggestions to help her cope.

Gregg hung up the phone, practically delirious. "We have to *wait*?" He couldn't believe it.

He scurried down the hall and fetched blankets. After covering Grammy, he flopped onto the floor next to her and tried to take her hand again, this time very gently.

She groaned with every breath and the pain in her face was extreme.

Gregg stroked her grey, bristly hair and quietly begged her to stay alive. "I still need you."

Grammy's expression seemed a jeer.

He remembered what it was like after the man in black had left him in the open grave to die alone: the pain, the numbness and the clear awareness of bodily systems shutting down,—one after the other—leading him to impending darkness. Gregg didn't want that for Grammy. Not now, not like this. If only she could heal like Gregg did.

"Don't die!"

Grammy's eyes kept sliding shut.

"C'mon, don't you dare die!"

Her body writhed and her lips quivered. "I love you. I always have." Her eyes crept open and after a moment of staring straight into Gregg's, they flashed on something and seemed to drift inwards. Her hand twitched in Gregg's grasp and bits of blood discharged from her mouth as she forced out the words, "Look behind you!"

Gregg's head veered in time to see a dark shadow approaching.

The man in black had come back.

Chapter 28

Released

"Go away!" Gregg barked, guarding his grammy.

The man in black, Damianos, instead went to his knees and shuffled through the heaps of books scattered across the floor.

"Where is it? Where is *The Book of the Nornir*?" His voice was threatening, his movements intense, yet he kept his distance. As he rummaged through the debris, he kept glaring at his damaged hands. "Damn it, boy! Why must you be so stubborn? Our people were once united against the same enemy, the enemy you're now trying to protect!"

"What, Jody? She's not the enemy. She's just a girl." Gregg's heart was pounding.

"Yes, and you are just a skinny, love-sick boy," Damianos scoffed. Suddenly his eyes widened and his sullen expression lighted into glee.

Oh no, the book!

"This must be it!" Damianos snatched it up and inspected the front with obvious delight. Turning it over, he halted, stymied.

Gregg felt a surge of malicious satisfaction. The dragon lock. The freak couldn't open the pages either.

Gregg watched as Damianos, glaring at it dubiously, stroked the dragon with a probing finger. The dragon's eyes began to brighten and, with a startled cry, Damianos yanked his hand away.

Clearly thinking better of carrying on his investigations there and then, Damianos stood up to leave.

"Stop!"

There was no way Gregg was going to let him walk out with that thing. Not after what that bastard had done to Jody and Grammy, never mind what he'd put Gregg through.

Gregg left his great-gran and jumped at him.

The struggle that followed was a blur, punctuated by their grunts and the staccato ruin of more of Great-grammy's things. Gregg was managing to hold his own with the man-in-black's wounded hands giving Gregg some leverage. His confidence growing, Gregg pressed his advantage.

The fight had brought them close to the fireplace and Gregg angled Damianos in that direction. Maybe he could fry the monster's backside for him.

Intent on his plan, Gregg failed to anticipate the danger.

The fireplace toolset within reach, Damianos grasped the long-stemmed poker and lunged at Gregg, swinging.

The iron implement nailed Gregg's right arm and then his left kidney.

His lungs stalled and he fell to the ground writhing and desperate for breath. From the corner of his vision, Gregg saw the scoundrel make to impale him with the poker's large fishhook. He reached up just in time to grasp the rod and wrench it from his attacker's failing hands.

Stumbling to his feet, Gregg steadied himself to strike. Damianos, however, was clearly a swift thinker. He latched onto the fireplace shovel and heaved burning wood and red-hot ash from the open fireplace into the room and at Gregg

Gregg ignored the pain and the embers scattering onto the sofa and rug and charged. He beat the bastard down, but the damage was done. The floor had started smouldering again and Gregg could only fight one enemy at a time.

Gregg tried to finish Damianos with a perfect blow, but his focus was divided and with every passing moment he knew his great-grammy was in increasing danger.

Where is that damned ambulance?! The flames were growing and Grammy wasn't moving except for her contorting face.

Gregg dodged a lunge and accidentally flung the poker over the couch. He dove for the fire extinguisher, lying discarded near his feet, pointed, and pulled the trigger. Only a brief, meagre cloud of white stuff shot out.

"Crap!" It was empty.

Frustration pounding his temples, Gregg spotted Damianos across the room. He evidently took the opportunity to retrieve the book and was trying to sneak away. Gregg clenched his jaw, gripped the extinguisher tightly, and threw it. Score! It hit Damianos hard and launched him straight out the back door onto the porch.

Gregg scurried after him, catching his great-grandmother's soft cry for help as he went by.

"Where is Jody?" Gregg's breath was fiercely hot as he head-locked the weasel and squeezed. "Where?!"

He was losing control, and it felt good.

Damianos gasped and choked, but gave no reply. Gregg tightened his hold. He'd happily keep squeezing, but a moment later Damianos's concealed claws slashed his legs. Reflexively, Gregg let go.

Damianos picked up the book and smacked Gregg upside the head with it before running across the meadow like a gazelle away from a hungry cheetah.

Gregg was about to shoot after him, but stopped when he heard Grammy fussing back in the house. He turned to see the living room rapidly becoming a death trap.

"She'll burn alive!" he told himself, not because it was obvious, but because he needed to hear it louder than the cries inside his head: *he's getting away! If you lose him, you'll lose Jody forever!*

He stood there, feet nailed to the porch's wood-plank floor while his head veered from the burning house to the darting shadow in the tall grass, unable to choose.

The heat simmering in his core intensified, making everything around him appear smoke-like. His space wafted and bulged like thick clouds surging in a turbulent sky. It swelled from his insides, deepening his world into a setting lit more by blushing molten rock than a dimming afternoon sun.

Gregg's heart and mind raced, these bizarre changes less fearsome than the knowledge that every moment slipping by worsened his chance for success. He grasped his head and pulled his hair, screaming!

Then, quite abruptly, his resistance vanished and the heat overcame him. He was aware of flying across the meadow directly at the man in black, like a bird of prey. He couldn't tell if he had in one way or another forgotten his body altogether, but there was such a freedom of movement, it was like nothing he'd known before.

Damianos's expression as he looked over his shoulder was one of pure terror. Gregg swallowed him in a nebulous mist and, without feeling exerted in the least, shook and threw him badly, finishing him off with a terrible thumping against the earth. Leaving the heap that had been his former nemesis, Gregg retrieved the book and returned to the porch where his sights returned to normal.

His eyes opened as if from a dream. He had his body back and held neatly under his right arm was the book Damianos had wanted so very much. Somewhere, hidden in the meadow's waving green blanket, were the broken remains of the man in black, likely dead.

How in Hell did I do that?

But before he could ponder it further, his great-grandmother's agonized call stirred his attention and Gregg hurried into the burning house.

Chapter 29

Demigod

"Grammy?" Gregg leapt across the room aware of, but disregarding, the burning furniture close-at-hand. He knelt beside her, his heart beating so fast and hard he could scarcely speak. The 9-1-1 dispatcher had been very clear with him. His great-grandmother should not be moved under any circumstances before the paramedics arrived. But that was before the place started burning again.

What the hell is taking them so long? Living in the boonies had its negatives.

"Greggory?" There was so much pain in her voice. Her hand twitched, reaching for him.

"I'm going to get you out of here."

"No," her response flustered him. "I can't feel my legs." He grabbed her.

"No!" she commanded and then sagged from the exertion. "Please, there isn't much time. In the cellar is a dark leather sheathe and another crate like the one that held the book, only smaller and tired looking. They are from Jody's mother and must not be lost. Find them first and bring them to me."

"What?" Gregg's head was spinning, his puzzled thoughts giving him fits, but his great-grandma cast her all-powerful glare at him and he committed himself to doing what he was told.

He jumped over her and headed for the basement door. His feet streaked down the steps where he spotted the cache. He grabbed the items and carried them back upstairs with the idea to take them to his Grammy. As he skipped by debris into the living room though, he noticed a menacing patch of fire drawing ever closer to his great-grandma's feet.

If she can't feel her legs, she can start burning and not even know it!

The vision made Gregg drop the stuff and do whatever he could to keep the flames back. He waved at them, kicked them, even used a few books to try and shovel the fire away but in the end he couldn't think of anything to keep the inevitable from coming.

He knelt by his Grammy, took her hand despite her grimaces, and told her he was going to pick her up.

"I'll be careful. Trust me."

A few awkward moments later he felt like he had a fairly good grasp of her doughy girth and put his newfound strength to the test.

Lifting, he heard some awful cracks coming from his great-grandma's body and her entire frame went frighteningly limp. The wind blew out of her, making a terrible sigh, and Gregg lost the stamina to hold her up.

His legs buckled and they both crashed back onto the floor.

Gregg squeaked like a guinea pig when he missed reaching for her head in time and saw it thump hard against the solid wood planks.

"Oh, my God! Oh, my God! Grammy?"

He took her hand anew and looked into her near-lifeless face. The gloom was washing over her. The end was near. "Oh, my God!" Gregg howled, "I killed you!"

Beyond the hungry churning of the rising flames, Gregg could finally hear the sound of an ambulance's siren. At last help was on the way.

"It's too late." He gripped her hand in his, knowing she couldn't feel him. "Why?" he blurted. If only she could heal herself, like him.

He held her much too hard, praying for her to get up but there were so few signs of life left in her. "C'mon, get better!" he shouted. "I want you to be fixed so you can get up and get outta here!"

Amazingly, his grammy mumbled something.

Gregg lowered his face to hers, still clenching her hand, refusing to let her go. "I'm not leaving you here." He feared these were the last moments anyone was ever going to have with her. He couldn't bear the thought of her dying alone, not ever alone.

As hard as the situation was to accept, he thought he should say something brave, something kind before her ears closed permanently. He considered things he'd like to have said to his real mother, Samantha, if he had a second chance. Like *I love you* or *thank-you*. But in the end he only whispered, "I wish I could make you better."

His great-grandmother moaned, her eyes mercifully shut. Then she managed to utter a response typical for someone so old and warm-hearted, "I wish you could too."

The magic that followed was something befitting only to Gods.

Chapter 30

Spent

Gregg knew something was different that very second. It was like a seal had burst at the end of his arm and the swelling of heat that simmered so intensely in his body spilled through it, into Grammy. Akin to a plug being pulled at the base of a full bathtub, Gregg's essence flowed from him and he watched in a state of puzzled vertigo as a faint shimmering radiance came forth where his hand grasped so strongly onto his great-grandma's.

Her body became flushed with what could only be described as, life. Her pinching face relaxed and her eyes slowly opened, cloudless and sharp. Gregg even wondered if old blemishes and spots were mysteriously sinking back into her smoothing skin.

Grammy shifted her head and peered around with a perplexed expression. Her feet jerked and her legs moved under her, lifting her body into a kneeling position. With her free hand she examined herself, probably verifying the authenticity of her experience.

"What's happening to me?" she said at last. "Greggory, what are you doing?"

The approaching ambulance sounded as if it was coming up the driveway. Surely the paramedics would see the smoke wafting from the house, if not the fire burning within.

Gregg watched in awe as the dizziness made him slump. The heat that had fuelled his ire was fading, dangerously so, and his Grammy must have sensed it. He could feel her trying to jerk her hand, her connection to him, free.

"Greggory?" she kept calling, confusion and worry in her voice. "What's wrong? Why won't you let go of me?"

His hold was like a lock. Although his mind was still able to heed the contact and perceive the peril if the bond was not broken, he couldn't wield his body the way he wanted.

Grammy must have gotten up to her feet and was putting much more backbone into freeing herself. "Gregg!" she was shouting, "Gregg! Open your hand! Let me go! Let me go!"

The siren stopped. He could hear a diesel engine just outside the house. A second later there was crashing at the door and people were coming inside. There was yelling and calling, choking and gasping, his Grammy and the paramedics.

It was all fading from Gregg's ears. Darkness filled his eyes and he became eerily aware of the nothingness for the second time that day.

Chapter 31

Prophecy

In the darkness, Gregg noticed the molten ball of heat appear, swelling, throbbing, seeing it with his mind's eye as a hovering red droplet of liquid metal.

What is that thing supposed to be?

He thought of the warmth that had risen so sharply from his belly when his stress had been high and his urgency acute. It had churned inside him until his battles peaked, then it left as if swallowed by some grim hole hidden in his core. What he looked at now, brewing and stirring, had been washed out of him last when he saved his great-grandmother.

His ability to reckon things flowed easily this time in death. Or whatever this venture was. Ideas formed instantly, without the hindering disquiet of uncertainty. The moment Gregg wondered about the strange object, he realized that yes, this amazing sphere was the basis of his life.

It was a single brightness surrounded by smothering, unexplained dark. He was looking at his very essence, restoring itself, becoming larger and intense. He could feel it.

Suddenly, the nothingness around him oozed into raw and lurid, unnerving things. And he didn't want it to stop.

A befuddling haze washed over him, becoming a dazzling white. Shapes began to appear. He had the ability to move again, and something in the fog moved with him.

Jody, he hoped.

Gregg was lying down, looking up, and Jody was there leaning low over him, her skin lingering just above his. Delight overwhelmed him as he gazed into Jody's shimmering blue eyes. He shuffled to a sitting position and pulled her close for a deeply needed hug.

"Oh God," he whispered. "I wish this was real."

Jody resisted and pulled back. She stood, enveloped by the same indistinct white void from top to bottom. Gregg couldn't tell if they were in the centre of a tiny room or the middle of a vast universe. There was nothing that revealed their place at all, except for the perfect white table from which Gregg's feet now dangled.

He stared into Jody's smooth face, adoring her magical smile, noticing with a sideways glance that the long winding twine that ran so brightly from him did not exist on her. He fought hard not to get caught in the illusion.

"This is a dream," he insisted. "I still have to find you."

She looked back at him, sultry as all get-out, one hand softly pressed against his naked chest while the other traced the contours of his nose, chin and neck.

Gregg tried to think clearly, but it was hard. Gregg knew, as wonderful as it was being there, that he needed to find his Auntie Sam, *er... mom.*

Gregg waited and waited. "Why is this taking so long?" he finally blurted. Then the speedy, effortless manner of his thoughts engaged with solutions and fed him a surprising realization.

Jody's hands were all over him, her smile entrancing, yet the last time he was here he could not return that affection even though it was what he wanted most. Perhaps there was something to be learned in that.

Gregg quickly reached for her, putting a hand on either side of her head so she couldn't get away. He pulled her into him, although she resisted, shut his eyes, and puckered his lips.

As expected, his face didn't reach hers. He opened his eyes to see her a short distance from him, looking back with a pained expression. The white beyond around them closed in, becoming shaded, hardening into a long, stone corridor.

"Don't leave me!" Jody cried, stepping back toward a bend in the damp, cold hallway. "You promised me!"

"I'm not going to leave you," Gregg said calmly.

"Gregg!" Jody reached for him, desperate. The man in black, his hands grasping her flimsy clothing while flashing that insanely polished smile, stood behind her. His movements were smooth but screaming fast, ripping her apparel away, just as before, and digging under her skin with gouging fingers. Jody's blood gushed as Damianos pulled her skin from her body with the ferocity of a beast.

Gregg fixed his gaze onto her back, eyeing the gore and trying to understand how the odd hunks of muscle and blood-stained clusters of blanched filaments had gotten there and what they might mean.

Jody's screams were nightmarish and Gregg fought the urge to jump to her rescue. *This isn't real*, he kept telling himself.

Above him a white cloud emerged and from it a reaching hand clamped onto his shoulder.

"Chasing the illusion is what It wants!" Samantha's voice called.

"I know," he answered as Jody's cries shrank into an abyss of silence.

"You do?" Sam sounded surprised. "Then what are you doing here? Are you ready now?"

Bewildered, Gregg looked up at the brightening cloud within which Sam's face was visible. "Ready for what?"

She peered at him queerly, finally gesturing at the lighted cord. "You're not! You can't overcome the darkness like that. Hasn't Grammy helped you?"

"She tried."

Recounting the bulk of his day, he noticed the different expressions in Samantha's face. She appeared so much more normal now that she was dead. He could even see her quirks as if they were stamped straight from his own face.

"How could I not have caught on before? I didn't think you were anything but my crazy, scary aunt."

"I'm not scary!" she half-joked, "And I hope you can appreciate why I did what I did." She gestured toward the empty hallway. "Now you must stop this partly-dying nonsense, for Pete's sake! You're clearly not prepared."

"For what?" Gregg demanded. "What should I be prepared for? And why?"

His mother twitched unhappily. "I haven't a clue. You need to figure that out."

Stuck for words, Gregg peered nervously down the freezing hallway.

"You must face It, I suppose," Sam offered. "The darkness."

Gregg sighed. "The darkness..."

Strangely, the mystery of this looming problem did not grab his attention nearly as much as the questions that persisted about himself. "Who was my father?"

His mother looked aghast. "Your father?"

"I want to know what I am and the answer rests with him. Didn't he almost kill you?"

"Well, he did actually. But it was an impassioned fury that overcame him, nothing sinister. He also blessed me with a voracious sense of ecstasy. Everyone that saw me afterward saw only the wounds. He sent me to heaven, Gregg. And from it, I received you. How could I not love him?"

Gregg worried. "But he hurt you!"

"It was also him that saved me. He brought me back from the brink much the same as you saved Grammy just now. He, like you, has the ability to kill and also the power to heal. The catalyst is consent. You don't need it to put someone to death, but you gotta have it to revive 'em. Freewill is such a bizarre thing when you think about it.

"It was during my brief death that I became aware of this place and discovered the real monster that is hunting us all."

"Hold up," Gregg interjected. "Grammy said it was Jody's father that saved you."

"Yes, that's what everyone believed. I was so confused by it all that even I wasn't sure what had happened at first."

Gregg became aware of a bewildering presence wrapping itself around him like a heavy, stifling blanket. He glanced to the bend in the stone hallway and wondered what was lurking at the other end.

"Is that the darkness?" he asked.

Samantha glared at the bleak corridor. "It exists in the belly of The Beast."

"The man in black?" Gregg was confused. "I'm not afraid of him anymore."

"I told you, this is an illusion. It's a trap arranged to bring you to It. This is what It does to all those who are disoriented by their body's end. The darkness pulls them in before they can find their way home. Lost souls come here where It entices them with worldly desires. They follow through those halls never afraid of the blue fire that awaits them.

"At the end is a short ledge that sticks out high above a raging channel of piercing, cold lava. Spirits fall and become trapped in the numbing flow until the current brings them to a rocky beach where the darkness feasts on them, ingesting their light."

Gregg considered the spot where the dream-Jody and Damianos had disappeared, scared.

"It almost had me," Samantha confessed. "But I heard dear Lucy's voice calling for me and I felt him reaching, from where I did not know. I answered him and received his warmth. I became alert, standing on one of those many ledges, peering over the icy Hell that had nearly consumed me. I ran back into the hall as soon as I saw Him."

"Who?" Gregg had an ominous feeling.

"The darkness's shell, thundering into that hardened air. The dragon..." Samantha looked lost for a moment, reliving the nightmare. "Your wonderful father saved me. I know that now. It took me a long time to remember.

"He pulled me back and when I told him what I'd seen, he said the strangest thing. He knew. He didn't believe until after it happened, but he knew what I had gone through because someone had foretold it to him. He let it slip that there was more to the prophecy, but it hadn't made sense before. But since the first revelation had come true, Lucy was convinced that the others would also. Among them, that our child would be charged with protecting the dragon's enemy, so that she might rise up and lure the darkness from Its thickened scales."

Gregg gaped. "What?"

"Lucy warned me that the Beast can reach us in our bodies. He listens to our thoughts, asserts Himself in our minds, drives us to do things we know we shouldn't. All to bring us here, to this place, making *It* stronger."

"Temptation? Are you talking about being led into temptation?" Gregg recalled the things he had learned as a kid about the artful ways a certain villain tricked good people into doing bad things. But he had grown up convinced they were only stories.

Can this be happening? He couldn't turn his gaze away from the empty hall.

The answer that came to him seemed unbelievable.

"He found me. He knew me because I had been so close to Him here in His realm. I spent the rest of my life fighting Him in my head, keeping you and Jody a secret as well as I could. But He drained me. Jody in particular was always in danger. I'm sure He knew you were both near-at-hand. The fabrication that you died while still in my womb couldn't fool Him. I couldn't take it anymore. I felt Him, and the darkness that dwells in Him, always coming closer... I had to do something.

"I remembered what it was like being here, in this purgatory. I think freely here. The brain's barrier is not present in this place and He can't hoodwink us as well as He would like. I was sure I could protect you here.

"You mustn't go any farther, Gregg. Your place is with your body, not here in this trap." She reached for him. "If not for your father's genes, you'd be cooped up in this place, like me. You have the gifts to do what needs to be done. Without them, Jody won't make it. Go, my son. Find her now and keep her safe until you both figure out what you must do."

"Do you know where she is?"

"I know nothing from your world anymore."

"But how will I find her?"

Sam ducked her head toward the hall. "That man in black seems to be the answer. The dragon uses him and Jody to bait you for a reason. He knows what you held most dear in life and the greatest threat to your having it.

Whether you are aware or not, that wretch is it. Find him and you should find Jody."

"Great," Gregg sighed, grasping his tightening cord and feeling a sudden jolt lift him. "The one person I need to find Jody just happens to be the one person I've already killed."

Chapter 32

Revived

Gregg felt heavier and his thoughts raced in all directions. *Where am I? What's happening? Why can't I move?*

He was back in his body and he twisted and jerked as his vision slowly returned. He made out a voice in the blur around him.

"What the hell?"

Someone was touching him, pushing under his neck and pinching his wrist.

"Jesus! I don't believe it!" Whoever it was must have been a heavy bloke because Gregg could feel the world beneath him rock and shake when the guy moved and abruptly hollered, "Ben! Ben! Get your ass in here! Now!!"

The fog over Gregg's eyes gradually cleared. "What's going on?" he murmured.

He was lying down, strapped into a tight and narrow bed. Bright lights shone in his face, metallic white walls surrounded him and shelves protruded to his left and right. He lifted his head and glanced toward his feet. They felt cooler than the rest of him. Looking down he could see the open ambulance doors and beyond that, his great-grandmother's house.

Firemen in yellow reflective gear were cleaning up from their assault on Grammy's living room. Deflated hoses snaked across the ground and the flashing red lights from multiple fire trucks reflected off everything in the early evening backdrop. A tough-looking old guy with a bushy, grey moustache, dark blue uniform, and a red stethoscope draped around his virtually non-existent neck came leaping into the truck.

"What is it?" He didn't sound like he appreciated jokes too much. He froze, gaping when he noticed Gregg looking back at him.

"I can't move," Gregg complained. "Let me out of here!"

Ben and the EMT who'd called him gawked at each other before Ben finally blurted to his partner, "What did you do?"

"Nothing! I swear I was just sitting here filling in the paperwork when he started squirming."

"Well I'll be...!" Ben grunted, the lines on his face deepening in amazement. He turned his attention to Gregg. "Where'd you go, young felluh? You had us all scared as Greeks in the Public Sector." As he spoke, Ben and his partner carried out numerous checks on him, prodding Gregg in various places.

"I'm fine," Gregg argued. "I must have just blacked out."

"Blacked out?" Ben scoffed. "Young man, you weren't breathing and you had no pulse. Josh and I worked like the dickens to bring you back and failed. Pure and simple, you were what we in the profession like to call 'effin' dead'. Now," he went on, considering, as he pointed outside the ambulance, "your... who is it?"

"Great-grandmother," his partner helped.

"Right. Your great-grandmother is just outside with the Mounties, pretty devastated. I just left her by the squad car when I heard Josh chirping like a squirrel treed by a bear."

"Squad car?" Gregg's head felt as though it was spinning in the dryer.

"That's right." Ben put his big hand on Gregg's forehead and guided him back down to the pillow. "She's jabbering on about something or other."

"Where?" Gregg twisted under his restraints. "Jesus, let me outta here!"

"Whoa, easy!" Josh tried to calm him down. "Where's the fire, Chief?"

"Not here!" A man in a white fireman's helmet outside the door quipped.

"Look"—Gregg caught his breath—"I don't have time for this. I have to go and find the guy I killed and somehow make him take me to..." *Oops*. Gregg wished he'd bitten his tongue before he'd started speaking.

Ben and Josh watched him with the most puzzled expressions and Gregg strained to find a way to turn back the clock. Thank God a familiar voice started barking farther away.

"Have you seen my son? Gregg? Gregg? Where is he?"

On second thought, Gregg didn't know whether to suck in a heavy breath and call for Laura or to slump back and play dead. Of everything that had happened thus far that day, why was the presence of his mother, no — Laura — suddenly more stressful than anything else?

"She's gonna go bananas when she finds me in here," he sighed.

The EMT guys were still staring at him when his great-grandmother's distraught face came into view, leading Laura, Patrick, Dave and a Mountie in a flak jacket. Gregg actually considered going back to find Sam.

"So," Ben hesitated, "what's this about you killing somebody?"

Gregg cringed, unsure of how to handle the situation. He glanced from eyeball to eyeball, avoiding the policeman's as best he could, before he finally summoned the skill to focus on his prime objective.

"Grammy," he said—she sure looked a lot healthier now than when he'd left her—"I need the book. I know what I gotta do."

Chapter 33

Hell

Damianos was strangely cognizant of his body dissolving around him, slowly sinking into a sea of cold black ink. The pain was gone, the urgency had vanished, and the voice was silenced. There was nothing but an eerie sense of slow descent.

Powerless, recollections began to crawl in and out of his thoughts. He had been so close.

Perhaps his fervour for fairness had been doomed from the start. Quietly playing the role of judge and disciplinarian for the humans had appeared to work for centuries, but with every punishment he delivered and sense of accomplishment he achieved, there were always more tyrants out there unchaining their despotic deeds over the meek. Justice was the trophy he longed to grasp, but always it came as a puff of smoke, wisping away between his clenching fingers.

Then the voice had arrived and with it, new hope. Damianos gave himself over to the instructions he received, avoiding any thought of contention. At least, that had been his singular feeling on the matter until he first laid eyes on that half-breed jivita.

By then he couldn't stop the cause. Not then. His excitement had dulled his sensibility. He knew that now. He'd gotten sloppy with Gregg, making decisions to appease the voice in his head rather than to keep himself out of danger and alive.

His surroundings during his creeping fall changed. The black dissolved into a soft, sombre haze of flickering firelight, bare-log walls, and brown, rough wood furniture. Damianos felt his shape return and got up to look around.

Inside the old cabin were three simple beds, a modest kitchen, a small table with chairs and a crackling fire atop a stone hearth. Damianos ached at the sight.

He noticed his perspective was rather low, his stature small, such as that of a child. He sank to his little knees, his watery eyes wide, his voice breaking. He knew this dwelling. After stacks of years and heaps of misery, he had come back to the place of his birth.

Damianos was home.

It was just as he wanted to remember it. Warm, untroubled and safe. The cabin was set amongst the trees, next to a rippling creek, in a country strengthened by families of the same ilk, who put their faith in nature's temperament. A lilita's life was simple, living in tune with the world around him.

Damianos's spirit felt light, practically floating above his head. Suddenly he heard the clank and clash of the door and in walked his father, Acanthus. He was a towering figure with long, thin, dark hair that draped over his shoulders like a swelling stream at night. His eyes were black, wide apart and intense, and the powerful lines on his face made him seem majestic.

Behind him came Damianos's mother, Dosia. Her beautiful face was as bright and graceful as an early morning glow over snow-capped mountains. Her skin was smooth and pure to the touch and her carriage was proud and steady. Damianos's little sister, Lida, followed her in.

Lida's eyes had not darkened with age, still radiating a startling hazel-brown that practically smothered the whites. Her enormous cheeks were flushed, her nose small and button-like between them, and her long brown hair cascaded down her back like a shroud made of silk fluttering in the breeze.

Damianos was inundated with forgotten, joyous feelings as his family happily greeted him. His mother lifted him up into her arms as if he was a child again. At first it sent chills of uneasiness up and down his spine, but then the lifetime of memories he'd collected wasted away and he melted into her warmth, nuzzling into her chest and shutting his eyes, refreshing his mind to what life used to be like before the angoros came.

Something flashed and he realized he was standing again, inexplicably alone. He shot a look to the heavy wood door as it crashed open. A cold wind nipped his face and an icy chill gripped his heart.

Filing into Damianos's sanctuary like an advancing plague were stone faced angoros, their white robes and unclouded skin injecting the sting of pure terror into his veins.

Sick to his stomach, he watched as his father fought them and his mother struggled. Damianos knew he had no chance against the intruders as a thin-skinned child. He pulled Lida to a corner and hid with her behind a stack of firewood, under a tossed blanket. There he listened to the awful grunts and cries, reliving the horror that had haunted him for thousands of years, all the while doing his very best to keep his little sister from screeching and squirming. He didn't want it to happen again.

Be still! Be still! he ached to tell her, but he was too frightened to speak up. Fear, just as before, was paralyzing him.

Damianos heard his mother give one last despairing gasp and then, silence. Lida bawled and the angoros promptly swooped down and plucked her up, pulling her from Damianos's protective grasp.

"No!!" Damianos jumped, but he was only a child. The floor around him was bloodied, the place turned upside down and ahead of him, two angoros were dragging his dead mother and father away whilst a third held his crying sister tightly.

Not again! Not again!

His face was hot and tight. This had been the point in his horrific ordeal when young Damianos had made his fateful decision. When he'd thought only of escape.

He looked down at the wall behind the pile of wood where a small access door gave easy entry into a storage space outside. He had shimmied through it and ran away across the creek and into the forest, all while hearing his sister's frantic wails behind him.

Those cries had lived with him now for too long.

Not again!

The fireplace light faded and the walls around him broke into a cold, dark, rocky hall. The ominous cavern tunnelled around a bend where the angoros disappeared with Lida.

There was no stopping him. There was no way Damianos was going to let the nightmare go unchallenged another time. He would rather die.

He rocketed through a labyrinth of stone hallways. The dank stench and mouldy walls soon edged into a maze of biting chill. Damianos didn't slow. He could hear Lida's terrified voice ahead, even over the advancing reverberations of howling wind. He didn't let the rumbling tone of the place upset him. Lida was still alive and she was all he cared about now.

Damianos stopped when he came to a junction where an icy hue swelled, and he gazed cautiously to the end of the hall. The wind blew into his eyes, making it difficult to see. But there was a little something ahead, standing near the passageway's edge.

"Dammie!" It was Lida! "Help me!" her tiny voice shrieked. She had somehow evaded her abductors.

"Lida!" He moved toward her, but the cold was intense. "Lida, come back!"

"I can't! I'm too scared! Help me, Dammie! Please!"

Damianos kept pushing against the heavy air. Behind him, he could make out someone's faint cry, calling his name, but he tuned it out. He reached for his sister.

"Take my hand, Lida! I can save you! We can go back home, together!"

Lida screamed and Damianos's heart skipped. He peered ahead, "Why are you farther away from me? Come closer! Take my hand!"

Behind Lida was a gaping exit to a place of arctic cold. If she should step back only a few more paces, she would surely slip out of sight.

"Step this way! Come to me! I will keep you safe from the angoros, Lida. They will never hurt you again!"

"Dammie!" Her high-pitched voice cried ahead of him at the very same time as a deeper, boyish one called from behind.

It threw him and he jogged his head. Lida took another uneasy step back.

"No!" Damianos charged down the hall before the biting air stopped him. "Lida!"

"Damianos!" The boyish voice was coming clearer. It belonged to someone he knew.

It can't be.

Out of the corner of his eye, Damianos caught a glimpse of his little sister taking another ill-fated step back toward the dark chasm.

"Lida, no!" He ran to her with his hands outstretched, but he was too late. His sister slipped. "No!!"

His foot lurched over the edge of an overhang and he barely reached back in time to keep from falling down a steep cliff-face. Beneath his dangling feet was a sea of molten rock. Only it was blue and glacial looking.

"Damianos!" The other voice followed him even over the roar of the wind.

To his left and right was a sheer cliff studded with rocky bulges, similar to what he now clung to. Above was a clear black sky, sprinkled with faraway stars and shadowy, meandering silhouettes. Ahead was a pebbly black beach strewn with frostbitten bodies, and looming above them was a colossal dragon.

The towering monster angled over the beach and spread its mouth wide in a chasmal yawn. The effect was like a vacuum and bodies everywhere rose up and flew into the dragon's long throat.

Damianos stared at it, paralyzed.

The giant horror gnashed its fangs while a torrent of blue fire and white smoke ran between them, wafting angrily up and around its long, beastly snout as it tossed its head. The huge eyes, gleaming an abyssal cobalt blue that seemed to swim in shades of black, turned and searched over the great icy bath.

Damianos was stuck, trembling, barely holding on to the ledge, terrified the monster would spot him. Suddenly a blood-curdling roar shook the place and Damianos risked a quick glance. The dragon had settled on his beach and was glaring right at him. Then, sounding straightforward in Damianos's head, came the voice.

"You failed."

Chapter 34

Cliffhanger

Damianos's hold of the ledge was weakening. He could not last long against the frigid air and frozen rock. Below his dangling feet waited bubbling cold lava.

"What is this place?" His tone was weak.

The dragon let out a blast of smoke and ice from its nostrils, sneering. Damianos's resolve waned. After a lifetime of pursuing vengeance for his murdered family, he was about to join them in death, unfulfilled. He let go and slipped off the ledge in woeful acceptance of his everlasting punishment.

But something held him up.

"Damianos!" It was the half-breed. "Come back!"

Damianos looked up at him, disbelieving for the longest time. Gregg appeared as a mere shell of his being, like a blank wax figurine. His face was vacant, his eyes empty. Even his flesh felt curiously lifeless. Yet his hold on Damianos was strong.

"Damianos! I can't keep this up. Follow my voice. Follow my voice!" Gregg's mouth didn't move.

An arrogant chortle lingered over the liquid glacier. Damianos glanced at the huge dragon, its curious stature almost smug.

"The half-breed is a halfwit. His day of reckoning will come."

The mighty beast sprung enormous black wings that flexed high into the sky.

"Damianos!"

The cliff-face began to crumble, sending a shower of rocks over him. He reached for Gregg's arms and heaved as hard as he could, pulling himself back into the tunnel from where he'd fallen. Standing up, he realized the boy was gone. Inexplicably, he stood alone and from his belly, a strange blue cord darted deep into the mouth of the stoned hall from whence he'd come.

He glanced back and the dragon's flooded eyes locked on his.

"Set me free and have your vengeance on the angoros!"

Damianos turned and ran, careening from one hall to the next while a white haze appeared around him like a growing cloud and the twine that shot from his belly stiffened. He felt himself pulled into the mist and, just as the brightness became blinding, he heard the voice.

"Your jivita has handed you a second chance. There will be no third."

Chapter 35

Escape

Damianos gasped, taking in the cool evening air, feeling heavy. He sensed his return to his body and shot up, only to be overcome by light-headedness. He stumbled while his eyes slowly focused.

He was standing knee-deep in the tall grass of a meadow, near the edge of the forest. The house he had left to burn had been invaded by fire-crews. Emergency lights flashed from the front and men in yellow jackets hovered throughout. Down the property's gradual slope toward the street, Damianos spotted more blinking lights: red and blue.

The fog in his mind was thinning and the ring of alarm bells took its place. He had driven Lois's car off the road around there. With all the attention the house fire had garnered, someone must have noticed the abandoned beater left in the ditch.

"No." He cursed himself for being so careless. How could he have let things come to this?

Suddenly he noticed several police officers rounding the house, following a dog. *They're looking for me,* he realized. Never before had he come this close to being discovered by humans hired to uphold their laws. This could expose him and his kind. He crouched out of sight.

He could fight them. He'd likely win as long as they didn't shoot him first. If not for the throbbing ache from the wounds inflicted by that rotten little half-breed, he would...

Damianos paused, slowly grasping something that should have been obvious from the start. "I'm alive."

He stared at his perfect hands. They felt amazingly fine and looked even better than before he'd burned them. His whole body was limber and statuesque again! *But how?*

He remembered fleeing with *The Book of the Nornir* in agony, then being overwhelmed by the jivita and left to die.

Was it real? He shuddered, thinking of the dragon and its storming rage. *A second chance?*

Part of him clung onto the hope it was all just a dream—a very, very bad dream. His head ached trying to make sense of it.

The police dog barked madly, practically dragging his handler into the grass. At least six other officers joined the chase, coming towards him. Damianos turned to face the woods, knowing the trees and brush would give him the best chance to take out the dog and humans without being seen by others. He had to get out of the open.

Alas, his attempt to hunker and run was stymied by a stiff blow to his side. Something collided with him and sent him flying. When he looked up, Gregg was glaring back at him.

"Don't you try nothin'!" he warned with a breathy hush. Then Gregg's face lit up strangely. "I can't believe I did it! Ha! I totally brought your ass back to life!"

Again, Damianos couldn't make clear sense of anything at the moment.

"I healed you and called you back." He seemed quite proud of himself. "And I broke the connection before I got all woozy again. Shya! Who's Superman now?"

Apparently, the half-breed was a quick learner.

"You saved me?" Damianos couldn't believe it. If not for the little schnitzel, he wondered what might have become of him. "The dragon..."

Gregg's expression shifted in an instant to stunned wonder. "What? You saw him?"

Damianos was about to admit the impossible truth and ask what Gregg knew about the huge beast when the sound of the approaching dog caught both their attention.

Gregg gasped. "Crap! What do we do?"

"We?"

Gregg threw him an impatient, dirty look then reached behind him for something rather large and shoved it hard into Damianos's chest. To his utter surprise, it was *The Book of the Nornir*.

"Take me to Jody!" Gregg demanded. "Or I'll send your sculpted butt back to Hell!"

Damianos at first caught his breath, keen to his limited options at present. "Very well." He filled his lungs again.

"If we are to do this together though, you must learn to stop hitting me!" He got up, being careful to stay low, and gestured toward the forest. "Come. We can take care of them in here."

Gregg followed. "What do you mean, take care of them?"

Damianos knew he was going to hate breaking this kid in. "I mean kill them!"

"Kill them?"

"Yes." They scurried over the gnarled roots of a tall cedar and ran through the bush. "And here's something else for you to learn. I hate repeating myself."

"Repeating yourself?"

The little skunk's teasing was going to be a real challenge. Damianos tried to ignore him. If he was lucky, he might be able to outrun and lose Gregg without having to fight anyone.

Damianos moved fast over the darkening landscape, using his agility to skim by trees and brush and hustle over the uneven ground. *I don't hear him,* he grinned.

He kept glancing farther ahead, looking at the treetops and wondering if his luck could be more perfect. To think, the voice had brought him to this far end of the world without being able to pinpoint the girl's whereabouts exactly. But Damianos had picked the spot to make camp, preferring the shelter of thick woods, and now it seemed he might be closer to his hideout than he knew.

He snuck a look over his shoulder and didn't see anyone behind him. *Ha,* he thought and slowed his pace to catch his breath. He held the book adoringly in his hands, safe at last. But how much more fictitious could the feeling be?

The sight of the dragon sprang to his mind. "Set me free and have your vengeance on the angoros!"

What was this book and did he really want to set a monster like that loose? *To do what? And if the dragon was imprisoned, why and by whom?*

"Why can't I hear you?" he softly called into the forest shade. No reply sounded in his tense, overwrought mind. He didn't know what to do. "Why won't you speak?"

Catching him by surprise, another voice chirped loudly in his ears, "Because, I've been having fun with the dog!"

Damianos spun around so fast he almost kept going, like a top. "What?" He tightened his grip on the book.

Gregg shrugged and nodded in the direction they came. "While we were running, I remembered how your girlfriend—Lie, was it? She was peeved that I snuck by her at the cemetery this morning. All I know is that I really wanted to sneak up on you and Jo. So, I wondered if I could do the same thing with the cops. I stopped running and stood there waiting for them, wanting to be hidden. They made tracks right by me!"

"Of course they ran right by you," Damianos snarled. "They're looking for me!"

"Yes," he agreed. "But you don't understand. They didn't see me and the dog didn't smell me. Nobody knew I was standing there right in the open. Sooo, I started chasing them." He had a look of mischief gleaming in his eyes.

"I swear I've never run so fast in my life! It was like I wasn't me anymore. I caught up to the dog and started yanking the thing's tail. You should have seen that mutt crash into a huckleberry bush, yelping. I kept doing it and the poor pooch didn't know what the whoop was going on.

"The cops thought the dog was going insane and weren't sure what to do about it until finally I screamed like a banshee in its ears. It took off in the other direction and the police followed."

Gregg chuckled, clearly amused with himself. "I'm pretty sure they heard me shriek too because, man, those cops jumped. But they didn't see anything. Their eyes were going all over the place. I bet they're telling each other these woods are haunted now. Everybody's going to remember this forest again."

Apparently, the boy was able to pick up some of a jivita's talents all on his own. This wasn't necessarily the best news Damianos had gotten that day. He feigned relief. "Then, no one is following us?"

Gregg proudly signalled no. "I could get used to this. Girl's locker rooms, here I come!"

"How entertaining for you."

"Mhmm." Gregg took hold of Damianos's arm and resumed their walking. "And by the way, I've got something you should learn too. Don't try to run away from me. You remember what happened the last time you did that?" He slowly let Damianos go. "Jody better be okay."

Damianos felt as if he was being ambushed from all sides. His mind raced to find a way out.

Chapter 36

Fear

Ligeia gripped her belly and grumbled, "I need to eat." But syrēnes did not make a habit of packaging the leftovers from their meals. They preferred devouring what they could from a fresh kill and looked forward to the next hunt when the craving came again. Humans, it's not like they were hard to find.

Her problem now was keeping her composure around that befuddling girl. "Grr, where is he?" she complained. "How long can it take to find that dumb book?"

Ligeia was becoming increasingly convinced this venture was going to push her to her limits, a place she did not want to go.

The day was ending, meaning the temperature was getting even colder. She stood alone in the tent's shadowy gloom, watching with little amusement as misty clouds gently rose. She contemplated igniting the propane heater again.

Ligeia suddenly realized she hadn't heard Jody's pathetic whining for some time. *I wonder if she's dead.* The thought brought a grin to her face, but then she quickly adjusted her thinking. "Not without me, she doesn't!"

She went out and paced around the tent in the forest twilight. Above, the stars began to shimmer and blink in a clear blackening sky. Feeling confoundedly obliged to do what Dammie had wanted, she sealed their tent shut and opened their prisoner's.

Ligeia looked through the dimness, seeing only stillness in the unlit room. Suspicions crawled through her mind and she glanced over her shoulder as she slowly stepped in. *Why am I worried?* she told herself. *She's only a girl.*

To be honest, she wasn't sure what Jody was. Not yet.

Finally, Ligeia spoke. "Where are you?" she spat.

"I'm right where you left me," came Jody's shivery, sarcastic reply as the shape of her head lifted from the pillow. "Where did you think I was?"

Ligeia hissed. She didn't like this dopey girl, not one bit. "I was afraid the cold might have killed you."

"You're not fooling anyone, beauti-foul." This little witch was mocking her. "Just do what you gotta do with me and let me go or kill at will. Just get it over with because I'm tired, I'm cold and I am friggin' hungry. My body hurts, my heart is broken and my spirit wants to spit in your pretty bitch face."

Ligeia remained standing a short distance away in the dark, not wanting the girl to see her grin. It was a rare thing for Ligeia to come across a male victim that showed such grit; she hadn't thought it existed in females.

When she had more control of her facial expression, she went and lit the kerosene lamp. It created a soft, warm glow in the otherwise cold and stuffy tent. Jody's skin was creased across her face from pressing on the pillow, and the rest of her bare skin was covered with unsightly goose bumps.

Yet there was still beauty. Tragic. Granted, her gorgeous platinum hair was a mess, but Ligeia still had a hankering to run her fingers through it, to feel its glossy soft strands and smell their flowery contours. She imagined mounting the girl and grabbing her from behind, pulling her head back by that wondrous hair and tearing into her fine neck.

Ligeia shuddered. She was getting much too hungry.

Her eyes roamed over Jody's back. It looked absurdly gruesome compared to the rest of her. "What happened to you?"

Jody jerked as if she had fallen fast asleep only to be surprised awake. "What?"

"Your back. It looks awful. What happened to you?"

Jody let out a murmur then turned her head away.

That response only irritated Ligeia. "Answer me!"

"I don't know. It's been like this for as long as I can remember." She seemed to sag deeper into the mattress. "I don't know."

"It's ugly."

"Thanks for noticing."

"How have you managed this long with such a disfigured body?"

"Hey!" Jody's head swept back and she glared. She looked as if she wanted to say something, but changed her mind and instead curled her nose, snarling, "That which doesn't kill me, makes me stronger, right?"

Ligeia thought for a moment. "That's stupid. You should get that mess fixed. Human doctors can do that, you know. See how strong you become when you're beautiful, like me."

"I don't like doctors. I've never been to one and I never will."

"Are you a loony? If you've never been to a doctor, how do you know you don't like them?" Ligeia snickered. "I like them plenty..., especially when they're just out of med-school. They think they're so smart." She really needed to eat something soon. Perhaps she'd try changing the subject. "Who was that boy you were with last night?"

Jody looked exhausted. "What? You mean Sean?"

"Sean," Ligeia chimed. "Yes, that's him. Do you love him?"

"How did you know about Sean?"

"We were watching. He wanted to have sex with you." Ligeia couldn't help but shudder, thinking of the girl's revolting flaw. "Why didn't you?"

Jody looked appalled. "What, why? Are you nuts?"

"Was it because of your back?"

The question seemed to throw the girl off course. She apparently had something to say, but again bit her lip and didn't answer.

"It's okay. I'd be much less likely to exhibit my womanly traits if I had marks like that. Sean didn't give me the impression he was stimulated by them. I can see why you keep yourself covered there."

"Would you please shut up?" Jody whined. "What is this? What are you doing here? Is this your girl-time or something? If I insisted that my back was definitely not the reason why I didn't have sex with Sean last night, would you show me your sweet backside and leave?"

"Then, why?" Ligeia hated beating around the bush.

Jody growled and thrust her face into her pillow.

The reaction confused Ligeia and she watched, trying to understand. She had never done that to any great extent before, although Damianos often recommended it. He believed it made him a better hunter.

Suddenly a thought entered Ligeia's head. "Oh, I know." She felt rather proud. "It's your jivita, isn't it?"

"What?"

"You know, Gregg. You have an odd relationship with him."

Jody deflated at the mention of Gregg's name. "Had," she corrected. "Oh God, I can't believe he's dead. You monsters."

"Do you love him?"

Ligeia thought she had got the obvious answer when Jody's eyes welled, but the girl's tongue seemed pasted to the inside of her mouth. She observed Jody's odd body language for some time before the girl finally rolled an awkward glance her way and said, "He was a friend."

Ligeia felt her face twist. "A what?"

"A friend. My best friend. There's a difference between what Sean and Gregg were to me. Gregg's always been there for me, for as long as I can remember, treating me like a princess one minute and tangling with me like a wrestler the next. He knew what I needed and when, even when I didn't."

"Like last night?"

Jody sighed. "Leave me alone."

"Sean was right," Ligeia goaded. "You are a tease." Jody flung herself up between her restraints and threw her a horrified scowl, but Ligeia wasn't buying it. "You've never told Gregg, have you?"

"Yes!" Her voice was adamant, but something in her demeanour faltered. "Just... maybe not directly."

"What does that mean?"

"What am I supposed to say?" Jody argued. "Every time I get too close to a guy, they turn around and leave me! Every single one! I never wanted that to happen with Gregg. I couldn't live without him. He was... he was..."

"Your friend?"

"My *best* friend. He's the only one I've ever shown my scars to, willingly," she added with a grumble. "My adoptive parents have seen them, of course. But not since I was really young. I don't know. There's always been this connection with Gregg. I felt safe. I knew I could just be myself and he'd still put up with me. He was the only person in the world that would never ever hurt me, no matter what. Lots of boys have tried to be what Gregg was to me, but it always ended the same. Tits and ass, that's all they really wanted and when I didn't give it to them they left me, calling me names, being mean.

"I've found ways to get over it because Gregg was always there to pick up the pieces, to listen to me cry, or tackle me to the floor and blow into my ears." Her smile was tremulous and her shoulders shivered. "God, I hated when he did that. But that never stopped him."

If she didn't like it, then Ligeia had a hard time figuring out why Jody looked like that all of a sudden.

That manner soon vanished though. "And now he's gone, too."

Normally Ligeia cringed at the mere idea of having a conversation like this with anyone. Maybe it was okay at the moment because she was starving and looking for a distraction.

Her mind flashed on Damianos and the relationship they'd shared over the years. For a long time, their bond had been fireworks. Her whole world had revolved around him. But after a while she'd become more aware of his strange attraction to justice and started to feel less important. She couldn't remember really telling him how she felt.

Bleck! What an awkward talk that would be.

Come to think of it, they didn't converse much at all anymore about meaningful things. Throughout this entire search for his 'benighted child' Damianos had never been fully clear on what he intended to do next.

Perhaps it wasn't food or a distraction that she craved for, after all. "What's it like to be left?" Ligeia asked.

Jody didn't look like she wanted to have this talk.

"No one has ever deserted me." Ligeia couldn't help but sound at least a little pompous, even to her own ears. "Anyone who bows out of my life does so because I wish it."

Jody suddenly glared. "I don't believe it," she gibed, staring at Ligeia's face.

"It's true. In fact, I've dined on my previous mates."

"That's not what I meant, and you're disgusting. It's just... if I didn't know better I'd say there was something in your eyes just now."

Alarmed, Ligeia started rubbing them. "What? What is it?"

Jody grinned. "Don't worry. It's something I've been looking at in the mirror for years... it's fear."

Chapter 37

Afoot

Gregg followed Damianos through the forest. How the guy knew where he was going was a mystery to him. Never in his life had Gregg periled a trip this deep into The Whispering Woods. There was always something that seemed amiss here.

When Gregg and Dave were smaller, there were a good number of times when they'd run like hellhounds back into the open meadow, sure they'd heard voices speaking from the high perches around them. Every time they looked back however, no one was there. Grammy never believed them, determined it was just the wind blowing between the trees.

Shya. While officially the place's name was acknowledged as The Woods, Gregg and Dave made the unilateral decision to add the 'Whispering' bit.

Gregg sure appreciated his great-grandmother though. After he'd awoken in the back of the ambulance earlier, all he'd wanted to do was get the heck out of there and find Jody. His Grammy had made a clear path for him to sneak away by making the excuse in front of the family that she had left important parcels in the house that she had to find. She wanted to give one in particular to Gregg as quickly as possible. As soon as she was allowed, she started rummaging and asked Laura, Patrick and Dave if they would help.

It was a simple but perfect distraction and Gregg took full advantage of it, dashing for the last place he remembered seeing Damianos.

It was hard at first, grabbing hold of a dead guy's cold, stiff hand. Gregg had to swallow down the creeps and clamp on tight. Then he closed his eyes and imagined searching for the man in black.

He didn't yet understand how it worked; it was more like an obscure sensitivity than clear sight. He supposed it was like following a trail, a fine strand of that twisting whirling fibre. Once he had a hold, he just kept following it. Cold and slight at the start, the strange rope became warmer and more robust the farther he went.

In time he heard sounds and noticed shades of darkness and light. He called over and over until he could hear Damianos's voice and, at last, he could feel the villain's grasp. In that moment, Gregg felt his heat draining into Damianos's body through their connection. The corpse's bleak inflexibility seemed to melt away, giving rise to warm life again.

When Damianos's eyes opened, Gregg knew it was time to break their bond. Unlike his experience with Grammy, Gregg managed to make it work just right this time. What he didn't much like however, was the shock he got from breaking the hold.

Light-headed for moments afterward, Gregg had soon felt pretty stoked about what he'd done. It was an amazing feeling and he had the growing impression he might be invincible, even better maybe than Superman.

"I suppose I should thank you," Damianos said, without turning around, as he bounded over a fallen log in the middle of their trail. "Despite the fact that it was you that took my life, you were also the one that gave it back. A second chance. And you did it even though I had awarded you such hardship earlier."

He threw Gregg a backwards glance, suspicion in his carriage. "Half-breeds and their parents are caused great displeasure where I come from. It's not natural for races to mix. Because of that, it's not really known what happens when the traits of one species are combined with or subtracted by another.

"I can tell you this, young man, there is no chance a pure jivita would have brought me back. Your human derivation apparently brings either compassion or stupidity to a jivita's raw will to overpower his enemies. I wonder if you really are a halfwit."

Gregg wasn't sure how to take that and Damianos didn't stop to see any humble or royally pissed response Gregg might have had. Instead, the walking shadow continued to lead them deeper into the forest.

"You said you saw the dragon." Gregg was curious.

Damianos paused, looking as if a weight had been placed on his shoulders. His breathing was heavy and his eyes seemed to be looking inward.

"What do you know?"

Gregg took in a deep breath. "I know it's a shell. Inside is the darkness."

Damianos shrugged. "There is darkness inside us all."

Gregg felt a little awkward. "I guess so. But I'm supposed to protect Jo from this particular darkness because she is going to destroy it."

This declaration got a rise out of Damianos. "Destroy the dragon?"—Gregg could see through the forest gloom that the guy's mind was brooding over something—"Are you sure?" Damianos looked at Gregg, as if calculating.

"When I died today because of you, you turd, I came to in this white space. Jody was there with me and we"—Gregg stumped himself, his face feeling redder suddenly—"did things, you know. Anyways, the whole scene changed and suddenly I was in this cave with a narrow hallway at the end of it. You were there. You hurt Jo and then ran off with her down the hall.

"I didn't follow. It's a trap that the darkness uses to catch souls on some rocky beach at the end of some channel of glowing cold lava. It eats them and grows stronger."

"You didn't follow?" Damianos appeared to be speaking more to himself than to Gregg.

"Did you see it? The lava and all?" Gregg didn't wait for an answer. "It's not just in death that It reaches us. It's like the bible-thumpers were right, man. The Beast gets into our minds and makes good people do bad things. It leads you into temptation! Is that why you took her?" Gregg asked.

Damianos stood motionless, unreadable.

"That's it, isn't it? It's in your head. My God. What would make you sell your soul to the devil?"

"Keep your God and Devil out of this!" Damianos flared. "I despise the notion. Any deity that allows so much pain and misery is no better than the Devil in Hell. Don't try to play me for a fool, boy. And don't pretend to know what impels me to do what I do. Look closely." He pulled up the burned sleeves of his black coat. "Do you see any strings? I make my own decisions in this life, free of any meddling by fictitious monsters that lurk in the hereafter."

Gregg thought for a minute while Damianos pushed on amidst the undergrowth with determined steps. "So, why Jody then?"

The man in black held up the book and gave him an unflattering look.

"What is it?" Gregg asked.

Damianos responded with an impatient sigh. "Aside from the obvious, I don't really know."

"Well, where did it come from?"

"I don't know."

"What do the symbols on the front mean?"

"I don't know!"

"Then what good is it to you?"

"Damn, boy! I don't know!"

"For a guy that takes such pride in making his own decisions, you don't know very much." Gregg was feeling the strain in his mind. He wanted answers. "How did you know this book even existed?"

Damianos stopped and grumbled something and flashed his menacing black-orb eyes at Gregg.

"A voice came to me one night as I stood next to a church altar in Italy. It told me everything I wanted to hear and more, making a promise to me in exchange for a service. It was the voice that told me where your dear Jody bides and of the book that should be near her. It was all too *tempting* to ignore.

"I've come this far. I've made it this close. Be it destiny or good fortune that I still breathe in front of you now, I will not blow this!

"You look at me like a gambler whose bluff has been called. You think you can control me, much like the voice that guided me here. Yet here are the facts, boy. I possess something you deem fully necessary to your life's purpose: Jody. I also possess something the voice regards as indispensable for *Its* aspirations." Damianos flashed the book. "The voice pledged the realization of a long awaited justice for me as compensation.

"Now," the prick curled his perfect nose and seemed to speak out the side of his mouth, "I challenge you, dear halfwit, to tell me what you can possibly grant me to quicken my pace to your missing girlfriend?"

Gregg wasn't going to waste any more time with this crap. He approached Damianos, fire lighting in his belly, and the man in black took a short step back.

"I can remind you that it was I who sent you to meet your voice in the first place."

Damianos seemed to chew that one over in his mind. "Let us walk then," he said smoothly.

"What'd the Beast promise you? Money? Power? Everlasting life?"

Damianos pushed undaunted through the blackening forest and chuckled.

"Genocide."

Gregg's belly churned. Damianos said it in such a relaxed, natural manner. Was he joking?

What seemed like such a clear-cut plan to find Jo and save her was suddenly feeling iffy. He glanced back over his shoulder more than once, watching, almost hoping for the police dog and bounding Mounties to come back.

As Gregg kept pace with the scoundrel, going deeper into the unknown, he hoped he wasn't making the biggest mistake of his life.

Chapter 38

Returned

"It must be blocked," a hushed tone muttered near Jody's ear. "We must get back to the light!"

The quiet babbling that carried on all day around her had become more of an annoying white noise as Jody trembled and agonized on her cot.

In addition to the shivering cold biting her naked skin and the stabbing ache in her heart and mind, Jody's stomach had now begun wrenching. She was sadly convinced she was losing the will to live, lying in the dark, weak and defenceless, at her abductors' mercy. *What good will possibly come of this?*

The winged woman had left minutes earlier, making a big scene about whatever, and since then Jody's ability to withstand the misery kept sliding away into some deep abyss. No one would find her in time. No one.

"You're stronger than this. Don't you give up."

In Jody's dazed state, she said the first thing that popped into her mind. "Mommy?" It came out more as a slurred whimper than anything else.

She lifted her head, trembling above the moist, funky-smelling pillow and looked around. Not surprisingly, she was alone.

"Help us find the way back. We want to go home."

"What? How?" she asked, keeping her shivering voice down. Her body shuddered, making the bed's joints squeak.

"Shut up in there!" Ligeia was lurking outside the tent.

She'd been so still, Jody hadn't realized the bat-winged witch was near. Jody wondered what she was doing out there, being so quiet.

Ligeia shifted and the tent's flaps separated as Ligeia stepped in. She lit the kerosene lamp and, with a strangely stoic expression, brought her face close to Jody's.

Jody's eyes welled up for the umpteenth time that day as her captor began stroking her long white-blonde mane. She shook, and this time it was not from the cold. There was anticipation in Ligeia's eyes. Something was going to happen and Jody had the awful feeling it wasn't going to be good.

The witch's sleek voice cooed, "He's back."

Chapter 39

Found

A masked golden glow ahead guided Gregg and Damianos through the smothering night. It appeared as if out of nothing in a treeless basin.

"What's that?" Gregg asked.

"What do you think it is?" Damianos sounded elusive.

As they got closer, it became obvious they were approaching a tent, perhaps two, with a lamp lighting one from the inside. Sudden excitement kicked Gregg's heels into high gear.

"Jody!" This must have been the spot where Damianos was hiding her. How bizarre that it was so close to his grammy's house, nestled deep inside The Whispering Woods. He never would have guessed to look in here.

Gregg ran ahead until a tall full-figured shadow emerged before him, with black wings spreading wide. He slipped to a stop at her feet.

"What's this?" Clearly surprised, she blocked Gregg's path, wearing some one-piece sweater thingy that was out of this world.

Damianos stepped between them. "What do you think it is, Lie?" He walked by nonchalantly and muttered, "Honestly, you both speak much too soon and far too often. Observe first, find understanding, and confirm your suspicions for yourselves. In short, think before you validate your weaknesses in front of others."

Gregg and Lie frowned at each other. Her face and hair, her entire body exuded sex in a way that left Gregg weak in the knees. He realized that he was staring at her like Dave eyeballed the girls he found online. She was inspecting him too.

It wasn't easy, but Gregg snapped himself out of it and tried to dart around his curvy obstacle to make a beeline for the tent. Finding Jo was the most important thing now. He couldn't let himself forget her like he'd done this morning. Not again.

Unfortunately, Lie grabbed hold of him, gripping his arms as if she had pincers instead of hands.

"He's different this time," she decided. Cautiously, she brought her face closer and sniffed. "I can smell him."

Damianos looked unconcerned.

"That's brilliant, Lie. Whatever would I do without you?"

"He didn't this morning."

"I know."

Lie licked her charcoal lips with her amazingly long tongue. The sight froze Gregg in a heartbeat, a very fast and dizzying heartbeat. She slowly brought her mouth close to his and touched his lips with her tongue, taking her flirtatious time.

The feel of her touch was warm, melting his resistance until he felt like goo in her grasp. She kissed him and Gregg became suddenly aware of the one part of his anatomy that most definitely was not feeling like goo.

He couldn't help but kiss her feebly back, though he did it with a stubborn smattering of guilt. He both wanted her to stop and keep going, on and on. It was so confusing.

She finally pulled back, looking reluctant to do so and at the same time pleased about what the experience had done for her. "I can taste him too."

There was something dribbling down her lusty lip and over her chin. She collected it with her finger and sucked it off in her mouth, grinning.

Gregg shivered, feeling drained and dazed. Something warm was puddling behind his lip. He drew a sharp breath when he realized it was blood.

"Jesus! Did you bite me?"

Lie chuckled.

"Marvellous," Damianos muttered. "Any less subtle, my love, and you'd be having the bastard's child."

"Of course," Lie murmured, a peculiar gleam twinkling from her dark eyes. "I like your smell," she whispered softly to Gregg. "And you taste like…"

She finished her sentence with an odd gesture. She flared her teeth and gnashed them together, curling up her nose to boot. Gregg couldn't tell if she was super horny, or darn hungry.

He carefully shook himself free and scuttled next to Damianos. "She seems nice," he lied. "You two been a couple long?"

He sighed. "Very."

Gregg managed to focus his attention on the tent, seeing the light that radiated from inside dance and flicker. Something in there moved.

"Jo?" he called, keeping one eye on the black-winged dominatrix.

Damianos appeared amused and glanced at Lie inquiringly, "Well, my love. Thank you for not eating the child. You didn't *nibble* on anything, did you?"

Lie glared at him, "I demand more glory for my efforts. If you had any idea how difficult a day I've had..."

"Yes, yes. It's always about *your* day," Damianos interrupted grumbling. "I'd wager my soul that mine outdid yours." He gestured towards the tent. "I see you left the light on." His eyes turned skyward. "Pray the police helicopter does not fly above us soon. I shall give you more than glory should our camp be found thanks to your shining beacon."

Lie scowled and huffed something incoherent.

"Who's out there?" a meek voice fussed. "Hello?"

Lie massaged her face and groaned, "Please, tell me I can kill her now?"

It was Jody's voice, Gregg knew it. She was alive! Not waiting for permission, Gregg went to the entrance flap and opened the way in. What he found both relieved him immensely and choked his heart's every beat.

"Jesus, you black-hat-wearing lowlife! What have you done?"

Chapter 40

Serenade

Ligeia came to Damianos with an irked look upon her face. "I don't get it. This morning I had no idea that the half-breed was anywhere near us. Now, I knew you were coming ten minutes before I could see you. What gives?"

"Surely you can figure out he has a jivita's knack to hide in plain view, should that be his desire. What's interesting to consider is, did he figure it out before today?"

"So, why isn't he hiding now?"

"Once he knew it was just him and me in the forest, hiding was no longer a concern. The forest keeps us all well covered. His ultimate infatuation has remained, however."

"And that is?"

Damianos chortled. Ligeia could be so simple-minded. "To save his love, of course."

Ligeia glared at the tent with a clearly begrudging expression. "And behold,' she quipped sourly, "here he is. He's good. So, what do we do when his greatest desire is to kill us and set the bitch free?"

Damianos shifted under his coat, deciding not to answer. "Tell me you found something spectacular in your little book of spells."

Ligeia grew a peculiar smile. She drew a deep breath and let out a series of brilliantly soft musical chants, becoming gradually louder to the ear.

Over her voice, Damianos could hear commotion inside the tent. Crying, examining, asking and answering. There were so many emotions ballooning on the other side of those canvas walls, Damianos wondered if the seams might break apart.

Ligeia's song rose up, unchallenged. Damianos doubted Gregg and Jody even realized they were being serenaded, and wondered what effect it might have. Peering through an open part of the tent flap, Damianos watched as Gregg knelt down next to Jody, visibly shaking, his hands hovering over her bare skin, to her tight restraints and back again. Without a doubt, the stupid boy didn't know what to do first.

"I will only numb his senses from here," Ligeia warned. "I must sing into his ears alone so that the verse's power is most effective, and you are not... *risked*."

Dismay knocked on the fringes of his thoughts. Damianos had never known a syrēne enchantment that required such a close proximity to communicate. But then, he had not heard of a syrēne successfully baiting a jivita before either.

He decided that if Ligeia made it work, then he could quickly kill Gregg and win the day. No one else was going to stop him. If Ligeia failed, then Gregg would probably kill her first. In either case, one of his problems would disappear.

Damianos grinned holding the book tightly. In only a short time, he would have the advantage again.

Chapter 41

Torment

Jody's world stopped. Her eyes bored into the pillow and her mind rushed to find meaning. That tone, that delivery... *that's Gregg!* It couldn't be. It was impossible. Those animals were playing an evil trick on her!

But then, what if it was him? What if Gregg's voice had joined the others, whispering, calling, searching for the way home? A startling thought crossed her mind. What if she was already dead?

"Jody?"

Gregg's cry strangely lit her insides and her fixed concentration broke.

"Oh my God, Jo!"

There was rustling beside her and she flung her eyes up to see.

"I knew I'd find you! I knew it!"

To her confounded surprise, there he was, standing right beside her. "Gregg?"

She was stunned. *He came back. He came back!* His face poured over her with a medley of stirred emotions. Excitement, horror, relief and pain. It was all there.

Gregg fell to his knees, looking like he wanted to hold her, maybe kiss her or something. But as she watched his eyes and hands roam awkwardly for a spell, she knew he must have changed his mind. He growled, "I'm getting you out of here!"

He reached over and tried to untangle the cords around her wrists. The experience hurt, and that rattled her because up to this point she had really not been thinking clearly. Was she proper dead, or was Gregg in fact alive? Which made more sense?

"We're leaving. No one is going to hurt you anymore."

This was a very confusing delusion. "Is this happening?" If it was, then Gregg was sure fumbling a lot with her restraints. And it was strange that he took such awkward pains to avoid touching her.

Jody was no fool. She knew Gregg had always tried to get closer and cuddle in his way, or cop a subtle feel here or there. What was different? Was it because of her back? She couldn't help but shrink in front of him.

A moment later, the monster stepped into view and the dream was over. The nightmare had returned.

"Good evening," the black demon said, his words spreading almost hypnotically over the gloom like an amazingly warm blanket. Something about his voice was numbing her, which it hadn't done before.

It must have been grace inside that gave her the valuable sense to resist, but she was very weak. *Oh, God! Fight it, fight it!* She kept telling herself, shutting her eyes and gritting her teeth. She didn't want to be seduced, not by him.

The winged woman came also, her dark eyes staring intently at Gregg. Jody's lungs froze, watching her sleek advance. Ligeia pressed herself into Gregg in a most curious way, urging him to look at her. But he kept brushing her aside.

"I'm going to get Jo out of here. You're not going to give her to that Devil, you freaks! I won't let you."

The man in black stood there with a gnarled snicker on his face in obvious amusement. "I didn't really expect you to." He raised his voice, looked at Ligeia and asked, "Why do you hesitate, my love?"

Ligeia threw him a dirty glare, and then wrapped herself around Gregg like a straightjacket. It all seemed too surreal. What was going on? Gregg was dead, she'd seen it happen.

Ligeia brought her face closer to Gregg's and started humming something, her melodic voice throbbing while he tried with obvious difficulty to shake her off.

"What are you doing?" Gregg complained. "Get off me before I witch-slap you!"

"It's laughable," Damianos said. For the first time, Jody noticed the big book he held tightly in his hands. "You're labelling Ligeia and me as freaks. Animals. Monsters..."

He stepped around the cot and coolly whispered into Jo's ear, "When it is the both of you that are the anomalies. We live by nature's way. Your parents transgressed it."

Gregg threw Ligeia off and growled, "I'm getting her out of here, now!"

He reached down and tried to untangle the cords around Jody's wrists again, with greater success this time. But without warning, he stopped and gripped his head tightly. Something about Ligeia's melody was hurting him.

His eyes draped over Jody's head and body with a look of pure agony and he glared like a mad wolf at the man in black. "I'll kill you again for this!"

He lunged, but Ligeia got in the way and shoved Gregg to the ground. She dragged her body over him like a twisting snake, practically smothering him, all the while singing, "Tribuo mihi vestri pectus pectoris," over and over, louder and louder.

The sight rocked Jody. If there was a Hell, surely she was in it now.

"Gregg? Gregg? Oh my God, how is this happening? Help me! Help me!"

"Whatever are you trying to do, Lie?" Damianos didn't sound happy. His typically smooth voice was riled. "This is no deathly curse!"

"Shut up!" Ligeia gnashed. "You have your ways, Dammie, and I have mine!"

Gregg twisted and turned to get out from under the singing temptress, but his resistance seemed to be withering.

"No!" He kept looking away from Ligeia's face, his free hand reaching for Jody. Slowly, though, his demeanour changed. Gregg's eyes lost their fight, his look slipped into a state of submission, and his struggling came to a halt. He no longer tried to ward off Lie's advances. Instead he showed signs of welcoming them.

Ligeia's musical laughter took the place of her singing and instead of wrestling with Gregg, she started caressing him. Her fingers combed his messed hair and she lay on top of him like a satisfied lover. It was as if Damianos and Jody didn't even exist anymore.

"Gregg?" Jody agonized to bend her neck enough to see his face. "Gregg!"

Ligeia cast her a slanted, condescending look while Gregg caressed her. "Sorry, my weakling child. Your hero wants a stronger woman now."

Chapter 42

Torn

Gregg's arousal was as inspiring as a leap off lakeside rocks, the thrill of flight as the water drew near akin to the tingles he got holding Ligeia in his arms, hearing her magical voice and admiring her fathomless dark eyes. Awaiting was the sting of the freezing bath, that acute blast of sharp, piercing coldness that collapses lungs and hardens muscles, triggering one's awareness that he is without a doubt, fully and completely alive. It was what Gregg wanted so much to feel, drowning himself in Ligeia's love.

His hands and lips were moving faster than he could think. Touching, fondling, groping, he wanted to tear that snug dress-thingy off her glorious body more than anything in the world. He didn't care if he wrecked it. He had little concern for her overall safety in fact. Right then, it was all about him and his desires.

He latched onto Lie's clothes with cruel intent.

"Yes!" she cried. "Take me! Make me yours!"

"Lie, what have you done?" another voice demanded.

As if in a nightmarish dream, his breath still heavy and his hankering still rife, Gregg snuck a crisscross glance around Ligeia's thick black mane. To his surprise, they were not alone. A tall, broad-shouldered man sat behind a ratty looking cot whereupon stretched a half-naked girl. She was beautiful, enchanting, yet tied down and obviously abused. She kept looking at him with stunning blue eyes as if pleading while she lay there exposed, belly down with her limbs tied to the four corners with taut cords.

Her face was worn, exhausted, marked by red creases. But her eyes held him prisoner. They hearkened an allure that both confused and provoked him. Her expression was startled, frightened and all things terrible, and it gripped Gregg's heart.

He had the sense he should be feeling something, something that was apparently missing. The inkling made his carnal throbbing for Ligeia slip.

"Gregg, what are you doing with her?" The girl looked hurt, as if it was his fault. "Won't you help me?"

Gregg only stared.

Ligeia swung her long dark hair in the way, blocking his view, and forced him down to the dirty ground. Putting her legs on either side of him, she got hold of his shirt and ripped it down the middle.

"He's mine!" she growled, guiding Gregg's hands up to the v-neck on her dress, demanding he tear it away.

Gregg eyed her unshackled flesh beneath the fabric and his hunger quickly returned. He reached for her cleavage while she moaned, grinding her hips into him.

"Lie!" the man raised his voice. Gregg didn't care.

"You can do what you want with the girl, Dammie," Ligeia said. "And you can chase your justice to the gates of Hell for all I care. Did you think you could leave me just like that? Do you think anyone leaves *me*? I should never have been so willing to help you!"

"You're mad! Of all the... so, this is how you react? You're going to make the jivita believe he loves you? This monstrosity is going to replace me?"

"Jealous?" Ligeia sneered, pulling Gregg up to meet her slate coloured lips.

The kiss sent shockwaves of delight straight down to his toes and he roughly ripped her top away to her navel.

The tall dark character let out a forceful breath. "You are a fool and you'll damn us both!"

Gregg wasted none of his time gawking at Ligeia's heavy breasts. He was about to push her to the ground and go for broke when he heard the girl's despairing appeal, "Gregg, don't do this! Please! Can't you see me? It's me, Jo."

Gregg glanced over his shoulder. That man in black looked hazily familiar. He drew closer to the girl, about to put his hands on her bare scars, a poisonous grin broadening his face.

"I never lose without a fight," the fellow quietly affirmed.

That *feeling* was coming back. Seeing that guy near the girl was doing something to Gregg. It was like a vibe and it was close. He could almost explain it. Almost.

Ligeia grabbed Gregg's face and plastered his lips with a mind-blowing kiss. Then she reached down and started massaging his groin, his awfully confining pants still in place.

This of course, pretty much kicked the crap out of any distraction Gregg had with that other girl. He quickly responded by pushing Ligeia down and climbing on top of her. He stared at her heaving body below his, blown away by her dramatic coos and musical meows.

"Oh, that's my boy. Come to me and be mine forever! Take me! Take me!"

The promise in her charm seemed everlasting. The fantasy had all the aspects of eternal bliss. Soon, very soon, he would experience heaven. But like a hazy flashback that could have been real or dream, that strange girl's soft, quivering sob struck deep inside him and wouldn't leave.

"Gregg, you promised me. You promised you'd never leave me!"

Chapter 43

Lilita

Jody's soul was falling apart. The abysmal torture she was forced to bear—powerless to escape, unable to stop it, and incapable of blocking it out—was destroying her. Now, being forced to watch Gregg do the unthinkable, propping himself over another naked woman with a look of fierce passion in his eyes, made her heart collapse in her chest.

Oh, God! Why are you doing this to me? She'd thought she had no more tears to shed, but the ugly tragedy playing before her conjured up a steady stream of agony's rain.

Everything about this was wrong, especially after what they had been through together. Their lives had been so wonderfully intertwined for so long. How could it end like this?

An unanticipated touch upon her bare back surprised her. Without a second of thought, she knew whose hand it was, and her body started shaking. *Oh God, no.* She felt his warm fingers brush over her naked skin and she couldn't help but whimper.

"You are very beautiful when you strain your body this way."

Jody tried to turtle when the monster's voice whispered like a quiet hymn next to her ear. "Perhaps I should ravage you."

The mere idea made Jody pull on her bonds so hard it felt as if she might lose her hands and feet. He chuckled and combed her hair with those skilful fingers.

"You wouldn't dare," Ligeia spoke up.

"No? If you sink yourself to this level, why shan't I? I would not be the first to mix his seed with a lesser creature."

Jody did her best to pull away, but it was no use. "Who are you people?"

He seemed to pause, then slowly leave her. "Yes, introductions. We haven't done that." He came around and bowed before pulling up a stool to sit between her and Gregg.

The carnal sounds behind him lessened. There was an odd tension. Jody stared at him. She couldn't help it. His beauty was hypnotizing. His face was so comforting, so full of... warmth. His skin was smooth and flushed, his teeth were immaculate and the hair that settled around his shoulders looked ethereal.

She had to keep telling herself that this guy was a killer, that he had kidnapped her and was holding her captive in this horrible place. And he was, above all else, not human.

"I am the son of proud parents and the brother of a trusting sister. I lived in a realm of peace, far from other people's war-mongering, with a family contented to live out their days hunting and gathering, maintaining an enduring way of life of freedom and understanding. I am of a race condemned by yours to suffer encroachment, villainy and all manner of injustices. I am a lilita," he said with a haunting expression. "My name is Damianos, and I intend to make things right."

Chapter 44

Contrast

Ligeia kept an attentive gaze on Damianos as he stroked Jody's long white-blonde hair. He got up and eyed her back with a nasty scowl.

"You cannot seduce a jivita."

"He is only half jivita," she acknowledged, petting the boy like he was a dog.

He was perhaps a little clumsy, but Ligeia thought he still deserved to be recognized for his effort. The half-breed seemed to be fuddled by something, though.

Ligeia suspected Gregg was a virgin. If so, the fun of being a jivita's first sexual experience was very exciting. If she were to succeed and make him enter her until done, the spell would win him over and bind him to her forever.

"It's worth a try."

"Is it?" Dammie sounded like he'd hoped she'd say that. "You seem to have forgotten who I am. It's as if something has blinded you."

"Blinded? Blinded? Me?" Ligeia's chest was heaving, she was so irate. She stood up, leaving Gregg at her feet as she rubbed the boy's slobber from her breasts. "There was a time, Dammie, that you would have wreaked havoc on me with my chest slickened this way. Now you don't even care. You turn your eyes the other way! Tell me, who is blinded?"

"There is more to life than satisfying the body. With this girl, I now have something that should help me with that," he said, turning to Jody.

"What?" Ligeia sulked, deflated.

Damianos slid his head and took a breath. "Those mysterious calls that brought us here. I have a face to go with that voice now, and it is not a cheerful one. It grieves me to admit this to you. I am more confused now than I ever have been. Yes, I am drawn to the girl. But it is more an insatiable curiosity than an erotic attraction.

"This anomalous child is somehow pivotal to forces of which I was not previously cognizant. There is a competition for her in a realm beyond our own." Damianos went to the book and gently placed his hand on the cover. "I have leverage. Yet, ultimately, I do not understand why."

Ligeia peered through the dimness to where the flickering lantern light fell upon the large book's muted silver colour. The embossed designs cast small mystifying shadows, their peculiar dance captivating her eyes.

Damianos laid his index and middle fingers against a confusing mass of what appeared to be a tangled skein of yarn and Ligeia stared, incredulous, as she caught a glimpse of something moving on the book's cover.

"What is that?" She drew a sharp breath.

The shadows blinked and flitted in such a way that the small, winged lizard embodied on the book's frontispiece seemed to suddenly be scaling the knotted mound of silver yarn, heading straight for Damianos's hand.

"Watch out!"

Damianos pulled away as if he had been jolted.

"What is it?" Ligeia asked.

Damianos appeared to be considering things. "My love, if I was not entirely sure of my mental processes, I might think myself mad. All this time, since my family was taken from me, I have despised all considerations of gods and spirits, deities that somehow rule over us mortal bootlickers.

"Frustratingly though, my mind has continued to venture into possibilities of an afterlife, despite my cynicism. The hope for something more, something greater, persists at a level of consciousness that I have not yet mastered. There is a stubbornness ingrained in me, and I dare say us all, that searches for deeper meanings to our experiences. To life.

"Today, I fear I might have encountered first hand what lies in wait. Fear and misery. Damnation. This confirmation has changed me, as it should. I have been given a second chance. But what should I do with it? Do my actions here influence my experiences in death? Can I escape my own doom?

"Alas, I am left with only faith to answer my picking brain. But still, I am comforted by at least this one unarguable piece of logic. On this Earth, in our space, alloyed with everything we know, there is always contrast." Damianos paused a moment and then resumed, "From left and right, up and down, in and out, justice and injustice. Always, there is contrast."

"So?" Ligeia challenged.

"So, when I grappled with the sight of that dragon across his bay, that obstinate part of me threw an assumption around my head that I could not ignore. If after life there awaits this beast of bitter cold and evil ambitions, then logic dictates there is the inverse, somewhere.

"But where? Why has it not kept me, and others, on a virtuous path towards it? Faith has left me alone and despairing while the voice has filled me with hope. Who is right? Who decides? It is as if God in his kingdom has forgotten us."

Ligeia's mind was boggled. Never had she heard Dammie speak like this. This whole bizarre quest was nearing its end and still, it flabbergasted her. Her eyes fell upon the book and its incredible artistry. She peered at its odd dragon-faced lock, highlighted by the lantern's yellowed glow, and she realized something that confounded her even more.

"This thing wasn't made by humans, was it?"

"No." Damianos looked at it as if daydreaming. "I doubt it was written by any culture we know." He sighed.

"*The Book of the Nornir*...?" He looked at Jody, speculatively. "What do you know about it?"

She did not answer.

"Nothing? Is it an animal? Some mystical, godlike creature? Is it a title for some great well-received position in society? What is a Nornir?"

Jody cowered. "I don't know anything."

Damianos exhaled heavily. "No, of course you don't. I forgot. I shall have to find the answers myself. Think, Dammie. Think!"

Ligeia didn't like the fact that Jody was still a mystery. Add to that Dammie's bewildering hiccup with spirituality, and there was a whole lot not to like. But at least she had Gregg on something of a leash now. With a few swift moves, the jivita half-breed would be her greatest possession. With him, she could have lifelong companionship, someone to dote on her every whim, someone to keep her safe for all time, someone to fulfil each of her many fantasies without exception.

She glanced over her shoulder at him. He was watching Jody, just staring with an odd, puzzled expression. Ligeia bent in front of him in an effort to solidify her hold and she cupped his chin, guiding his eyes into hers. He seemed to react woozily, which was good.

A moment later, though, he shook his head and blurted something surprising. "Norns?"

If Ligeia didn't know better, she would think that little bugger was knocking off her spell already. Restless, she started singing again to try and bring him back.

"Stop it!" Damianos shouted. He was glaring fiercely. "Stop your damned witchcraft and let the boy speak!"

Ligeia threw up her arms, incensed. "Shoot!"

Gregg kept staring at Jody. His mind must have still been fuzzed over. "The Norns," he said slowly, as if drunk, "I've heard of them. In school. Weren't they like... the Fates? Women who controlled the destinies of men?"

It was as if a light bulb had been turned on over Damianos's head. "Norns? Nornir... why didn't I think of that? In myth, they come when a person is born to decide his or her future. Could this book be about them? How strange would it be if the stories were true? What if the pages therein have been written by them?"

He inspected the dragon lock from a distance, then went to the side of the cot and knelt next to the girl, looking her over. He glanced up at Ligeia.

"If that's the best your little witch book came up with to nullify a jivita, you are in for trouble. Now then"—he switched gears—"Gregg mentioned Jody has a destiny of sorts."

He returned his attention to the girl, gently lifting away stray locks of hair to see her tear-reddened eyes. "There is a hidden monster that wants very much for you to come with me, my sweet child. Did you know that?"

She responded with an impugnable glare, but nothing more.

"There is a dragon-headed device on this book. I can feel it repelling me. I shall assume that I need a key to get past it, yet I see only an open hole in the lock's mouth and I dare not inspect the darkness within it too closely. Do you know how to open it?"

Jody slowly moved her head side to side, hate shooting from her eyes like daggers.

Damianos was getting agitated. "As expected. Why would you know anything? Stupid girl. I have walked upon this earth for some two thousand years. There are few human languages that I do not speak or have the ability to read. Add to that the experiences I've had on

Sarion, and I am left aghast why it should be that you, a brainless, limp, weak little child is endowed with such an invaluable treasure. And why are you able to interpret a spell that no one else can?"

Jody avoided looking back at him. "I am not weak." She pulled on her arms and legs until the resistance became too much and she slumped back onto the mattress.

Ligeia noticed Gregg's breaths getting more excessive, carrying with them a low, unnerving rumble.

Jody spoke. "I don't know anything about that book or your stupid magic voodoo crap! If I did, I'd wave my wand and make the whole lot of you disappear. What stupid spell do you need interpreted anyways?"

"What spell, indeed?" It was evident that Damianos was working hard to figure it out. "And where is it? This salvation, as it is called." He drummed his fingers on his lower lip as he spoke almost secretly. "You are to go where your delusion began, without waking up. To a place hidden in the darkness, beyond the walls of your finite universe."

He paused, staring at Jody in deep thought. "I wonder. I positively wonder." He kept turning from the girl to the book and back again. "Things being what they are, one would gather that a scheming Norn has planned special things for you, child."

Damianos leaned closer to the girl's back and she flinched in obvious anticipation.

"What shame would it be then? Is it even possible? If I should do something that no Norn could predict?"

Chapter 45

Decisions

Jody shook violently as Damianos came nearer.

"It poses an intriguing prospect" he grinned. "If you are destined for greatness, then that would mean all manner of failure is sure to be averted. Otherwise, how could you possibly achieve a divine ending? And if something should happen to keep you from fulfilling your goal, then how could you have had the destiny in the first place?"

Damianos pointed to the book's creepy lock. "Do you see that face? It is the face of certainty. That beast is in your future, in triumph or defeat. Sadly, it also appears to be in mine." His palm pressed down on the back of Jody's spine, making it gradually harder for her to breathe.

"If I help the dragon, this darkness as your lover calls it, any notion of you rising up to kill it would be dismissed and the world that was predicted to come would be forever lost." He eased up, considering. "But what if your failure was predicted? What if the dragon is supposed to free itself? Hmm, what would be better? Do I risk alienating a monster, or stay on the safe side and cooperate with it?"

"Stop it," Gregg's surly voice grumbled.

"Gregg," Jody pleaded in growing torment. "God, won't you help me?"

"I have asked that question myself, child, many times," Damianos declared, showing broadening amusement. "I'm afraid the answer is always the same..." he pushed down so hard Jody thought her spine would soon press against her navel. Her lungs collapsed and her eyes bulged. "Silence!"

Gregg exploded as if shot from a cannon, colliding with Damianos and crashing with him over the top of the cot to the other side. There they fought while Jody struggled to regain her breath.

Beside her, Ligeia watched, hesitant when Damianos called for help.

Gasping for air, Jody glanced nervously at Gregg as he fought tooth and nail with that dick dressed in black. Suddenly, a different hand rested against her skin. Her head swivelled around to find Ligeia, her face showing an unsettling determination. The winged woman curled her fat lip and flared her teeth.

"And who shall I associate with; the tall, dark, handsome one with the impressive vocabulary but frustrating demure, or the young vibrant one with the firm *character* and undersexed virility? The answer should be obvious, except for one small, whiny problem. The jivita's heart still belongs to you."

She reached under Jody's chin and, Jody, powerless to stop her, lay helpless as Ligeia climbed on her back and proclaimed, "I hate competition!"

Chapter 46

Hindrance

Damianos was insanely fast with those clawed hands of his. It took everything Gregg had to avoid being sliced into oblivion again. He got in a few good licks, but he couldn't understand why he wasn't able to overpower Damianos the same way he had a few short hours ago.

Everything felt easier last time. He remembered being angry and how his body had just seemed to react to every little thought without impediment. Something was different this time.

As Gregg managed to duck away from another one of Damianos's lightning strikes, he realized that Ligeia's singing voice was still echoing in his head. It was impeding his ability to think, and more importantly at the moment, to fight.

He threw a small, empty propane canister at Damianos and it smoked the guy in the head. The freak fell atop a pile of boxed supplies, looking dazed. But before Gregg could leap over and beat his opponent down for good, he caught sight of a peculiar shadow reflecting off the canvas walls from the lantern's flickering light.

Ligeia was on top of Jody, her teeth bearing down on Jo's neck.

"No!" Gregg flew off his feet and tackled the winged woman, dumping them both hard onto the dirt ground. Gregg heard Ligeia's breath whoosh out of her.

They fought until she directed a timely kick and sent him flying. He managed to land on his feet and in nothing flat grabbed the lit kerosene lamp. His sights were clean. One swift throw and that bitch was going to burn.

She must have known it too. There was nowhere to spin and run, not enough time or space to get away. She looked up at him, clothes torn and ragged, her wings half folded and her hair shabby. She was at his mercy.

All Gregg had to do was throw the lamp. But when he saw her, near naked and vulnerable, his temper seemed to collapse. He glanced over his shoulder and looked at Jo, tied down, half naked, and crying, he realized he couldn't do that to the chick with wings. As much as he tried to make himself angry again, that heat that had felt so important in his belly fizzled.

Ligeia examined him, appearing confused at first, then hopeful. "You"—she shifted—"you're not going to throw it?"

Gregg's grip on the lantern tightened. He threatened, but in the end he found himself shouting expletives and slamming the stupid thing back on the folding tabletop. He stared into Jody's defeated blue eyes, almost begging for forgiveness. "I can't. Why?"

He heard Ligeia get up, her voice sounding as confident and seductive as ever.

"I know." She came to him and smoothly extended her hand. He spun and swiped it away, glaring, but Ligeia grinned. "You love me."

Gregg shuddered and he balked. "What?" That couldn't be it. It was probably just some dumb hormonal thing, or maybe it was something deeper even than that.

Ligeia approached him again. "My spell did work after all."

"No!" Gregg shoved her. His head was rolling with that harlot's voice and he just couldn't shake it.

He heard Damianos clamouring up from the corner behind him and knew the moment of escape was passing rapidly. This time he went to the cords at Jody's ankles and ripped them away without any concern for the pain it might cause her.

Obviously, Jo wasn't expecting the pain and she wailed from the hurt. The second her legs were freed, she pulled her knees into her chest and coiled into a ball, sobbing. "Oh God, make it stop! I want to go home! Please, just let me go home!"

Ligeia hissed behind him. Her attack was unexpected and Gregg stumbled as she leapt up and wrapped herself around him, digging in with her claws and thrashing to knock him off balance.

"I'm sorry, my little destroyer," she said. "I can take it back later. If you promise to behave."

Ligeia began to sing again and her song enveloped him, making his body itch and shiver like something was scraping him clean from his head to his feet.

"Racksana asta. Prazamana vyapaya."

He resisted desperately, their fight sending them both careening this way and that. For a horrifyingly split second, Gregg spotted Damianos standing over Jo. If only he had taken advantage when the lantern was in his hands. If only his stupid conscience didn't make him think so much! He could have avoided this. He could've been running through the woods with Jo in his arms this very second.

Instead, as bad as things had become, Gregg feared it was all going to get much worse.

Chapter 47

Defiance

"You cannot deceive me, Damianos. No more than you can deceive yourself. I am in you."

The voice was back, aggravating Damianos's already disconcerted mind. "Who are you?"

"You know."

The Devil was the most likely answer, but Damianos long ago had recognized that as a human fantasy, a means for a few cunning people to take control over many.

"You're being narrow-minded. Do you not pride yourself as a disciple of the Age of Reason? Think clearly, Damianos. You have found yourself, in life and theology, at odds with the perceptions of the Ultimate Do-Gooder and His opposite. Why, in human bibles God is depicted as both light and darkness. They are the same."

Damianos did indeed pride himself on learning as much as he could. Religion, philosophy, all things to do with spirituality and its meaning were sources of his interest. He remembered a passage he had read from Thomas Paine, an 18th century philosopher who wrote, "Whenever we read the obscene stories, the voluptuous debaucheries, the cruel and torturous executions, the unrelenting vindictiveness, with which more than half the Bible is filled, it would be more consistent that we called it the word of a demon, than the Word of God."

"Fascinating irony, isn't it? In your searches you've read a great many books, queried a great many clerics and deep thinkers. You know the God rendered by men. I can be 'very pitiful, and tender of mercy' and I can be cruel, wrathful and swift to exact appalling vengeance for even the most minor provocation.

"There is no Devil, Damianos, and there is no God. *There is only me.*

"You had the answer long before you asked the question," the dragon prodded coolly. "You dream about contrast as though one end of the spectrum is somehow disconnected from the other. The ultimate truth is, there is no disconnect. Everything is tied in to everything else. Even me. In the scope of things, Damianos, *there is only me.*"

"You're lying," Damianos argued. "You are not the absolute. You're a deceiver. Who could have possibly imprisoned you, if you are all there is? And why would you need me to set you free?"

Silence followed.

Damianos stared at the way Jody's tightening skin fashioned itself over bone and muscle. The typical undulations over ribs and spine were mangled, producing an image that should not be.

"Remember..." the dragon's voice was bolstered by its apparent stranglehold on Damianos's grief. "Open the book and find the way. Decipher the galdor and have your revenge!"

Damianos's hands curled, his claws scratching Jody's back. Her eyes flashed open as she squealed. No amount of thrashing would save her now.

She twisted and fought with the cords around her wrists, even gnawing at them until Damianos retracted her legs and forced her flat onto the mattress. Despite her pleas, he dug his knee onto the base of her spine and pinned her there.

"Do not kill her!"

He could feel himself turning wild. Damianos lunged, slitting Jody's back, making her scream louder than a burning syrēne. The sound invited more rage. "There is no God!"

"Damianos!"

Chapter 48

Venom

Hearing Jody's piercing cries gave energy to Gregg's will and he launched free from Ligeia's grip.

"My God!" he yelled, suddenly seeing Damianos using his claws like surgical tools to peel back Jody's skin and peer inside at peculiar, bloodied white fuzz. "No!"

Gregg's eyes flashed on the kerosene lamp. This time he grabbed it without a second thought and hurled it at Damianos. The man in black raised his arm and the lantern's glass base broke apart on impact. The liquid fuel sprayed over his black coat and ignited.

Damianos stumbled, flailing. He moved like lightning to get his burning clothes off while Jody writhed and trembled on the cot.

Ligeia got up, licked her lips and pounced at Jody's wound. Gregg grabbed a folding chair and beat her with it.

"Get away from her!"

Ligeia drew back, cowering as Gregg forced her right out of the tent. He threw the chair after her and scurried back to Jody, waving his hand at the choking air, black with smoke.

"Oh my God, Jo!" he whined, fumbling with the unbelievably tight restraints.

Her lips were getting pale, her whole body was shaking and her wonderful eyes weren't focusing on anything. "

Jesus, I'm gonna get you outta here. I promise you, Jo! Just hang in there! Damn these cords!"

His bellow was cut off when he spotted Damianos rising on the other side of the cot. Behind him he heard Ligeia groan. "I took his power. Hit him!"

Damianos lifted the big silver book and swung, hitting Gregg on the head. Gregg's whole world sparkled behind his closed eyes and his ultimate crash to the ground came slow and bluntly across his body. His perceptions blurred and his mouth went dumb.

Gregg heard Ligeia's voice as if she was talking under water. "I cursed him. He's only human now." He fuzzily made out the inglorious grin spreading across Damianos's face as the creep knelt down beside him, the book still in his hands.

"Then the boy can help me." Damianos gestured to Ligeia. "Open the flaps. Get some air in here!"

He placed the book on the folding table, then took Gregg's limp hand and singled out his index finger.

Everything in Gregg was worsening as Damianos spoke. "If it is destiny that beckons you both to rise up and destroy the Beast, then this book must be part of it. What mysteries lie in wait, I cannot fathom. But surely, I believe, the messages are for you and your precious pig girlfriend, and to keep them safe from prying eyes, the book's maker used this enigmatic lock."

Damianos brought Gregg's hand closer to the tome, causing a strange electric charge to spread up the length of his arm.

"Now, an idea is rattling around in my head. If I were to make a book of important secrets that I didn't want anyone else to know about, particularly a crafty dragon that manipulates a good person's mind, then making a scary, keyless device to clasp it shut would be brilliant."

The fixture's eyes were slowly lighting up, shining a spooky crimson red.

"It would need blood. But not just any blood. Your blood. The blood of a perfectly rare breed of creature. A mix of human and jivita."

Gregg could feel the lock's power inside him, reaching and tightening his every muscle with prickling electric charges. His tendons and ligaments all pulled, fighting against one another, intensifying.

As Damianos worked to bring Gregg's hand to the dragon's head, the fearsome thing started to move.

"I had an inkling to try it myself," Damianos said. "But the response it gave me inspired a walloping suspicion that perhaps whoever made this book did something else, so as to punish any fool, and the beast behind him, who tried to sneak a peek.

"So, your finger will either open the lock or, I'm supposing, it will reject you and hurt you in some wildly creative way." Damianos's tone was full of eager expectation. "In either case, I'm looking forward to what happens next."

Damianos stabbed the dragon's mouth with Gregg's finger. The device's snout closed around like a spikey-toothed vice and stabbed through his jittery digit.

Paralyzing shock and terror instantly filled him. Gregg could only scream as the venom's icy pain coursed up his arm and throughout his body.

Damianos chuckled and let Gregg's hand go. "It might even kill you."

He didn't sound discouraged.

Chapter 49

Ill-fated

Ligeia leaned carefully over Gregg's motionless frame, staring at the very strange book from which an unsettling sulphurous odour wafted up her nose. She identified it as the smell of ozone and nitric oxide, the gas produced when electrons are ripped from atoms, like what happens after a lightning strike.

She gave Gregg a shove with her foot. "Do you think he's really dead this time?"

Damianos had returned to Jody's bloodied body, his breathing hungry. "Close enough."

Jody kicked and shuddered, but Dammie kept her in place.

"She's lost a good bit of blood, but here and there the clotting has begun. Her reaction's slower than I would have expected. When vessels are damaged or wounds appear, angoros platelets set to work instantly to stop the bleeding, like a plug. Proteins move in an intricate chemical reaction, like a rushing wave, to bring about a shield of fibrin strands which reinforce that plug and allow healing to happen."

"So, she's an angoros after all?" Ligeia was confused. The spell she used on the girl earlier should have brought it out.

"Yes, but not fully," Damianos explained. "Hence the inconsistency in her response to my incisions. My previous suspicion of her mongrel status was correct."

"Half-breeds," Ligeia sighed thoughtfully. Her confidence in the syrēne's book of spells lessened. What effect would the charms she'd placed on Gregg have in the end because of the unknown factors in his mule DNA?

Damianos meticulously examined under Jody's skin. "These muscles are underdeveloped. I doubt she could even hold up a pair of wings with this hybrid human body."

"Half human..."

Damianos sniggered. "Keep up, Lie. It would seem humans possess some genetic sequence that makes them tantalizing even to the angoros. These naked monkeys can make the most cultured breed sink to forbidden domains for gratification. I must admit, this girl had an effect on me earlier that had me imagining things."

"There is something about them, isn't there?"

Ligeia turned her eyes toward Gregg, pondering. She didn't like thinking he was dead, mutt or not, and she couldn't help but imagine being with him. Despite everything, she realized, she still wanted to find a way to win the jivita's affection. She gave Gregg another hopeful nudge with her foot, attempting to show disdain for Damianos's benefit.

Gregg's brows rose slightly and Ligeia felt her prospects improving. Perhaps she would swing things around and give back his ability to heal, so he could recover from whatever the book had done to him. Since only the one who cast the spell could remove it—either freely or because the syrēne no longer lived—Ligeia had total control, and she savoured the feeling. Yet, before she'd do anything of the sort, she'd have to be very sure that she'd get her way in the end. Jody had to die so that Ligeia could swoop in and latch onto Gregg's broken heart before anyone else had the chance to.

"They are sentiments misplaced," Damianos grumbled. "Love with another kind is a pitiless, immoral violation of nature's way."

"I beg your pardon?" Ligeia drew a sharp breath. "And what have we been doing for the last two hundred years?"

Dammie rolled his eyes. "You cannot be serious, Lie. Lilitas and syrēnes are practically the same. Save for the wings and the perplexing self-regard, we are more from different social classes than different species. Honestly, do you think me a lilita or a horse when we make love?"

Ligeia nibbled her lip and didn't answer.

Damianos dipped his finger into a small pool of Jody's blood with a wily expression on his face. "The smell is intoxicating. I have tasted angoros before, but never this." He looked as if he was straining to resist. "Bring me the book."

Ligeia knelt down by Gregg and heard a faint, agonized moan. She took the book in her arms and cautiously lowered her lips to Gregg's ears.

"Be still," she whispered.

She got up and watched anxiously while Damianos collected Jody's strewn, bloodstained hair and placed it over her shoulder to keep her back clear. The girl lay on her belly, her teeth quivering and body trembling. She was losing her colour and looked utterly exhausted.

"Please... I just want to sleep," she whimpered

Damianos winced suddenly and stood bolt upright gripping his head in apparent distress.

"What is it?" Ligeia asked.

"Hush!" he growled. "The voice!"

What followed completely surprised her.

"Who was it that confined you to that place? Why?" Damianos shouted like a defiant child. "I am the one with power now. Your freedom depends on me!"

He lowered his face and breathed in Jody's scent before moving his finger angrily through her spilled blood. "You're lying." Ligeia stared, watching him obviously have a conversation with someone not standing in the tent. "I don't believe you!"

His features hardened as his eyes skimmed the girl's naked skin in a way that strangely aroused Ligeia. The smell of Jody's blood was exciting enough as it was, throw in the strong emotion thundering from Dammie's every breath and Ligeia itched for gorging and lovemaking.

A voracious hope surged in her that the hunter in Damianos would come bubbling back to the surface like a long awaited rebirth. She loved seeing it, admiring the seasoned killer savour his closeness with his moored captive.

He took another breath, his smile menacing.

Jody started thrashing again, panicking. "What are you doing now? Oh God, please help me! Stop!"

No matter how hard she tried, the girl couldn't turn her head enough to see the torture.

Damianos must have found a good place, near where one of the girl's humerus bones should have been attached to the scapula, and paused for closer inspection.

"The muscles here have been torn. Angoros muscles. Yet, her shoulder blade is too petite. It, and by the feel of things, her vertebrae are undersized human bits. It looks like someone made a botched amputation here. That's where her scars came from. A hack job."

Ligeia was reminded of Jody's loathing of doctors and sensed a strange emotion bewilder her thinking. She wondered if it was even possible for a syrēne to feel pity.

After observing Jody a moment longer, Damianos shuddered and his eyes darkened. He brandished his smooth tongue and slowly licked Jody with it. The girl's back arched and Ligeia's womb sang.

"Stop! Oh God! Please stop!" Jody cried.

"Keep going!" Ligeia appealed, a skyrocketing sense of desire tingling between her legs. Shivers fluttered up her spine. Seeing Damianos linger over his victim with such control, such discipline was fabulously erotic.

Ligeia's mouth watered, her aroused hands smoothly stroking herself, as she imagined Damianos following up their potential feast with a ferocious romp together, just like in the old days. The mere idea made her weak.

"Pray, child," Damianos groaned into Jody's ear, "that your God is listening, for both our sakes!" He stood up and raised his bloodied hand, staring at it like a biologist inspecting cultured cells in a petri dish. "Until then"—he glanced at Ligeia with a sly grin—"I shall do what I must to keep life equitable."

Damianos brought his bloodied hand close to his mouth and deftly licked it while Ligeia watched, fully enthralled at the sight. His shoulders jumped and a look of satisfaction lit his face.

Damianos moved his bloodied hand towards the lock on the book. "There! It does not push me away!" he was almost hysterical.

"The dragon needs the secrets inside this book revealed, and the only one who can make it happen is a half-breed that by all accounts should never have been born. It's not jivita blood at all! To unlock what could be the greatest puzzle ever imagined, perhaps guarding from mortal persons the words that reveal the mysteries of life and purpose, of God himself, requires nothing less than the combined blood of two different breeds of people, emerging from our two different worlds!"

Damianos's hand went closer still to the dragon lock and the thing's red eyes throbbed to life and flickered to a deep, haunting blue.

"It's absolutely brilliant. A fine answer."

As he brought his hand to the dragon's mouth though, Ligeia noticed Damianos begin to shake and falter. He seemed to be fighting something and his face cramped.

"What if I'm wrong?" He tried to pull his hand back, but it was too late. The dragon's eyes beat red again.

Provoked

"Dammie!"

Chapter 50

Destiny

"It knows!" Damianos shrieked as Ligeia watched his reddened finger approach the lock's gaping mouth. The thing seemed to emit an inaudible rumble that churned up and down Ligeia's whole body, keeping her at bay.

The moment Damianos's outstretched finger was inserted, the dragon's mouth shut. His body constricted and he gasped for breath, almost expulsing his dark eyes from their sockets before the lock's snout finally opened again. Damianos fell to the ground, smelling as if he'd just been blasted by a storm's fierce wind.

"Dammie!" Ligeia hurried to him.

"It saw through my trick," he said slowly, his head bobbing as if on a spring.

Ligeia helped him up and Damianos cast an apprehensive look at the now dormant lock.

"It knew." He glanced at Gregg's still body and then at his hand where Jody's blood was now mixed with his own.

Before Ligeia could say a word, Damianos put his finger in his mouth and sucked. The result had him nearly flattened on the ground again.

Ligeia jostled him. "What is wrong with you?"

He shook his head and took several breaths before attempting to speak.

"When I was a child," he mused with a trembling smile, "my mother filled me with stories of old brews lilitas used as folk medicine, based on blood from different species."

Damianos gradually rose, leaning on Jody's cot. Something peculiar was happening to him, Ligeia could tell. His eyes brightened, his skin regained its colour, and his stature was strong. Ligeia realized, dumbfounded, Damianos had a peculiar, intense look of desire lighting his face.

"A sample of shyntaur's blood mixed with a hint of angoros makes a remedy for albinism. A mayavin's put together with a rasva's in just the right quantity makes a lilita faster and stronger, and so on. Fresh blood delivers substances such as nutrients and oxygen to a body's cells while carrying metabolic waste away. Each variety of animal has needs that might be uncommon to another, giving their blood unique qualities"—he lowered his face to Jody's back and followed his nose—"like smell."

Ligeia's loins started throbbing, seeing Dammie's hungry eyes skim over the girl's naked body.

"It is as if all my otherworldly concerns have somehow wilted away,"—he murmured, as though to himself—"benumbed by the effect of my blood polluted with the girl's. In its place is a perverted hankering for physical relief." He grew a wide, boyish smile and took a deep breath. "I rather like this."

Damianos leaned over Jody and found a shallow depression where her blood had pooled and not yet congealed. He dipped in his finger and gently stirred.

"I believe I have found a most intoxicating medley here," he said. The girl's sobbing was relentless and Dammie's smile widened.

A long moment passed while he pressed his own blood onto Jody's back. The girl cringed, screeching, as Damianos lowered his face just above her skin and breathed deeply in.

"It's strange," he explained. "None of this seems real suddenly. I know I should be anxious. My life is in danger and I've learned that the part of me that lives on is quickly heading toward a much scarier situation. Yet, I feel... wonderful. It's as if I found my juvenile sense of immortality again. My hormones must be running rampant, and with that has come an insatiable yearning for sex!"

He paused, panting. His eyes swung to the folding table.

"It's that book! It did this to me," he growled. "As ridiculous as it sounds, be it my drugged way of thinking or not, that damned thing must have known what was to come! The half-breed's blood mixed with mine inside that lock's blasted mouth. Never before in creation has such a soup been concocted! Is *this* destiny? Was it meant to be?"

Ligeia didn't care. Dammie's comment about sex was singing through her head and she just wanted to get on with it!

But Damianos seemed to have forgotten. He looked again at Gregg, seemingly lifeless on the ground where he had fallen. "Despite my efforts, my adamant belief in my free will, have I followed a path inexplicably laid out long before my time? And if the book's will has shunned me in this way, what has it then done to the jivita?"

Chapter 51

Passion

Although any more chatter about destiny and free will threatened to undo Ligeia's hankering for ecstasy, the excitement she felt watching her great hunter's performance was something from which she could not turn away. Mystery of the book be damned, Damianos looked like a real killer again!

He went to the spot on the girl's back where his blood mingled with hers, and he lowered his pursed lips into the mix. Another unbearable minute went by, disturbed only by Jody's sobbing while he lapped up and savoured the warm liquid.

The sight made Ligeia want to explode.

Damianos pulled away, excess blood trickling from the side of his mouth. His eyes were fully blackened, his nostrils stretched, his lips quivering.

"Can you imagine, my love, the self-control needed to keep me from devouring this young creature? This is a challenge no lilita can prepare for. So young, so helpless and so valuable."

Damianos gestured to Ligeia, grinning, and she went to him feeling as if she was floating, charged with anticipation. She wet her lips and her heart leapt in her chest.

He dragged his fiendishly skilled finger into the vital remnants on the girl's back and shuddered, as if the simple touch of it was somehow euphoric.

Ligeia desperately wanted to taste the half-breed, to experience her. She couldn't help but grip the girl, almost clawing her, waiting for Damianos to share the bounty. The child cried out and Damianos pushed Ligeia back, instead offering her his finger drenched in rich red blood.

"For you, my love. A taste of the divine!"

Ligeia salivated at the gift, opening her mouth and stretching her tongue for his approaching appendage. Her belly twitched and her loins tingled, all with the promise of impending rapture.

The girl's desperate whimpers rang in Ligeia's ears like distant church bells. Damianos's finger hovered over her waiting tongue until finally, a slow-building drop let go.

Starting where the blood rested on her taste buds, a wave of excited heat surged through Ligeia's body. It sent thrills down her spine and shivers through her womb. She gasped for air, clenching anything she could as her entire being flooded with ecstasy.

Ligeia seized onto Damianos's hand and stuck his finger in her mouth like it was a child's pacifier. In a few intoxicating seconds there wasn't a trace of angoros blood on his skin and Damianos quickly pulled away.

"My heart still needs what's left." He gestured to the bite mark the book had given him.

"But I want more," Ligeia shouted, descending on Jody's bloodied back, sweeping her thirsty tongue over the girl's skin and into her wound, famished.

Damianos dragged her off the screaming child.

"I want it! I want more!"

"You cannot!" he warned, overpowering her every swipe.

The forcefulness of his actions, the intensity of his emotions was a frenzy that energized her lusting to a level she hadn't experienced for more than a century. Before she could clamp her hands on either side of his face to pull him in for a maddeningly needed kiss, he was already mauling her.

"Dammie! Oh, Dammie!" She opened herself to his frantic assault.

"It's the book! I can't stop myself!"

Ligeia was perfectly delighted to hear it. "Don't you dare try!"

She forced his face into her breasts, moaning at the pleasure of it.

"I mustn't," Damianos cursed. He sent a drugged, suspicious glare at Gregg's motionless form. "This is happening for a reason. Something is afoot!"

Ligeia riveted her gaze on Dammie's eyes and fastened her lips on his. Her take-charge passion had its desired effect and she sensed Damianos's resistance fall by the wayside.

His strong hands and arms, Damianos grabbed Ligeia's bottom and forced her up to ride his hips out of the prisoner's tent into the open night. The cool air sent shivers up and down her naked skin, but the heat welling from within demanded release.

"I will have you!" Damianos could barely get out the words, his hungry lips busy tasting hers.

"Not without a fight you won't."

Ligeia wrapped her legs tighter around his waist. She was going to enjoy this.

Chapter 52

Wounded

He could hear her whimper, but Gregg knew better than to jump to the rescue until the animalistic sounds outside the tent moved farther away. As hard as it was, Jody had to wait.

While he lay there, appearing as dead as he could, his mind hammered away at what the lock had shown him. Everything had happened so fast, the dragon's bite sending blasts of numbing pain rippling under his skin in a paralyzing blur. Yet there was something riding along with that sting.

They were pictures, figures..., reflections of things he loosely sensed were real, though he had no way of knowing for sure. When the lock let him go and he blacked out on the ground, those images stayed with him. A grass meadow rising high above the shores of a restless sea. An angel, her white gown blowing in the wind. And a menacing cloud, its shape like that of a monster.

There was also the dark stone corridor, brightened only by a distant arctic glow. In the belly of the passage ran a man, chasing a light that drifted ahead of him.

A strong, soothing male voice Gregg recognized echoed in his mind, its edict curiously repeated outside. "Be still," it and Ligeia's silken speech warned him together.

Now, at last, those weird noises Ligeia and Damianos were making sounded far enough away for Gregg to sneak a quick peek. His peek turned into a glance. Then his glance turned into a full scanning of the tent. Amazingly, his playing possum seemed to have worked.

He carefully got up and moved to the cot. What he saw made his lungs cave in and his shoulders slump.

"No!" He had never seen such horror.

Jody's body lay awkwardly, her legs strewn, her head between her bound hands clumsily swaying left and right. Her back was splattered with blood.

"Oh my God!" Her skin was pulled up in places. Gregg didn't know what to do, where to start. "Jesus!" he tried to keep his voice down, but it was hard.

His teary eyes swept over her, his heart pinched and his mind fell to pieces. He locked onto the odd configuration of her shoulder blade. Holding his breath, Gregg leaned closer, seeing past shrouds of red flesh and clotted blood to baffling tufts of stained white down.

Jody shuddered. "I'm so . . . cold."

Her voice rattled Gregg. and he did his best to concentrate, but this was a nightmare beyond imagination. He had to get them out of here.

He thought he could untie her wrists and carry her out of the woods to find help. He should be able to with his newfound strength. *My strength!* He suddenly recalled his status as a half-breed-something-or-other.

"I could have stopped this." How stupid he'd been, lying on the dirt like a useless pink tutu-wearing pansy. "I'm such an effing idiot! I could have helped!"

Help. The rational thought calmed him. He had to get Jody away and to help.

He went to the cords and finally undid them. Jody pulled her wrists under her body and coiled up, but the wounds on her back must have hurt so much that she yelped and immediately moved her sore frame into a flattened position.

Gregg approached her with the ambition to heave her over his shoulder, or maybe it would be best to cradle her in his arms. Either way, it would probably hurt like hell. Should she scream, or even fight him, Damianos and Ligeia might choke off their creepy idea of kink and come back. How then was he going to get Jody out of there?

He didn't know where to put his hands, worried about touching Jody pretty much anywhere. He paused. "Don't be a moron, man." He decided to take off his shirt and place it gently over Jo's back.

She bounced violently and shrieked as it made contact and Gregg quickly removed it again.

"Shh! Jesus, Jo, shh!"

New blood was rising, spilling onto the crusted mattress. There had to be something else he could do.

He weighed his options, fearing that at any moment Damianos and Ligeia would return. If he had to, he'd fight the both of them; maybe try to turn into that cloud thing like he did before, when his Grammy was down and out. Then something that should have been obvious from the start sprang to his mind.

"Wait! I can heal you!" Gregg placed his hand clumsily on Jo's bare skin.

Jody gasped and bucked like a pissed-off mustang. "Don't touch me!" she begged. "Please!"

"I wish I could heal you." Gregg's voice didn't sound very confident, but there was a lot on his mind just then.

He figured the easiest thing to do would be to repeat his experience with his great-grandma. All Grammy did was respond, saying, "I wish you could too." That must have been all the acceptance Gregg needed.

"You can't!" Jody complained. "No one can fix me."

"I can. Just say 'I wish you could heal me too' or something like that."

"Let go of me. God, just let me die."

"I won't do that. Tell me you want me to heal you!"

"No!" She was emphatic. Her intensity must have hurt and she cringed, relaxing only after several slow, careful breaths. She looked at Gregg with those wounded blue eyes. "It's too late, Gregg."

"Now you listen," he protested. There was no way on God's green Earth he was going to accept that. "I didn't come back here to watch you die!"

Gregg's mind was so frantic that he hadn't noticed the flow of blood on Jo's back had lessened and now reduced to a mere trickle. He watched, astonished when the last few dribbles actually stopped. Stunned, he stared awestruck at Jody's exposed flesh, following her muscles' rise and fall with each shallow breath, considering the surprisingly wondrous workings of the human body beneath the skin.

"Why are you here?" Jody's weak voice asked unexpectedly and it took a few seconds for Gregg to answer.

"To find you."

"No." She fussed at first, and then stopped. "I mean, why... aren't you dead?"

"Oh, you mean from this morning?" Gregg didn't really know how to shovel that whole mess in a clean, speedy sort of way. "I guess I'm not the average, run-of-the-mill type of guy you thought I was."

Jody's body bobbed a little and Gregg thought he heard a faint snicker.

"I never thought you were run-of-the-mill."

He wasn't sure, but she sounded like she was kind of roasting him there. It made him smile.

"Do you love her, that bitch with wings?"

"What?" Gregg suddenly felt like a criminal. "No!" He did his best to demonstrate aversion, but fumbled. "No way. Good grief, she's *so* not my type."

He really wanted to stop talking now.

"She's very beautiful," Jo said, her tired voice becoming distant, "and confident, and strong."

"So are you."

"Stop it," she scoffed.

Gregg hated when she did that. "Damn it, Jo. What's with you? You are the most beautiful girl in this whole stupid world!" He gently patted her hair as he spoke. "You may not be the most confident, but you're definitely strong."

"Now you're just being an idiot."

"Are you kidding me? If you could only see what I'm looking at right now. Jesus Christ, Jo. How many chicks can lie on a rotten bed in a stinking cold tent, have their backs mutilated by a God-forsaken-monster, and still take the time to ask the neighbour kid if he digs the dark-skinned woman with the big boobs? You're one of a kind."

Jody managed to wave that off too. Instead, for some mind-numbing reason, she said, "She does have nice boobs."

Gregg was flabbergasted. Was there a right way to respond to this? "They're okay," he grudgingly admitted. "But she has those freakish wings..."

Judging by Jo's nominal shift in body language, Gregg should've just kept his mouth shut.

"I'm kinda freakish," she admitted dolefully.

Gregg focused on Jody's back, his belly feeling full and ironically empty at the same time. He slowly placed his hand over her head again and smoothed her hair before lowering his forehead next to hers.

"So am I."

He felt Jody warming to his touch and wished the moment could last forever. Finally, she spoke.

"I wish you could heal me too."

Chapter 53

Amour

His hopes rising, Gregg waited for that wonderful heat to pass through his eager hands on its way to making Jody better. He could scarcely keep himself composed, thinking how brilliant it was to have this amazing power to heal. With this one wonderful trait, he could make Jody better forever and ever.

He was, though, increasingly concerned when nothing seemed to be happening. There was no sudden opening-of-the-gates and no rushing of heat. There was simply nothing happening at all.

Jody whispered finally, "What are you doing?"

"I don't understand," he said. Her horrible wounds remained, her colour still pale. "Do you feel any better?"

Jody responded behind a slow, achy breath, "I don't think that's going to happen anymore."

"Don't be ridiculous. Just give it another minute. Maybe my batteries need recharging or something."

Jody's body hitched and she growled through her gritted teeth. "You're not supposed to make me laugh. It hurts too much."

"I wasn't trying to be funny."

"Do you ever try to be funny? I think it's just a quirk with you." Her face pinched and her limbs drew together. It was as if she was trying to shrink in front of him. "Why haven't I died yet?"

"You're not going to die. I won't let you."

"I shouldn't have to ask your permission," Jo moaned. "God, everything hurts so much."

"I don't understand why I'm not making you better." In fact, though her face appeared more peaceful, Jody's wounds were looking worse.

"I'm glad you're here," she said. "It would have been sad to die alone."

Her voice was breaking and Gregg noticed a tear glide over her pale cheek. The sight of it made Gregg want to scream.

"Stop talking like that. I'm going to save you."

Only, he really didn't know how. He decided to grab onto her and lift her up, but Jody resisted and her damned twisting overwhelmed his balance.

"No!" Soreness made her whole body spasm and Gregg had to let her be. The brute force he thought he had seemed to be missing. He felt awfully normal. There was no disputing it then. Jody couldn't be moved.

"I'm sorry, Greggo." She made a meek effort to reach his hand with hers.

"Jesus, you're freezing!"

Jody nodded dimly. She was looking worse. Her lips quivered. "I'm glad you're here."

Gregg's mind pressed for a solution. They were in the middle of a dense, old-growth forest and the fastest way out of it was a good thirty minute hike over roots and mossy ground in the dead of night. There was no way around it, Jody wasn't going anywhere.

"Jo?" Gregg held her hand tightly and stared into her tortured eyes. He knew this was going to be the hardest thing he'd ever done. "I have to go."

She responded with a look of pure dread. "What?"

"It's the only way to get you out of here. You can't walk, I can't carry you. I have to get help."

Although Jody's face and colour had been more and more wrought with signs of imminent darkness, her grip on Gregg's hand was instantly vice-like.

"No. You can't. You can't leave me. Not now. You just can't."

Her reaction was so pure it felt as if Gregg's heart had split in his chest. All his life he'd dreamt of hearing Jo speak in such a way to him, to want him, need him. He had never cared about anyone like he did Jody. It only cemented his determination.

"You are not going to die. I promise you, Jo. I'm coming back for you."

"But I don't want to be left alone!" she cried. "They're not done with me. Can't you see that I can't do this by myself? I don't want to! Oh God, I'm so scared. Why don't I die?"

"Don't talk like that. I told you I'm coming back. I always come back. Jeezuz!"

"Oh shut up! You don't know what it's like to be me. To be left alone!" Choked with emotions, it took her a few suffering bouts of wheezing before she finally calmed down enough to speak again.

"I know I've told you that I don't remember anything about my parents. That's a lie. I have one memory and it's one that I wish I could forget.

"It was the night of the accident. I remember being wet and cold. It was dark. There's this hazy image of my father kneeling in front of me, kissing my forehead. He said something, but his voice was stifled, probably from my own sense of panic. 'Throw the... layo into the light.' It was so long ago, I just can't remember."

She paused, taking in a long wavering breath.

"I didn't know where we were, what was happening, nothing except that I wanted to go home and get warm and feel like everything was normal and safe again. But that didn't happen.

"The next image fixed in my mind is of my dad running headlong into the river. Into the darkness. He left me *alone*. I never saw him or my mom again. I don't know how long I stayed there shivering, terrified, but it's the worst feeling I've ever had." She looked at Gregg weakly. "I can die right now and it'd be okay because you're here with me. I don't want to be alone, Gregg. Not now."

Crap. Gregg knew he wasn't going to win this. But he also realized that he had to.

"Look," he said, measuring his words. "Those freakalations won't let you die. They won't even bother you until I come back." He went to the folding table next to the bed and warily picked up the book. "Because I'm taking this. As soon as they realize this book is gone, they'll be fast-tracking into the forest to find me."

Jody lay exhausted, her face a sight of misery. "Please..." she beseeched. "You promised me. You promised you'd never leave me. Don't go!"

"Dammit, Jo! I don't want to, but if I stay then you are going to die!"

She didn't look like she cared much about that.

"Don't go, mon amour."

Gregg felt winded hearing the words advance so softly past her lips, as if lifted by her lungs' last breath. He could have crumbled to his knees and stayed by her side forever, worshiping her body as a holy relic up to his own day of ruin.

He seriously considered it.

Maybe there was nothing more he could do, or should. There were no guarantees he'd be able to find help outside the forest, or that he'd be able to make it there and back before Jody passed away. How could he live with himself if he returned to find her already dead?

If there was any hope left to saving her, to get her out of this horrible place, then Gregg knew he had to go. He *had* to.

With an uncertain determination forcing him on, Gregg went to Jo and leaned down to kiss her head. Her whimpers were becoming hysterical. He couldn't hold back his tears, hearing her cry this way, seeing her face crumble. Still, he managed to bring his lips to her ear and say the one thing he had wanted to for practically his entire life, but had never had the courage to.

"I love you."

Chapter 54

Peculiarities

Ligeia revelled in the racy orientations they made, bumping and grinding, twisting and thrusting. Damianos's body was like a furnace against her skin and her blood felt like it was going to boil. And then, fantastically, his penis found just the right spot and its touch laid the foundation for another of Ligeia's powerful orgasms.

Digging her nails into the cot's sheet and gritting her teeth, Ligeia cried out her elation and madly swayed and bucked, rocking and rolling hard into his girth, giving her even deeper stimulation until she happily felt him throbbing full of force, filling her at last with his climax.

He clung to her, pushing intensely while grunting and shaking, until at last his stature slumped and he was left gasping for air. Ligeia did the same, delighting in the rippling effects of their lovemaking. Damianos fell to the cot by her side, the look on his face revealing how completely spent he was.

Ligeia lay naked in his wake, at ease with the sticky wetness clinging to her skin, feeling more satisfied than she had in decades and thinking she could close her eyes and sleep for days.

Before long however, Damianos turned his back to her and she noticed his body was becoming more rigid against her gentle touches. Undaunted at first, Ligeia stretched and cooed, "I haven't hurt like this in years."

She stroked his muscular back and shoulder, but it only seemed to annoy him. Ligeia loathed the idea of losing this wonderful experience to more of Damianos's peculiarities and tried to woo him by wrapping herself around his hip so he could feel her naked breasts. The effect was not what she'd hoped for.

Damianos shifted roughly and with a look of disdain muttered, "Shouldn't you clean up?"

"Why?" she asked, flaunting herself before him. "I've been perfectly ravaged. And I know how much you like it when I get messy."

He grumbled, "The devil is latching onto my soul and you think only of what good the carcass brings. If I could just move my complacent body with more urgency!"

Damianos made a few rather feeble attempts to throw off the blanket and get up from the confines of their warm cot, but it seemed the cold night air kept shoving him back in.

He kneaded his face, complaining, "The book's play on me is finished. It must be. Now I must think more clearly."

"About what?" Ligeia asked, disappointed once again.

"About my soul, for starters," he barked. "And yours too, and everyone's. Honestly, have you never once wondered what lies ahead of us?"

"I am much more concerned with what 'Lie' is currently doing in this bed, whose thrilling high is being quickly sapped by the silly esoteric ramblings that seem to spill almost uncontrollably out of your ridiculously handsome head."

Damianos examined her closely for a spell, then sighed.

"It's true. I haven't believed in such things for most of my life, but faced with my struggles today I don't see how I can deny them anymore. There is a part of me that lives on, and I am left as scared as an overly inventive child that there is something frightening waiting for me on the other side of the closed closet door." He brooded. "That door is what separates this reality from the next. I have to wonder, the owner of the voice that has guided me so long and so far... what is it?"

"Your conscience?" Ligeia stared up to the tent's dark ceiling, fingers tapping her thigh impatiently.

"No, it can't be. You see, I know what my conscience sounds like, muttering on during my daily routines, analyzing, debating, giving opinions, some of which I speak out while most I keep hidden. This voice is different. It's one that asserts itself all on its own. It is the voice of a dragon, lurking in some icy hell that seems to be his prison."

Damianos made another attempt to get out of bed, but Ligeia wasn't about to let that happen. She rolled over, practically smothering him, and stroked his long hair.

Sure, it was a desperate attempt to save what little enchantment might be left in the air, but damn it, it was worth it.

"Rest now," she said softly. "This scary monster in the closet cannot get you here. This is your life, Dammie. The hunt is over. We have an angoros with blood that is without doubt the most compelling aphrodisiac in the history of creation, and a jivita who, if we can break him, can be our slave for all time. And they're both waiting powerless for us to do whatever we want to them. They, like your scary lizard, can keep waiting." She tried to laze on top of him, but Damianos shifted out from under her.

"I am done deluding myself," he said. "At first, I had an absurd attraction to you. I must admit I was infatuated. Syrēnes are engaging at so many levels that even I could not turn away. You became an obsession that overshadowed my hunger for revenge. I loved you.

"But I was younger then and alas, witnessing your hither and yonder plays, emotional simplicities and ceaseless efforts for self-indulgence has exposed a deep fault in that forbidden love. A syrēne and a lilita were never meant to hold an eternal flame together. In the end, our emotions get burned and our purpose is reduced to ashes.

"We are so different, you and I. And now, I need to grow up."

Ligeia threw off the blanket, the air's chill not nearly as biting as the anxiety swelling in her belly. "So you admit it then. You think of me as a child not worth loving!"

"How can I love anyone when my heart is so consumed with hate? It is my purpose that keeps me alive, that excites my passion. We are here because a beast that lies in the realm of death is desperately trying to escape! Some might run in retreat, but for me, it is evidence of my ultimate function. This is the *why* in 'why am I here!'"

He ran his fingers through his tousled hair in agitation.

"Think about it, Lie. Have you never wondered? I know now why I am here and need to understand what I must do about it."

Ligeia's throat closed in around her voice. For the last two centuries she'd thought she always knew why she was anywhere. She was born because her mother had sex with another syrēne. She stayed alive because she hunted and ate. She enjoyed life because she had love. But that had turned out to be the biggest lie of all.

"This dragon pretends to be as great as God," Damianos pondered aloud, apparently oblivious to Ligeia's crumbling heart. "Yet, it has been imprisoned. By whom, I wonder?"

Ligeia had feared losing Damianos for some time now, quietly fretting that this moment would come. Gregg's arrival into her life could not have materialized at a better time and her hopes for him continued to rise. Still, this hurt.

"The Nornir?" Damianos carried on, completely ignoring her. "And what were the reasons behind the captivity?"

She'd had other lovers before Damianos, but male syrēnes were such a disappointment sexually, and humans... well, she wasn't prepared to be intimate with her food. At least, not until recently. Teasing them was fun. Luring them into her trap gave her a high she couldn't explain. But humans always seemed so fragile. What an arousing delight it was to find Gregg, a human boy mixed with the get-up-and-go of a Titan.

She still needed to lure him though, and that made everything feel a little cheaper. Two centuries ago, attracting an admirer had been effortless. Love was easy. Too easy. She thought Damianos would be her last, her immortal beloved.

"But it is not to be," she told herself, watching him think so seriously about his stupid dragon delusion.

Maybe this was why syrēne's killed their parents, because the older people got, the crazier they behaved. She used to hold lilitas in such high regard, had even considered having a half-breed child with Damianos, if that should have pleased him.

But now this whole nightmare, of which she reluctantly had become a part of, seemed to be turning things inside out.

"Perhaps it is time that I grew up too."

Chapter 55

Appeal

Goosebumps fluttered over Ligeia's naked skin the minute she rushed out of the tent. "Damn it! Damn, damn, damn... grr, Damianos!" She stomped her feet into the moss-laden earth, having left that ancient, feebleminded Damianos to fantasize about all the choice options he could think of for eternity.

She wanted so much to unfurl her wings and escape this miserable place, this *life*, forever. She would do it, if not for the blinding darkness around her and all those stupid damn trees leaning overhead, caging her in like a dopey bird.

"Ooh, I hate this place! He thinks and thinks and thinks! Why can't he just do? Why can't he be here, in the now, with me?"

She caught her breath, juggling the many emotions burning in her breast, when suddenly something stirred around the corner of Jody's tent. She paused and smelled the cool air, then moved closer.

An obvious scent finally filled her nose. She quickly bounced forward and grabbed the jivita half-breed hiding in the dark, forcing him to choke back his fright with her hand pressed over his mouth.

Something deep within her brought her lips to his face and she kissed him, thankful he was alive. She shuddered then, trying to keep composed as she pulled back, her eyes fixed on him. He held the book.

"You're running away, aren't you?" She scanned the area and sniffed. "She's not with you. You left your angoros bitch in the tent?"

"Let go of me." He was clearly doing his best to sound intimidating, the dear thing.

"Oh no!" She feigned concern.

Despite having lost his abilities as a jivita to her spell, Gregg still managed to peel himself free of her hold. Her frustratingly weak, sluggish response reminded her of the consequences of frantic lovemaking. Her stamina had been exhausted, making even a human boy a dickens to contend with. She had to be careful.

"Wait!" she pleaded in a hushed tone. She had to grab onto him to make him listen. "Take me with you." She couldn't believe she said it so harshly. "I can give you your powers back. I just want to get out of here, to someplace warm and open, where a woman like me can make a young man like you happy... very, very happy."

Her powers of coercion had reached an obvious low, judging by the boy's expression.

"Give me my powers back?" he said, and then something in his eyes lit up. "That's why it didn't work. I can't heal anyone now and it's because of you!"

"I cast a spell on you," Ligeia admitted proudly.

"A spell? What the hell? Now, on top of everything else, I have to be leery of stupid magic tricks? How did you...? Oh. Wait." He had obviously reached his own conclusion. "You sang your voodoo crap to me, didn't you? That's your thing. With that magic windpipe of yours. You're like a siren." Again, his eyes kindled brighter. "That's it! That's what you are. Jesus, I am having the worst day!"

Ligeia beamed. "Sneaky, isn't it? Now your abilities as a jivita are gone. But I can give them back." She went to him, tracing the lines of his jaw with a gentle touch. "I can help you, if you help me."

"You wanna help me? Then help me get Jody as far as possible from that friggity-fracked psycho that put a hole in her back!"

She looked at him, lips zipped while she pondered. She couldn't believe she was actually negotiating with him.

But before she could respond, Gregg jerked himself away from her grasp and pushed her aside. He ran up a fern laden slope into the forest's blackness.

"No!" she panicked.

Her mind wrestled with itself, looking at her tent. Inside was the person she'd thought was going to be her lifelong Romeo. It was disheartening to admit that her romance had become a tragedy.

Now, for the first time in her life, she had to gather what strength she could and fight for the love she longed for. She turned away from the tent and hurried into the bush.

Chapter 56

Pursued

I have to keep running! Gregg told himself as the cold night air burned inside his hot lungs. Hindered by darkness, low branches and a harsh forest carpet that hid sudden swells and deep gaps, Gregg thought his mad escape was like something from a horror film. *Run, run, run!*

Behind him, he knew Ligeia was coming. The book swayed heavily in his arms, making his balance even more difficult to control, so when his foot sank under the moss unexpectedly, he fell and crashed onto the rugged ground. He looked back to see a black shape getting nearer.

"Get up! Get up!" he groaned between gasps for air.

"You're going to love me!" Ligeia blustered, sounding haggard.

He hurried by tree and stump into a brief open area where the stars shimmered brightly above him. He heard a frightening whoosh and before he could turn his head,

Ligeia struck his back and he flew forward. His chest whacked a thick branch that was close to the ground and he collapsed in a winded heap.

Ligeia, her breaths excessive, walked up to him. "Jody's a lost cause, Gregg. Nothing can save her now."

He knew he couldn't give up, despite the hurt. *Jody needs me! Fight! Fight!*

Gregg flung out his leg and slew-footed Ligeia to the ground. She fell on top of him and Gregg thought he heard his spine crack. They struggled, wrestling and panting, with neither gaining a clear advantage. Finally, Gregg head-butted her and she screamed bloody murder.

"Ow! You wicked little beast!"

Wheezing for air, she still managed to come back at him, clawing. Gregg accidentally slapped Ligeia's breast hard in defence, and she yelped again.

She rubbed where it must have hurt most, looking appalled, while Gregg waited guiltily. After a moment of recovery she got up with an odd look of arousal brightening her face, and Gregg suddenly realized her massaging had become rather fervid.

Her lips curled back, displaying her tongue making an exploratory journey across her scary teeth, and her heated voice, when it came to him, was flanked by a surprising sexual tension.

"That was... *mean*." She snickered and lunged at him, trying to kick him in the crotch.

"Hey! Hey! *HEY*!"

"Oh, stop being so coy with me. Take those silly clothes off and..."

Gregg surged back, bounding over one log, but tripping over the next. "Get away from me!"

Ligeia huffed and slapped at a prodding fern blade. "Do you think I fancy this sort of intrigue? I'm much more aroused when my lover battles to subdue me, not to free himself and run in the other direction."

A tall dark figure lurched from the shadows and Gregg's heart sank, knowing it was Damianos.

The man in black surveyed the commotion briefly, fixing his burned coat over his wide shoulders as he said, "Thank you, Lie. If not for your boisterousness, I would never have heard this mutt flee in time." He spotted the book lying on the ground and went to it. "Mutt... flee," he said mockingly while cleaning the book's cover.

Ligeia turned to him like she was about to say something heated, but Gregg had no intention of waiting to find out for sure. He took the sudden opportunity and kicked her in the back of her knee. She buckled and Gregg grabbed a nearby branch and bonked her on the back of her head with it.

She made an awful sound and floundered like a fish out of water. "You stupid boy!" she cried.

Gregg looked nervously behind him, but Damianos was walking away, cradling the book in his arms.

"Have fun with your new toy, my dear!" he called over his shoulder.

Ligeia hung her head and growled something under her breath. While the sight was naturally a curious one, Gregg knew to be watchful for anymore of her sly tricks. So when Ligeia shifted unexpectedly, Gregg was ready and pushed her down with his foot. He held the broken end of the branch threateningly near her chest.

"You wouldn't dare!" she snapped.

Gregg barely noticed the tear channelling down her face. He needed to be strong for Jody. "If I have to choose between you and Jo, then believe me, I'd dare."

Damianos was heading back to Jody now and it was because of Gregg's botched attempt to find help. His plan was falling apart.

"Dammie!" Ligeia called out again. "Dammie, help me! Come back!"

"He's gone, sweetheart," Gregg said, realizing that the siren's predicament wasn't so unlike Jody's. Damianos had left his girl in the hands of the enemy. The coincidence rattled him and he couldn't help but shudder at the sight of Ligeia's sad eyes.

Letting anything more horrible happen could be fatal for Jo, and would be eternally devastating for him. *What to do?*

He nudged Ligeia with the stick. "Give me my powers back!"

"Now? Are you insane? You've got a pointy birch on my tit ready to poke me as if I was a Lite-Brite."

"What choice do you have? Your boyfriend's given up on you. He's left you!"

The ache in Ligeia's dark face was clear, and very surprising. "What will you do?"

"Save Jody! Do you really need to ask?"

Ligeia hissed with contempt. "Not good enough."

"I'll kill you right here and now!"

She flinched. "Why? Why do you love her so much?"

"What...? ...Because! Because I do!" he blurted. "She's the only girl I've ever loved." It felt good to say it, to get it out into the open air like that.

Ligeia scoffed, "And she just happens to be living next door. That's convenient."

"It's the truth."

"You need to get out more. To be more cultured."

"Give me back my powers!"

"What if I told you that you're the only one I love?"

"What!?"

"Well?"

"I don't love you!" Gregg's insides shivered at the thought.

Ligeia sneered, "Not yet, but I'm a lot older than you. I've seen hordes of people, men and women, and I know exactly what love is. I'm the queen of culture, and Jody is nothing if not annoying, whiny, and about as feeble as any mall-rat that infests the western world. Really, what does she matter? Has Jody ever told you she loves you?"

"What?" Gregg was losing his focus here. "Not really. At least, not in English." He stopped talking. He needed to avoid another one of Ligeia's traps. "You know, this would be volumes easier if you'd just shut-up."

The siren laughed. "I suppose her having Sean as a boyfriend makes her feelings for you perfectly clear, does it? Do you think if you wait long enough, she'll come around? Just giving it time, are you?"

Gregg didn't answer.

"I think I should do the same. I'll keep your powers, thank you, until you come around."

Gregg spun the branch and clobbered her with it. "If I don't stop your asshole boyfriend, he's going to kill her!"

Ligeia's demeanour changed and she spun and slammed her leather wing into Gregg's side. He fell back, dizzied, giving Ligeia the opportunity to climb on top of him, snarling, "If he doesn't, then I will!"

Gregg struggled but couldn't free himself. "Why? Why didn't I just kill you when I had the chance?"

"It's not that I doubt your intentions at the moment, my dear half-breed, but I've added to your indecision by way of another spell I sang to you." The words escaped her sexy mouth as if heralded by tower bells.

"A very strong curse this one, it should have devoted you to me the moment you heard it. But the fervour that has swallowed your mish-mashed heart still beckons for her. It's so annoying, you have no idea."

Her facial expressions gave him a pretty good clue.

"As uncomplicated as it may be for you to hit me, you son-of-a-bitch, when it comes to really hurting me, I don't think you can do it. The seeds of love are there, it's easy enough to see. By the same token though, I'd bet the only reason you are not fully mine is because of that stupid blonde tied down in the tent. I can fix that, because when she dies, your wasted love for her should promptly die too, freeing up your passion for me. Forever."

"No!" He twisted and wriggled under her, but Ligeia only laughed, bringing her face close to his.

"You will love me." She let out her long tongue and grazed the end of his nose with it.

Gregg contorted his body to get free and managed to knock Ligeia off balance. Running was all he thought of doing now. *Go, go, go!*

Ligeia fussed behind him and he glanced back to see her putting a firm grip on a palm-sized rock. She snarled her fat lips and charged after him. Gregg slid to the left as she lunged to the right.

Another space under the moss opened up, this time below Ligeia, and it swallowed her knee. She squealed and cried out in obvious pain.

Gregg came back, unprepared for this fortunate twist of fate. It took him a moment to gather his wits, realizing that she was injured and vulnerable. Maybe this time he could do it. *Kill her!* He told himself.

He scoured the area, but the night hid most everything from sight. If only he had something that could finish her off quick and clean, like a loaded shotgun, a grenade, a bazooka . . . anything!

Looking around the dark side of a Douglas fir, he heard an odd scuffling of undergrowth behind him. He spun in time to see Ligeia ascend from the shadows, grunting with the rock still in her hand. She swung and hit him hard in the head and he dropped in a flash, the soft forest matting cushioning his fall. He noticed the rock resting near him as the deepest recesses of his brain exploded behind his eyes.

Ligeia screamed something chilling and threw her body upward like a victorious warrior, but then she yelped and quickly reached down to hold her ankle.

Gregg felt a warm stream oozing between the follicles of his hair and down the side of his head. His thoughts became incoherent and distorted. Voices echoed in his blurring mind, worries that badgered on despite everything. His body lurched, but without control and energy. He had to get up. *Jody!*

He thought of his mother, imagining her in that puffy white cloud. "Mum?" he said shakily. "I don't know what to do. Mum... I'm afraid."

He couldn't let himself stop. Jody needed him. That should be enough to get him going. Yet fear and exhaustion held him down, and he clung to the earth as though the world around him was turning upside down. His head throbbed intensely and it felt like the back of his eyes were being pushed out of their sockets.

Something stroked the back of his sore head and a man's voice massaged his mind. "It is good to be afraid," it said.

Gregg tried, but he could not focus. He was alone, save for a wisp of low-lying fog that had crept over him. It was strangely warm and felt good. Gregg relaxed and allowed it to take the edge off things.

"It is your mortality, and it is powerful. Let it incite the god in you." Was that the fog talking?

The little cloud bled away into the forest as quickly as it had come, taking with it Gregg's pounding headache.

"Get up and fight!"

Purpose refreshed, Gregg pushed himself from the ground until he stood wobbly on his feet. "Wait!" he called. The little patch of fog slipped into the darkness and out of sight. "Who are you?"

He thought of following, but spotted Ligeia's shape crumpled nearby. She hissed at him before slinking into the bushes.

His pain still lingered, his balance was amiss and, despite all the wonder and surprise of that day, his injuries kept trying to pull him back down. He hadn't yet determined which way to go when Ligeia's screams reached him from a dark distance.

"I'm going to kill that little bitch! I'm going to make her suffer! You're only a boy now. Human! And I'm not going to let you be anything else until she's dead!"

Chapter 57

Convergence

Moments slipped by and an eerie awareness came over Gregg as the night closed in around him.

The whispers.

Every time he spun his head to see the source of the voices, the oh-so-many voices, his dizziness sent him dipping and stumbling. The sky was blocked out by the trees' stretching limbs, smothering both stars and moon. The forest bottom was blotched in darkness with each and every possible landmark looking very much like everything else. In short, to his disheartenment, Gregg was lost.

Yet voices were coming, mumbling, grumbling, whispering. What were they nattering on about? It was horrifying and only helped to make his heart race faster.

Gregg staggered, his last view of Jody haunting him, without any idea if he was walking toward help, straight back to her tent, or worse, neither. In any case, he hadn't a clear plan of what he was going to do anymore.

Jo had begged him not to go, her whimpers beating against his soul with each awkward footfall as he ran off, leaving her in that wretched place. That single moment held enough blight in his being to plague him forever, and his unsteady mind fussed over his decision, wondering if he'd done the right thing.

Gregg needed help, but the idea of someone else, *anyone else*, rescuing Jo made him want to keel over and throw-up. There was no other option. It had to be him.

That was his purpose. Without understanding why, he knew it. Yet he was also violently scared.

His adversaries were not normal, not human, and the unreal powers he had only just discovered had already been taken away. He wondered disparagingly if he'd lost his testicles at the same time.

A sudden, wobbly wave of vertigo clobbered his senses and he fell upon a mat of thick green moss. He gripped his head and stared up at the trees, trying to escape his spinning mind. Lying there, wasted and wayward, his impoverished thoughts craved for clear answers.

The voices came louder, calling his name while he laid there, despairing. "Gregg! Gregg!"

Their cries blared in the dark quiet of the forest. Strange, careening shafts of white light wove in and out of sight, breaking through the blackness with growing frequency.

"Greggo!" That voice sounded downright familiar. "Dammit, Gregg, I am going to whupp your ass when I find you!"

Gregg lifted his hand, not sure whether to discount this strange experience or to jump up and cheer hallelujah! "Over here!"

A light flashed over his horizontal frame, striking his extended hand.

"Jesus, I found him! I found him!" A moment later, Daveyboy's light was glaring right into Gregg's eyes. "What the hell happened to you?"

Chapter 58

Insensitive

"Dude, you think this is time for games?" Dave shot Gregg a disapproving glare. "What the hell is wrong with you?" He reached down and helped Gregg back to his feet.

Gregg's balance had not yet returned and he leaned hard against the spine of a tall tree.

"Honestly, the minute we turn our backs, you take off! You're scaring the crap out of Laura. Grammy has been going nuts, dragging with her some secret heavy thing that she can't talk about and my dad and me are totally missing the 'Nucks game!"

"I have to get help," Gregg tried to tell him, but Dave was too busy ranting, as usual.

"And another thing, you dolt. I was going to meet up with Mike after hockey and go to the park." He looked really miffed about this one. "This girl's supposed to be going there with some of her friends and, gawd, she is only the hottest redhead I've ever seen! And now there's no way I'm going to make it, because of you, you busted cog!"

"I have to get help," Gregg repeated. "Jody..."

"Yeah, yeah," Dave cut him off. "She's still missing. And it's a bummer about her mom. Can you believe it? The police cordoned off our end of the street. I mean the whole thing! Christ, the stars are aligning, dude. The Universe is keeping me from Leah. Dear sweet, sexy Leah." He clenched his fists. "Why? Why me?"

Gregg did his best to ignore his stepbrother, but he really wanted to clobber the self-centred prick with the nearest baseball bat—if only he could find one.

"Greggory?" his great-grandmother's voice echoed closer, her approach foretold by the swaying beam of her flashlight. "Oh, thank God I'm not too late."

She sounded breathless and she was carrying something rather long and heavy. It made for a very strange sight considering how old she was and the rough terrain underfoot.

"I can't make sense of Grammy, man." Dave scratched his head. "There is something different. It's like she's Popeye's long lost sister or something, and she's been in the spinach, if you get me. Seriously, she's been moving like lightning out here trying to find you. I need whatever vitamins she's getting." He eyed Gregg again. "What have you been up to?"

Chapter 59

Help

"Gregg!"

He watched as more beams of light shot out of the darkness. Laura was coming and it looked like Patrick was with her.

"Your mom has been going psycho since you took off. Seeing the cops come running out of this place with their tails between their legs didn't help," Dave muttered. "They're still out there, waiting for the helicopter to come and check the forest from above. Laura had the bright idea you might be dumb enough to come in here and no one could keep her out after that. Are you bleeding?" Dave shuddered. His gaze left Gregg and scanned the tree tops. "This is so wrong. Why, oh why did you run away like that?"

Gregg was about to explain when Grammy came between them. "Greggory, I'm so sorry. I just kept getting interrupted. I wanted to do it sooner, but I guess I didn't realize the grimness of the situation. Until it was too late."

"It's okay, Grammy. I know where Jo..."

Grammy smothered his open mouth with her hand and peered at the blood along the side of his head. "There's no time for that!"

She got out a sport drink bottle and unscrewed the lid before dumping its contents down Gregg's throat. It was good and he gulped as much as he could.

Behind her, Laura and Patrick arrived. Gregg was surprised at how awkward it was to face the woman he had always thought was his mother.

"Oh, thank God!" She covered him with a huge hug and then noticed the blood. "Holy crap! What happened to you? What are you doing here? Why did you sneak off like that? Why are you bleeding?"

"Let him speak, Laura," Patrick interrupted. He was much more composed, even though Gregg saw an obvious glimmer of relief in his eyes. "Are you alright, boy?"

Gregg was going to tell them that no, in fact he was very much *not* all right. He had a terrible gash on the side of his head and he still felt woozy. Add to that, he'd found Jody and she was being held captive, half-naked, in a tent in some dark hollow by a handsome beast with fingernails like razor blades and a winged woman he was sure was a siren! But Grammy got in the way a second time.

"It looks like he's done some damage." She waved rather vaguely at his legs, missing his head altogether. "I don't think he can walk." She glared at Gregg as if to keep him in line.

Patrick moved in. "That's okay. I'll carry him out."

"No! No!" Grammy hollered. Patrick backed off, visibly bewildered. "You don't want to cause anymore hurt, do you? Isn't that right, Greggory?"

The way those steely blue eyes were looking at him, it was pretty evident he was supposed to nod and agree. Bizarrely, that's what he did.

"Ouch!" He feigned agony. "It's pretty bad."

"Well, thank God you're safe now." Laura gave him another hug, but it was hard for Gregg to return the gesture.

All the time he'd spent as a child loving her, confiding in her, running to her and crying in her arms, it suddenly felt like their special relationship had been a colossal lie.

She didn't seem to notice his discomfiture and simply released him, saying, "Let's find a way to get you out of here so we can put this horrible day behind us."

Disturbing voices started whispering all around him, just as they had when he'd dared venture too deep into the woods as a kid. "Don't leave! Don't leave! The root is stretching. The time is nigh!"

Gregg noticed Dave's face contorting, glaring restlessly up at the trees. The others, it seemed, heard nothing.

"You're right, Laura"—Grammy made a not-so-subtle attempt to separate her granddaughter from Gregg—"it has been a stressful day, particularly for Greggory, what with his feelings for poor Jody and all. But he's found now, and quite safe for the time being. Why not go ahead and let the police know what has happened and that he'll be needing a backboard or something. We don't want to snap his spine, do we? I'll stay here and keep him company."

Laura didn't look too enthused about that plan and eyed Grammy curiously. "Why not just call someone?" She pulled out her iPhone and read the display. "No signal," she grumbled, holding the silly thing in all sorts of directions. "Damn. Look, I'll stay with him and you go, Grammy."

"Uhm..." Grammy delayed, thinking. "But you could arrange things for when Gregg comes out much better than me. I'm just an old woman, remember? I get confused very easily."

Laura glared at Grammy and the mysterious object she guarded by her side. "You've been prancing like a ruddy gazelle, Grams. *Now* you're an old woman? What are you up to?"

"C'mon then," Patrick urged Laura impatiently along and gave Gregg a nudge before heading off. "No sense in wasting anymore time. We'll be back with help. Don't you move again, got it?"

They rushed off as fast as they could, considering the choppy terrain, but Gregg noticed that Dave had stayed and was standing next to him, scowling.

"You're not really bleeding," he asserted. "You never bleed. Just like you never get sick. What the eff is going on around here?"

Gregg was going to answer, but again Grammy barged in.

"He's upset, David. Jody has gone missing, her mother has been murdered; shouldn't you be worried for her too?"

Dave seemed rattled at first. Then his face hardened into a defiant expression as Grammy continued her lecture.

"I know you would do anything and everything to find Jo and keep her safe, just like Greggory. You two boys may be at odds often, but you're still chasing the same end. Don't you forget that."

Dave let out a heavy breath, murmuring something. His eyes flashed up at the trees again. "I don't like this. It doesn't explain why Lois's car is at the end of your driveway or what Gregg's been up to in this forest."

"I'll make this clear enough to you," Grammy offered. "You've a role to play in this, David. I've learned as much. And it will be your immaturity that holds you back and risks a great deal. Girls, booze, and attitude. You think that makes a somebody? I tell you, you can never master passion without feeling enmity. Your brother is hurt, both in body and spirit, and you sneer at him, trying to expose something, to make him feel smaller and you bigger."

"But I..."

"But nothing." Grammy waved her hand at him. "Go. Go and help the others and bring word if anything more is known about poor Jody. Go!"

Gregg watched, marvelling how his great-grandmother managed to send big Dave drooping into the trees. Those eyes of hers were practically shooting laser beams.

Thank goodness she reduced their intensity when she faced him again.

When they were finally alone, she handed Gregg her flashlight and fussed over the ragged-up-thing in her other hand. "Glory, I thought he'd never leave. How are you? All right?" She used some of the separated cloth to wipe the blood over his ear and down his neck. "God, how'd this happen?"

"You wouldn't believe me."

Grammy stared. "Really? After everything so far? Trust me, I am past all bias when it comes to the bizarre. I may be old, Greggory, but I'd like to think dementia would be more fun than this."

Gregg thought for a moment and then told her everything that had happened as quickly as he could, from the time he ran clear of the ambulance to his last confrontation with Ligeia moments ago.

"I think she's a siren."

His great-grandma flinched. "A siren, you say? Like those seductresses that lured sailors to crash their boats into rocks by singing to them?"

Gregg nodded, assuming she would sneer any second.

"And that's how the harlot took away your ability to heal? The same ability you used to save me?"

She seemed almost amused. "A spell? What, just by singing it?" She stared into the woods, deep in thought. "That's interesting."

"But it's been too long now," Gregg whined. "I have to go back!" He looked around with the flashlight for anything he could use as a weapon, knowing that trying to take out Damianos and Ligeia with only a stick or rock would be suicidal. "This is hopeless! I have to find help!"

"What kind of help would you like, my boy? Shall the police come guns-a-blazing to the rescue? What of Jo then? Hmm? They'll see her back. Surely you've thought about what they'll find? What if paramedics see too much? What then will they do with her?"

Gregg didn't know how to respond to that.

"It's true, isn't it? After what you've seen. . . you don't think she's, *normal*?" Grammy looked as though she was hoping Gregg would deny it, to keep the impossible truth... well, impossible.

"Am I?"

"Right." Grammy stiffened. "That settles it. I've got to clean you up and prepare you as best I can." She got to work, periodically scanning the forest's empty spaces.

"Wait, prepare me?"

Great-grandma paused. "To go back! There's no one else who can do it. Dave is much too childish yet and I've already told you the police will no doubt want answers for their efforts. Can you imagine what would happen if it got out that monsters really do exist?"

"I can't believe I'm hearing this. You're going to send me back in there?"

Grammy's glance turned devious. "It's what you want, isn't it?" Again, this astonishing old woman seemed to be reading his thoughts. She shuffled the last bits of cloth clear of the item she'd been holding and Gregg balked at what he saw. "But this time, my lad, you're not going alone."

Chapter 60

Hunted

Bitterness fired Ligeia up enough to sustain her as she crossed through the pitch dark woods, hobbling on a twisted ankle no less. She had a job to do and a score to settle. She would take great pleasure in killing the stupidly annoying girl, that wicked little pretender who had somehow managed to drive the last dagger into Ligeia's relationship with Damianos and had so far thwarted her efforts with the first jivita half-breed she'd ever seen.

As she came closer to the forest hollow, she heard Damianos's unmistakably enraged voice mushrooming from the home-wrecker's tent.

"I need you to open that confounding book!"

Ligeia stumbled down the embankment to the tent's fabric wall and listened, curious.

"Kill me! You murdering, torturing, miserable asshole!" The little cream puff was telling Damianos off rather smartly. "I hate you! I hate everything about you!"

Ligeia grinned, becoming conscious of how impressed she really was of Jody. Perhaps the little waif wasn't such a weakling after all.

"Sorry to disappoint you, Dracula," Jody's voice seethed with contempt, "but I don't know a damned thing about your precious book. And even if I did, the only way I'd open it for you is over my dead body!"

"You tempt me, angoros mutt!" Damianos's tone was fierce and there was the sound of a brief struggle. Even now, Ligeia quivered at the force in his voice.

"Do it," Jody taunted.

There were distinct choking noises on the other side of that canvas and Ligeia wondered if Damianos was strangling her.

"Why?" he eventually grumbled.

Jody gasped. "I don't want to live anymore."

"Don't be childish. You don't know what's waiting for you on the other side."

"I know you suck on this side," she spat.

A short moment of harsh breathing filled the silence and Ligeia leaned in closer, listening intently.

"Please, just kill me," Jody whispered.

"Release your hand." Damianos's tone was odd and Ligeia puzzled over why.

"I beg of you! Please! Let me die!"

"Damn it, child, release your hand!"

Another moment went by. "I did not see this before," Damianos sounded stunned. "The chain was hidden under your hair and the pendant between your breasts. If I had known..."

This conversation had taken an odd turn, Ligeia thought and she quietly shuffled toward the tent's loose flaps.

"The imagery... this is it!" he said with half a breath. "The key."

"I don't understand," Jody sounded frail again. "It's mine. It's from my parents. Get your hands off it!" Things got violent, with Jody's whimpers and gasps filling Ligeia's ears. Finally, Jody shouted, "Stop it! Stop it! STOP!!"

Everything went eerily still.

Ligeia manoeuvred her hands between the flaps, not quite believing what she was hearing. She paused as Damianos clearly sobbed.

"Damn you," his voice was faint. "That vile dragon, he says I am his best hope. But not his only. You, child, will be hunted for the rest of your days... however many you have left."

Ligeia glanced into the dim space, seeing only dark shapes as they moved. Damianos got up from his knees and advanced to the cot where Jody sat.

"Do it," the girl challenged. "I'm not afraid."

Damianos grabbed at something that was tied around Jody's neck. "You will be."

Chapter 61

Struggle

Gregg's murder, her abduction and forcible confinement, everything up to this point had given Jody the creepy notion that Damianos was always, *always* under some super-creepy sense of control. It was the way he held himself, back erect, head straight. His voice was devilishly steady and convincing. His movements were cocksure and seemingly unflappable.

Something changed all that when he'd caught sight of her pendant. His eyes had flickered and his lips had twitched, and in that moment she'd seen his madness.

"I will place this finery into the cover of the book, and you will put your finger into the dragon lock." His voice shook, its tone burning. "And your body will stay very much alive until I am done with it!"

Damianos yanked her from the cot trying to remove the necklace and she fell awkwardly to the ground, choking on the chain as if it was a dog's collar. "But I shall make it suffer, so that you will beg me to end your story! To cease your misery! You will do everything, everything, EVERYTHING that I want!"

The pain was excruciating. He was wildly cruel, pulling hard on her beloved necklace, pinching her windpipe shut. She struggled, but she was exhausted. In her mind she prayed for death to take her, but her appeals went unanswered still. So the agony went on.

"Damn this clasp!" He roughly dug at the fastener and fumbled time and again, becoming ever angrier.

On the floor with her was the book, the dragon lock facing her. When she looked, the device's eyes brightened and the mouth seemed to widen, sending new thrills of terror shooting through her chest.

The voices. The voices. They had come, rising, blustering like a frantic wind, collecting like rolling thunder. "The way! The way! Help us!"

Something was going to happen, she knew. *But what?*

Damianos wrenched her up from behind, using the choker pitilessly with one hand. "What must I do to free this obstinate piece of jewellery?"

He let go of her pendant and instead grasped her right wrist and pushed her fist toward the lock. Jody resisted, her knees digging into the soft earth.

"Perhaps there is a proper sequence of things that must be followed," he said. "First, I shall insert your finger. Then, I swear if this chain does not relent... I may grant you your wish sooner than later. I'll take off your pretty head!"

The voices rose up, "The way home! The way! The way!"

Jody balled her hand into a defiant fist.

"Open your hand!" he instructed, infuriated. "Open!"

"No!" It seemed there was still some fight left in her. Damianos thrust her closed fist against the dragon's head time and again.

He reached with his free hand, straightened the table, and placed the book upon it. Then he dug his hip hard into hers, thrusting her forward while drawing back on the chain so hard, Jody thought her neck was going to snap in half.

"The root is stretching! Can you feel it? It's reaching to take us! It's coming!"

"Open your hand!"

Staring unfocused at the tent's canvas ceiling, starved for breath, she did the only thing she could think of. She shimmied, stepping back hard against him, and knocked Damianos off kilter.

He puffed something incoherent and they both tumbled rearward onto the cot with Jody landing in a sitting position on his lap, and him holding her firmly in place.

That was when the tent flap rustled and in hobbled the winged witch, muscles tensed, fangs flaring, and her dark eyes burning.

Damianos let Jody go and she landed at his feet once again.

Chapter 62

Scorned

It was high time, Ligeia thought, for Damianos to learn a few things about life and relationships. The first thing she did was go to the girl and yank her away from him.

"Lie!" he barked.

"Don't you Lie me!" she huffed and glared at him, feeling more furious with every passing second. "Happiness with you has been a fool's hope, Dammie. A fool's hope! You can never be satisfied, can you." She wasn't asking. "No. If ever you should have been contented in your entire stupid life, it was when you were with me. Instead you relive horrors from the past and hunger for amends in the future, all the while missing the fantasy that you lived in the present. You expect me to believe any female lilita can outdo the likes of me? There is no one sexier, more passionate than me. If I cannot bring you bliss, then part the seas and jump into the deepest trench, Dammie, because heaven does not exist for you.

"I put my hand in yours..." She fought not to weep. Syrēnes never cried. "I was young and you charmed me to be your lover. I trusted you and gave you my heart. And now, having had your fill of it, you toss it back into my chest and expect it to beat on without you! You betrayer!" She couldn't help it, her vision blurred.

"And then you leave me out there in the cold night, running away into the forest like you did when you were a child, abandoning all hope for happiness."

"That's right!" Damianos barked. "I ran away as a child, because the angoros would have killed me also! I had no choice but to flee." He was fuming. "Perhaps if I had been just a little wiser I would have stayed. I may not have killed any of those bastards for what they did, but if I'd let them kill me..." Damianos spluttered for a moment and slid a brief look at Jody.

"Then maybe I would have been spared the torment of coping with the memories of that day, suffering that loss every single minute I exist.

"Calling it a never-ending nightmare would be appallingly wrong. There is no torture worse than this, to sleep each night and rise each day remembering how the love you once relied on so heavily, that you trusted would be there forever and ever, was taken in a few bloodthirsty minutes by people you supposed were friends!

"I live the loss, and *it* is my Hell."

Ligeia had heard this sob story more than once in her time and its effect had long ago waned. Jody however, seemed to be more responsive and there was a queer look passed between her and Dammie that Ligeia simply couldn't stand.

"And now karma has wrapped its inescapable arms around you, you louse," Ligeia jibed. "And what have you learned? You could have saved me out there, in the woods. If not for me, that book would be long gone by now. Yet, when the opportunity came to stand tall and fight for me—your lover only a short time ago—what did you do?" She dovetailed her seething remarks with melodic growls. "You picked up your precious book and took off!"

"I thought you had everything under control."

"You told me to have fun with my new toy!"

"Well..., did you?"

She pushed him, though he didn't move much. "You know what happens to us! You know how spent we get after we make love! He could have killed me!"

"But he didn't." Damianos sounded reassured, but Ligeia sensed he was hiding something. "Which means that, if you haven't managed to make him your slave, you must have killed him," he said with searching eyes.

It was her turn to act aloof.

"You did kill him, my love?" Damianos prodded, and then must have realized the truth. "You didn't."

"Don't call me 'my love'. I don't know what I am to you anymore."

"He's going to ruin everything!"

"He?" Ligeia drew a sharp breath. "*He's* going to ruin everything? What about you?" She dug her finger directly into his collarbone. "You're the reason that the half-breed keeps coming back. You're the reason we even found him. You're the reason we came to this lousy, cold, miserable part of the world in the first place! It's all you, Dammie. Everything that has happened is because of you!"

Damianos seemed to roll something over in his mind, then turned to the little half-naked wench on the ground. "He keeps coming back." He sounded worried. "You're right about that."

"What?" she complained. "What about the rest? Do you have any idea how pig-headed you are?"

Damianos plucked Jody from the ground. "He'll bring reinforcements," he uttered apprehensively. "They'll find us."

"Then let's leave!" Ligeia beseeched him. "Let's just pack up what we can and get ourselves far away from this depressing corner of the world and never look back."

Damianos snapped at her. "Our lives together are done, Lie! Isn't it obvious? I do not love you! If you are so determined to leave, then leave. If nothing else, it will put an end to your incessant howling and fussing so I can think with a clearer mind. Although I'm sure you're not done with that half-breed jivita quite yet, are you? Go and see if you can make *him* happy, my merry little whore. Go! You cannot flap those wings fast enough! Now, excuse me, I must open the book."

The sting of his words was like nothing she'd ever felt before. This kind of hurt was so foreign she hadn't a clue how to react.

Then, to her utter bedevilment, Jody started twisting and bucking again. That loser girl had more grit than Ligeia would ever have believed possible. As sour as she was, she found some pleasure watching Damianos fumble and grope Jody like a lanky teenager. He was obviously still rundown from the sex too.

Serves him right. Sex always seemed to take more out of him than her. *Dumb males.*

That realization sparked a wild thought in Ligeia's head. Damianos was probably weaker in that moment than she was. With her fingers twitching and lips trembling, Ligeia watched Jody, knowing that another opportunity like this might never come.

Chapter 63

Surrender

Damianos's efforts to move her felt much more anaemic than Jody had expected. Either that or she was stronger than she realized.

That clout however was shaky at best. If only Damianos would put this much work into killing her, putting her out of her misery, then she would likely sit back and oblige. But, faced with unreasoned stunts from headstrong, domineering types, Jody's stubbornness never yielded. She'd resist to the end.

Jody snuck a look at the dragon lock, lying in wait with those frightening eyes. The voices flew around her, calling and carrying on about some missing light and the way home. Whatever that all meant, it was clear now that this book had something to do with it and that she too somehow—however unbelievable—had a growing part to play in this whole crazy thing.

"Open your hand!"

Damianos, seemingly at his wit's end, punched Jody in the side of her head. The blow knocked her so hard and unexpectedly that she thought her brain had shot out the other side and hit the ground. Her limbs buckled and Damianos lost hold of her. The world had gotten fuzzy very fast.

Then something struck her again, this time at her back, and her eyes shot open. She screeched from the hurt that felt like a balloon of warmth had burst inside her. She gasped for air, as if the cold waves of death were pouring in.

"Lie!" she heard Damianos holler before he shifted to where Jody's sights could not follow.

Damianos kept shouting, "Get off! Get off!"

While Jody accepted the burning agony and fate to follow, the voices in the night howled, "No! The way must come! Save us! Save us!"

For Jody, the misery was almost over, forever.

Her ability to perceive the goings on around her was drifting into a pit of dimming twilight. The pain was numbing and the cries were thinning. She was hazily aware that Damianos was fighting with Ligeia, but Jody didn't care anymore.

Her prayers were being answered at last. She hoped.

Chapter 64

Fate

Terrified of what Ligeia could be doing to Jody at that very moment, Gregg tried his hardest to fix himself up and think clearly, to find a plan to save her. No matter the ideas he came up with, they were riddled with more holes than a sieve. He was ready to stomp his feet in frustration when his great-grandma removed the last of the cloth and unsheathed an awesome looking sword, its long gleaming blade flashing in a streak of moonlight.

"Whoa! Where'd you find that?"

"In the cellar, this morning." She sounded bothered. Tossing the cloth away, she showed him the weapon from hilt to tip.

Gregg stared with a frantic sense of awe. Its guard was lavish, seemingly made of pewter, or some such thing, and was teed with the busts of two snarly dragons. The exciting curves of a womanly angel silhouetted the grip, her bare beauty pleasingly affirmed by the placement of her hands: the left flat against her pelvis, the right flat beneath her ribs. Her striking wings extended outward, supporting the dragons' necks.

"What's it for?"

Grammy handed him the weapon and he anxiously accepted it.

The hilt's finish was amazingly smooth and though the sword's size and weight were considerable, Gregg thought he wielded it rather competently. While it was no cannon or howitzer, it was a big step up from sticks and stones.

"It belonged to Jody's father. He called it Deleo." She let out a deep, exhaustive breath. "Thank God David finally found you. I was supposed to give this to you earlier, but I kept hesitating. There's no denying anything anymore."

Gregg stood up carefully, not detecting any dizziness in his step, and he held the sword as he imagined a warrior should. Sadly, he had to admit his form was awkward, which did little to improve his sense of courage. Maybe with a little more practice.

He swung the blade this way and that, imagining Damianos and Ligeia getting hacked to bits. But all that make-belief had to end, because reality wasn't going to wait long in the forest hollow.

"One or two strange occurrences coming together as if purely by chance is believable." His Grammy sounded distraught. "But to have a day like this and even attempt to call it fluke is outrageous! It has to be by design, but whose?" She paused, as if struck by something. "The stranger at the door...?"

"Who?"

Grammy brushed him off, grumbling, "There's no time for that now. I had never seen that man before in my life, or since. How could he have known? Still, what if...?" she wondered aloud. "What if this has all happened before?"

"What are you talking about?"

"What if this is all meant to rouse something?"

Gregg gave his Grammy a queer look. He hadn't thought about it before, nor did he plan to ponder things further anytime soon. Ligeia was going to kill Jody and he had to stop her. That's all that mattered now.

He went to his great-grandma and, drawing a sharp breath, hugged her, feeling strangely like a sentimental child. "Thanks," he said. "Fate or freewill, I have to go."

"Yes, then go you must," she encouraged.

He took a few steps, trying to get his bearings and build up his timid sense of heroism. "I don't know the way," he had to admit.

"If it be freewill, then I'm afraid there's not much hope in this blasted darkness," his Grammy said. "But if it be fate, then you cannot miss. Go! Trust yourself!"

Gregg scowled then peered into the creepy forest ahead of him, shrouded in impenetrable gloom, and though he tried, he couldn't see anything that would give him a clue which way to run. "I don't have time for this!"

He finally put one foot in front of the other, sword gripped tightly in his hands, and he barked loudly, "Let it be fate!"

Chapter 65

Compel

Jody supposed intuitively that she was letting go. Somewhere around her she heard commotion still drumming on, but inside she noticed how heavy her body had become. With her eyes shut, she started slipping closer to the edge of some great, dark precipice and imagined leaving her ruined body behind in search of peace, wonderful peace.

At that moment however, something stopped her. An otherworldly voice rocked her. Louder, stronger, heavier than anything she had heard before. This voice rolled like thunder charging over high mountains and across low valleys. and it captured Jo's passing breath and pulled her back from the brink.

HEAR ME

Ironically, the first thing Jody noticed was the absolute silence that followed. It was not from some induced deafness from the booming cry, for Jo managed to detect the tiny rustling of the tent's walls shifting in the night's gentle breeze. As her tired eyes slowly opened and focused, she realized both Damianos and Ligeia were standing above her, looking utterly stunned.

"What was that?" Ligeia whispered harshly.

Apparently Damianos hadn't an answer.

All the outside sounds, too, seemed to be silenced. Frogs and crickets and things had shut-up entirely. It was as if everything in creation was suddenly and completely listening.

And then the voice drummed...

SEE ME

A great blinding flash of thrilling blue light blinded Jody and she pinched her eyes tightly shut while Damianos and Ligeia screeched together in a shared fright. When Jody could see again, she wished she knew better what was real and what was dream.

The darkness around her looked to be at war with dancing, stirring shapes that shone and turned and twisted everywhere above the ground. And with these bounding, illuminated figures came a torrent of cries and screams.

While Damianos and Ligeia ducked for cover, Jody suddenly understood. She was seeing the ghostly frames of the voices that had been filling her ears since she was brought into this horrible place.

They hovered and fluttered this way and that, calling and howling, "The root! The root is near!" Their bright shredded silhouettes kept hounding her, willing Jody to get up. "The way! The way must be opened!"

Behind her, Ligeia chimed angrily, "What's happening?"

"Spirits!" Damianos answered. "They must be!"

"Then go, you damned things!" Ligeia demanded. "Leave me and this place in peace and never come back!"

But the ghosts remained. In fact the glow of them was growing, illuminating an eerie blue haze outside the tent and pressing back the night's shade. The advancing throng huddled tighter together and their washed out, tormented faces challenged Jody to rise. But she only looked back at them, hunched over still, her body a beaten heap ready to die and join them in their swelling cloud of lost souls.

Then the grand voice rose again, exploding across the heavens and aiming her attention squarely upon the damned book lying before her, as if it had been waiting all her life to be noticed.

FIND ME

Then all Hell broke loose.

Chapter 66

Clouds

Dave bumbled his way through the dark maze of trees and their fallen pieces, flashing his light in an effort to find his way back to Grammy's field and as far away as possible from the damned Whispering Woods. That bizarre voice that had rocketed overhead left Dave feeling as if he had just been punched in the gut and the world around him had changed in an instant.

His skin crawled as an unnatural wind gusted through the trees and an eerie presence seemed to flash here and there. Dave did his best to discredit it all. He forbade all sense of fear from taking hold and refused even to consider who could have possibly amplified their voice so loudly over the treetops.

He grumbled to distract himself and tried to figure out why everything had to go to pot today. *Dammit!*

Sure, he could cringe and whimper, but that would go against his nature. It was easier to be angry than scared. And of course, he could be more empathetic with regards to Jody if he really wanted to. But it was easier to blame her because, if she hadn't gone missing today, then Dave would likely be at the park right now meeting the diabolically hot Leah Nasstics.

That girl, Dave realized, had managed to squeeze her way into his thoughts and stay there despite everything else, putting more of a spotlight on her than on Jo, or Jo's mother, or Gregg and Grammy and that damned haunted forest, for that matter.

Nothing else really seemed to be getting his attention and he wasn't sure if it bothered him or not. He just wanted to see Leah again, soon. And all this ridiculous hubbub about everyone else was getting in the way.

He managed to spot a clearing up ahead and he heard Laura holler at the Mounties to get their butts back into the forest to save her son. As the meadow emerged fully into view from behind a group of small trees, Dave noticed the police dog still cowering and whining behind its trainer while Laura and his dad tried to get the others to follow them with a backboard or something.

The police were clearly hesitating, pointing to something in the sky over the woods. Dave ambled toward them. He heard the police helicopter's unique high-pitched whine, but it was far off. He followed the gestures and stares directed above him and he couldn't believe what he saw.

Long, scattered wisps of white-blue cloud flowed like ribbons in the wind and collected overhead in a surging mass of haze that shone in the glow of the full moon and twinkling stars.

Dave moved faster to be with the others as the blasts of air got stronger. Laura was still arguing, "You have to help! My son is still in there!"

One of the Mounties kept barking on the radio about the strange change in the weather while another cop fended off Laura's advances.

"We're doing what we can, ma'am," he said rather meekly. "Air One has arrived and will see exactly where your son is and direct help his way in the shortest time possible. But the wind... You're just going to have to trust us."

Laura and his dad didn't look too reassured and Dave turned his attention back to the Whispering Woods and the massing strands of cloud above. They converged near the moon, coming together in a mysterious way that made an obvious and totally shocking image of a tree, its limbs stretching into the night.

Dave feebly pointed as he glanced at his dad and stepmom. They saw it too, and it didn't look like they had blinked in a long time.

"What is it?" Dave asked.

His dad groaned. "I don't think those are clouds."

Chapter 67

Returned

The dark forest flashed brightly from the strange, shredded clouds blowing around trees and twigs. Gregg gawked when he saw the windswept, suffering faces at the leading edge of those narrow blasts.

His heart nearly stopped as fast as his feet when some of those tattered wisps confronted him, staring him down with hollowed, empty eyes as they gestured restlessly at the sword he held.

"Who is this?"

"Help him!"

"He's not ready! And she hasn't hope in her bosom! Not yet!"

One of them jumped at him. "There is no time. You must come! Hurry!"

The strange things surrounded him like drafts of cold air, pushing him, urging him on.

"Heedful, you must be. Conscious of you and us... for we are the same, one and all. Hold on to wakeful thoughts when you sleep and beware of deathly ones when you wake!"

The assembly became larger and their light ever brighter until the seething mass of them swarmed high above the forest hollow where Gregg was ultimately led. At last, he was back. And although he had no mysterious powers to overcome Jo's captors, he did have her father's sword, Deleo.

Excited, he slid down a fern-laden ridge to the wall of Jody's tent and cautiously eyed the shadows inside. He saw Ligeia's wings and knew then the dark figure standing next to her must be Damianos.

Gregg gripped his sword tightly, filling his veins with fury and conviction. He pointed Deleo's blade at the tent's enclosure, hanging onto the hope that the beast in black would step a little closer. *Just a step more.*

"Come on." Gregg steadied himself. This time he was going to do it. This time he was ready. "Come here, you black-robed son-of-a...!"

Chapter 68

Stabbed

Ligeia knew she smelled him again. But the earth beneath her feet was jumping, the light was disturbingly bright and there were ghosts flying all over the bloody place. So when she saw Damianos cringe and tighten his stance to one side, she knew the jivita was to blame.

Damianos's hands clutched his waist and she noticed blood filtering over his fingers as he dipped to his knees. In the background was a sword's long smudged blade held wobbly through the tent's fabric.

Ligeia hissed, "Half-breeds!"

The bloodied weapon pulled away and a moment later Gregg barrelled through the entrance.

"Gregg!" Jo squealed. "You came back!"

Ligeia huffed and faced him. They stood opposite one another, Gregg with his sword and she with her semi-fanned wings and snarly teeth. He didn't seem willing to attempt the first strike.

"You remember what I told you?" Ligeia teased, flashing an eye on the girl. "With her out of the way, you'll have no choice but to be mine!" She made the first attack, breaking toward Jody.

"No!" Gregg shouted, and the fight began.

They kicked and swiped at each other, but there was little room in the tent for manoeuvring. Ligeia couldn't overwhelm him with her wings. Frustrated, she leapt at him and they both landed in the dirt somewhere on the other side of the tent's flaps.

That was when her skin crawled, seeing and hearing those awful apparitions fly all over the place, blowing her hair and harassing her ears.

"The way! The way!" they shrieked.

Ligeia had an awful feeling this night was not going to end well for her.

Chapter 69

Revealed

All the illuminated ghosts swooped and called in a great flurry, careening this way and that, giving birth to a brilliant performance of dancing light under the forest's dark canopy. Gregg heard them in Jody's tent, "Open the way! You must do it. Open it, open it!"

He shifted and managed to peer past Ligeia into the shelter. *The Book of the Nornir*'s lock was shining brightly in Jody's face and she was stretching her hand toward it. Except this time, the dragon's eyes gleamed blue.

"No!" Gregg bellowed as Ligeia attacked him again.

Gregg caught his breath and was fighting her off when something blasted from the side of a high ridge in the hollow. They stopped and gaped together at a large hole that had blown wide open, black and sunken.

Seeing Ligeia confounded, Gregg quickly tried to wrestle her to the ground and pin her there. Instead, she wiggled away and he threw himself to the left, just avoiding another of her angry swipes. He responded with a great swing of Deleo's heavy blade, its sheen spoiled in places by Damianos's red blood.

Damn! That thorny witch is fast!

It was a series of motions that repeated over and over—dodge, swing, dodge, thrust, dodge—until at last Ligeia's wing clipped Gregg enough to knock him off stride and she kicked him hard in his upper abdomen. Gregg nearly dropped Deleo, and perhaps a lung, and slipped over a fern. He recovered just enough to hold Ligeia off with the sword's sharp edge, as the whirling ghosts shot about brightly, singing in wild anticipation.

Another thunderous rumbling was building under the ground. Gregg shifted and speed-crawled along the dirt to the tent flaps through which he saw Jody's horrified expression as she tried to free herself from the grips of that damned book.

The wind grew violent, howling and whistling through the tall trees, and the earth's tremors became increasingly ominous. Ligeia seemed even more bothered by these sudden changes than he was, hissing and snarling distractedly over her shoulders.

Then the ghosts cried, "She's done it! She's done it!"

A great soundless boom blasted its way through Gregg's body and beyond like a mysterious, ethereal wave that felt like it was going to tear his insides apart. Ligeia must have felt it too. She clutched her belly as if she had only just gotten off a rollercoaster.

An intense beam of blue light shot across the hollow, emanating from the hole's deep, black throat, and a sudden gale of salty air blew over them. The brightness stayed strong, stretching rigidly from the opening, beating steadily as if it had some living pulse. Arcing fingers exploded outward, reaching and stretching for things, pulling them in. Then, as if retaking what it had given, that blast of wind changed direction and a ceaseless implosion began.

Gregg picked himself up and felt the hole's gravity for the first time. It was like he was standing on a steep rooftop with the wind at his back.

The hysterical ghosts cried and plunged themselves into that light, vanishing into its hidden depths. A continuous tide of white and blue shredded spirits streamed into that mysterious tunnel as if sucked in by a jacked shop-vac.

Gregg stared at it, wondering how, or if, it was even possible to plug that thing before he and everything else was inhaled into the abyss.

Gregg glanced behind him to see Ligeia leaning back, tucking in her large wings, and staring nervously at the shaft of light. "What is it? What's happening?"

Gregg considered helping her, somehow feeling compassion and a compulsion to act on it, even though he suspected her damned spell was the cause. Before he had a chance to, though, she launched herself and grasped onto his leg.

"If that thing takes me, you're coming too!"

Chapter 70

Bedlam

Gregg and Ligeia twisted and wrestled amongst the rushing clouds of spirits, freeing themselves from the worst of the hole's great pull. Ligeia also managed to avoid Gregg's admittedly feeble attacks. He was getting tired swinging the heavy sword at nothing but air, and he wasn't at all sure if his lack of success was because Ligeia was too fast, or if he was intentionally missing her.

On top of everything, both he and the winged witch had to jump and dodge those shooting lightning bolts that threatened to clamp onto them and force them into that perplexing abyss.

"Go ahead!" Ligeia teased just before knocking him down for the umpteenth time. "You can't kill me, remember?" She fanned her wings, jumped high and kicked him.

He fell, his noggin feeling like a rung church bell, and he barely realized the sword's grip was no longer in his hands.

Ligeia came at him. "I am so fed up with covering that lilita's ass. I should thank you for killing him. But turnabout is fair play. You kill my lover, I get to kill yours."

As if on cue, a hunched figure in black teetered out of the tent. Gregg watched astounded as Damianos, bloodied and weak, slowly staggered into the bedlam, looking strangely dejected and confused.

"I've got news for you sweetheart," Gregg announced. "Your boyfriend ain't dead yet!"

Ligeia snuck a disbelieving glance over her shoulder and growled, "It can't be!"

She seemed thoughtful for a second or two, and then put on a face of catty resolve. She wet her lips, steadied herself in the wind and began to sing.

"Tribuo mihi vestri pectus pectoris." Her melodic voice wormed its way into Gregg's mind , blurring his thoughts.

She knocked him onto his back, straddled his legs, and slyly moved the sword out of his reach. He made no move to resist, his will to fight dissolving into the magical currents that blew past them. And he welcomed it eagerly when she took his hands and placed them on her naked skin.

Ligeia eyed his tingling groin with a devious grin.

Chapter 71

Security

She knew she had him. Her spell had sent Gregg into a stupor like a drunk at an open bar. This time she would finish the charm before Damianos could get in the way and, should Gregg's unstable human side seem subdued enough, she'd give him his jivita strengths back to properly kill Dammie for good.

She started undoing Gregg's pants, without any resistance on his part. In fact, his hands were busy stroking her legs while she worked and sang. Everything was going beautifully until Damianos came staggering toward her with one hand still clutching his wound.

"The book is empty!" he cried, sounding ruined. Ligeia wished he was already dead. Things would be a lot easier. "The pages have no writing!"

That got Ligeia's interest. She shifted to face him. "No writing, you say?"

Damianos switched his gaze from her to Gregg, a puzzled expression flitting across his face. "What are you doing?"

"Never mind that! Your mysterious book has nothing written inside it! God, Dammie! You mean that we've come all this way, spent all this time for a book that doesn't tell us anything?"

"Why, Lie, are you sitting that way on top of that... that cretin? You're trying to make love to him! You're still trying to control the jivita! It can't be done!"

Something crossed her mind as she watched his lips shake. "Are you jealous?"

"All these years, I succumb to one indiscretion and you fall in love with my would-be killer! Was our search for justice...?"

"Your search!" she was quick to correct. "This has always been your search, not mine. And through it all, I have been faithful. I have been obedient and I have been more than patient. And what have I gotten in return, Dammie?

"Your blasted ridicule! You still see me as a stupid child, remember? I'm cramping your space, impeding your mission in life. You wanted me to leave! I am like your tool chest, full of useful endowments for you to build your damned fantasies, and when you don't need me, I get left in the dark ... alone and cold!"

"I don't have time for this..."

"I don't care! I don't care at all about awful ghosts and stupid afterlives because you know what, Dammie? It doesn't matter! We're not a part of that realm. Leave it be! What you see in front of your eyes"—she took his hand

and placed it onto her breast—"what you feel in your palm, this is what matters, the here and the now. Live your life today and worry about death when it comes. Which might not be far off for you."

Damianos faltered, his eyes appearing to search inward for something to say.

"It will never come for me. What I do with the half-breed will only assure it."

"He is my replacement," Damianos said cautiously.

Ligeia nodded. "I will never be anyone's second best."

Damianos had a mindful gleam in his dark eyes. "Your lust for him will be your undoing."

Chapter 72

Secrets

Gregg wobbled to his feet and slowly noticed Damianos's hunched frame shuffle for Jody's tent.

Get him! He told himself as a rush of anger burned behind his eyes. *How in Hell is that bastard still walking?*

Gregg fumbled with his pants, unable to think why they were undone in the first place. He spotted Deleo and staggered toward it, but that blasted Ligeia got in the way. And then he remembered.

"You crazy bitch! Move!" he shouted disjointedly. He realized he was slobbering. Another damn spell!

"Make me!" Ligeia hit him hard and Gregg fell back, gasping for air. She leaned over him, snarling, "You know, I don't like you shrugging off my songs so easily. Damn you! What's it gonna take to crush that exasperating human side?"

Damianos was entering Jody's tent. In desperation, Gregg did the first thing he could think of and tossed a mitt-full of dirt at Ligeia's eyes. She flailed and shrieked horribly.

Not giving Ligeia a second glance, he rushed to the tent and saw the most extraordinary thing. Damianos had Jody by the ankles and was yanking her hard as she writhed on the ground with her head and right arm fully inside the open pages of that weird book. Water splashed from it into the tent.

Gregg watched in total disbelief until Damianos bellowed, "Don't just stand there!"

Gregg ran to the book and struggled to set Jo free. At long last he and Damianos managed to pull her out. Freezing cold water sloshed across the dirt floor as Damianos's momentum sent him crashing right over the cot.

Without a second thought, Gregg went straight to Jo, his eyes travelling over her to reassure himself that she was all right. Although short of breath and dripping wet, she seemed well enough to hold him in her embrace with visible relief and pleasure.

She shivered. "Gregg, thank God! You won't believe what I've seen!"

As intrigued as Gregg might have been in that moment, the situation didn't allow for chatter.

"If there be a God, then please, cut this life out from me," Damianos grumbled, pulling himself upright. He looked like death was standing beside him. His face, so immaculate up to this point, had grown pale and fragile. He was leaning to the side Gregg had pierced, and his usually sturdy voice was breaking with the sound of growing despair.

His sights aligned on the book, its peculiar pages still opened as it rested in the muck, and a gleam of excitement came shining back. Gregg followed his gaze, taking notice of the water's rippling surface skimming right to the page edges, no longer spilling all over the place.

"This is impossible," he told himself, but by now Gregg knew better.

Damianos staggered toward it and suddenly a long, well-built arm reached up from the water, its hand open. Damianos stopped, looking as surprised as Gregg felt.

Gregg gasped and jumped to get Jody out of the tent in a hurry. "Holy Jeez! We gotta go, now!"

"Wait!" Jody held him back. She glanced at Damianos with a peculiar expression and Gregg noticed how fresh she looked. Her face was flushed with colour, her skin looked lively and almost glowing, and the gashes on her bare back had closed, though their unsightliness remained. It was an unexpected miracle that Gregg simply couldn't explain. But the answer, he suspected, must have come from the book.

Gregg watched as Damianos, appearing nervously inspired, stared at the reaching hand, comparing the mysterious appendage with his own. Finally, he clasped it.

The reaching hand grabbed tight and pulled Damianos hard. Damianos lurched forward with a startled cry and a few moments later his head was fully immersed in the book's folds.

Gregg looked on, incredulous. "Should I help him?" he wondered, but Jody held him back.

She was hesitant, then let out a deep breath. "For him or us... it's too late."

Chapter 73

Unfinished

It was unsettling to watch a man seemingly fight for his life, stuck drowning inside an open book. What made things worse was seeing Damianos suddenly stop.

Death. He imagined the feeling of his adversary's lungs finally opening up, burning for air, only to let the cold water flood in. What a bizarre way to die. He couldn't help but feel a stab of compassion because of it, even though he'd tried his darnedest to kill the bastard earlier, for the second time that day.

"C'mon." Jody tugged at his arm, grimacing. It seemed the pain still had a hold of her.

Gregg held her tightly against him as they hurried toward the exit.

"We need to get out of here," she said with obvious strain. "Before..."

The tent flaps tore away in front of them and Ligeia came barging in, her face speckled with bits of dirt. She wiped at her reddened eyes.

"I like it rough, half-breed, but not dirty. That's a game-changer."

Ligeia dove for Jody, tearing her clean away from Gregg and into the forest hollow. As Gregg rushed after them, she raised her hand, claws outstretched, and bent Jody's head to the side, exposing her neck.

Spotting Deleo on the ground, Gregg scooped it up and charged. His swipe sent Ligeia diving out of the way and split the two apart.

"Men!!" Ligeia screeched.

Gregg turned to Jody to see if she was alright. In that moment of distraction, Ligeia cleverly snatched the sword from his hands and swung it about as if she'd done it a million times before.

In the blink of an eye, she was in front of him using the flat edge of the blade like a clasp at the back of Gregg's neck with her hands holding tightly onto the weapon's grip and its central ridge, near the blade's point. He moved only a hair and Ligeia guided the sharp edge up to dig and cut into his flesh.

He was at her mercy and froze.

Ligeia steadied her stance and thrust his face into her chest, pinning him there so he could not breathe.

"Don't struggle," she said softly. "Or I will have no choice but to cut off your head."

Gregg held his breath, but time was running out.

"I don't want to do this, but I will. I've been having a very bad day. You see, everything will become much clearer in just another moment, when I bless our new love with your ex-girlfriend's dead carcass. But first, you need to go to sleep."

Gregg's lungs were burning. What air was in them slowly ejected, blowing in short, painful bursts against Ligeia's hot, mucky skin.

"Syrēnes don't like being alone, you understand. I've never been alone. Companionship is essential. I long to touch another and to be touched—sensually, fiercely… lustfully. Oh, I want it all!"

Gregg couldn't help it, he had to struggle; he had to push against the sword, to breathe.

"Two hundred years ago I chose Damianos. But I've gotten more condescension than orgasms for too long." She sighed, her chest still pressing painfully into Gregg's face. "But my efforts have at last reaped a fine reward, for today I will feast on fresh angoros and then…"

Gregg's lungs were squeezing out their last breaths as she finished, "I will win you."

Chapter 74

Tangled

As Gregg, slowly suffocated between her breasts, Ligeia became increasingly and pleasantly aware of how stimulating she was finding it. In an admittedly lecherous sort of way, the longer she did it and more frantic he became, the hungrier her womb turned inside her. He would soon die though, and she wasn't at all sure if that was a good thing at the moment.

"Let go of him!"

Ligeia glanced around, her reverie cut short, as that little half-naked Barbie doll with the perky tits grasped and scratched her from behind.

"Let go! Let go!" Jody shrieked.

Ligeia couldn't believe how enduring this cat was. She loosened the sword slightly from the back of Gregg's neck and he gasped and choked, spraying spit onto her glorious skin.

In spite of her recent passion with Damianos, Ligeia's hormone-fuelled imagination was going crazy. Sexual urges pulsed through her, overpowering every other thought in her brain, even with Jody slapping and pulling her hair. The whole scene, being caught in the centre of this wild commotion in the forest hollow with the lights and wind, ensnared in a fleshly conflict between inter-racial lovers, was pushing her close to the brink of ecstasy.

She hardly put up a fight.

Ligeia wet her lips and took a deep breath while forcefully guiding Gregg's face down the length of her torso before letting the sword fall to the ground and snatching the back of his head with her eager hands.

She made sure to keep him close, praying that he would get the right idea.

Chapter 75

Turnabout

The second Ligeia felt Gregg's tongue shyly stroking her, her legs wanted to melt beneath her and she struggled to stay on her feet.

She was blissfully pleased when he, in turn, grasped her shuddering thighs.

Despite the ecstasy however, she glanced around and noticed that Jody was gone.

Only vaguely did she heed the escalating pulse of the bright blue light and the accelerating closeness of its branching lightning strikes.

It was when one such strike slapped the ground nearby that Ligeia spotted Jody's silhouette flash before her with a hateful scowl spread across her face.

Something about it sent a tremor rippling up the back of Ligeia's neck, painting a sobering picture of fear in her mind.

Jody was holding the sword.

Chapter 76

Turmoil

Gregg's heart beat madly in his chest. It was as if his skin was on fire and his groin was... awesome. On some level he was aware of Ligeia's subversive influence, but it didn't really matter just then. All that did was how amazing it felt to actually be doing what he was doing, to a real woman.

His many dreams of this moment paled in the face of reality. The sweet taste of her moistened flesh, the way she shuddered with pleasure when he did the right thing and the feel of her phenomenal ass in his hands was sending him on a high no fantasy could project. He wanted to keep going. Forever, if possible.

But something cut into his carnal indulgence, making the hairs on his skin rise and body shiver. The blue light from the hole in the ground was surging brighter and brighter, its electric fingers reaching out and grabbing all sorts of things with greater obsession, dragging them away and out of sight.

His passion swiftly drooping, Gregg nervously peered around Ligeia's sinuous hips. The strikes were hitting everywhere, wildly, and they were getting closer. Gregg instinctively shrank back between the siren's legs.

Ligeia's frame stiffened in his hands and Gregg looked up to see her wings flare wide. She pushed back mightily just as Deleo's shiny blade made a clean swipe at her, its tip cutting her skin across her chest. The sword kept going, hurling to the ground several feet away.

Gregg heard Jody curse behind him, "Oh, damn it!" She was curling her lips at her open hands. "That thing is heavy!"

Ligeia had fallen to the ground, crying. Blood seeped from her wound over her breasts. "You she-devil! Look what you've done to me!"

A blinding flash hit Deleo where it lay and Gregg watched helplessly as a lightning strike took hold of it and dragged it toward the hole's gaping mouth. His heart nearly leapt clean up his throat and past his lips.

"Stop!"

He rushed to his feet and chased after it, daunted by the electric finger's potential to shock the hell out of him. "No, no, no, no!" He kept picking up small rocks and throwing them, not knowing what else to do. "Give it back!"

He chanced a quick look down the hole's throat, as much as was possible from his vantage point. Swells of spirits flowed in like smoke caught in a whirling vacuum. Now whatever lay hidden in the bottom of that cave was threatening to take away the sword, and as far as Gregg could tell, Ligeia was still a problem that needed solving.

"C'mon, c'mon...!" He hopped and jumped, looking for something he could use to get that blasted lightning bolt to let go. He raced up the embankment above the mysterious opening and picked up a heavy tree branch that was taller than he was.

Hurrying back, he slammed it down on the electric finger, breaking its connection with Deleo. He stood there looking at it, feeling quite pleased with himself until the hole charged ahead with even more lightning strikes.

Gregg darted carefully amongst them. Taking Deleo's hot grip into his hands, with many girlish whimpers, he hightailed it to a safer distance. He switched the hot grip from hand to hand. "Ouch, ooh, ouch!"

He ran to Jody, who stood watching him with relief, and stuck the blade into the ground before giving her a hug.

Confusing flashes jetted out around them and they tumbled and fell, trying to avoid being caught. Ligeia too, was having trouble, leaping here and there, shrieking and swearing as she did.

A particularly dazzling strike hit Jody's tent and ripped it apart. It moved and wound its way, reaching for something inside. To Gregg's bewildered gaze, it pulled a limp Damianos from the tattered canvas and dragged his wasted body across the ground toward the hole.

"Look!" Jody shouted. "He's still holding the book!"

Gregg peered. There, caught in the dead man's flopping arms was *The Book of the Nornir* and perplexingly, Jody's pendant seemed to be imbedded in its cover.

Gregg looked at Jody's chest to confirm. "Your necklace!"

Jody reached for where it should have been, nestled high between her bare breasts, and a look of full-blown dread plunged her eyes into their sockets. "Oh my God! It's still in the book! I used it to make the pages show me the water," she added. "That's how you find its secrets."

Gregg thought quickly. The sword was still hot from its encounter with the arcing light, whereas the wood branch seemed unaffected. He pointed to the sword. "Take care of this!"

He ran for the same branch he'd used before, colliding with Ligeia on his way. Undaunted by the bloodied vixen's threatening stance, he dodged past her.

Just as Gregg grabbed the branch, another electric finger shot out of the hole and smacked into him. He flew back, jolted and unable to see, hearing Jody's screams behind him.

Amazingly, the lightning bolt had not grabbed hold of him. Instead, as his eyes recovered from the brightness, he saw it drag the branch away.

"Gregg!" Jody cried, diving for cover. "Hurry up! He's almost gone."

Gregg located Damianos's slipping body, wrapped in charged white light. He got up to chase it down.

Damianos's face was dragging along the ground and his arms trailed behind with the book caught between them. He looked dead, with blood galore around his torn black coat where Deleo had cut him. He was wet, from head to toe, and the arcing fingers were leaving searing burn marks where they gripped his legs.

There seemed to be no way to save him this time, not that it bothered Gregg much. But grabbing the book was going to hurt like crazy, he knew, if he didn't get caught in the lightning bolt's hold and pulled off to God-knows-where.

"Gregg!" Jo shrieked.

"I know, I know!" He had to find a way to get that book. The hole's gravity was getting stronger the closer he got, and Damianos's body was sliding faster.

"No, help *me*!" she shouted again.

Gregg turned around and gasped. Ligeia towered above her as Jo held the sword falteringly in her hands. She could barely keep the pointed end up.

"Shit!" Gregg choked. He spun and threw himself like a shot at the book and immediately felt as if he had just stuck his fingers into a wall socket. Somehow, he grasped the old tome and tried to pull himself free when he noticed Damianos's head suddenly move.

The man in black looked up and Gregg gaped at his horribly tattered face, mauled by the rough ride along the earth. Any semblance of the beautiful features that were once there had been peeled away, leaving something horrific.

Damianos grabbed Gregg's hand with a fierce intensity. "The dragon will never stop, and neither will I!" He freed Gregg, his marred face lighting with an oddly disturbing smile.

Gregg watched, holding the book and shaking uncontrollably as Damianos was pulled into the shining light and disappeared. Damned if that mysterious brute didn't wink at him at the last moment.

The lights beat faster and with greater intensity still.

Gregg heard Jody's screams behind him, setting his sore legs on fire. Despite his condition, he quickly went to her, devoted to the end. Only, his efforts brought him no closer. Instead, he was slipping farther away.

Oh no! He watched his feet lose traction and skid over the ground and he realized he was moving backwards. He was caught in the hole's pull, and as every second went by, his hope of escape dwindled.

He slipped to his belly and grabbed at dirt and rooted plants, all the while clinging to the book. His heart was tearing a hole through his chest and his lungs wouldn't stop jumping up his throat. He glanced over his shoulder as his every attempt to stop ebbing away kept failing.

The hungry light grew brighter, engulfing him in its punishment.

Chapter 77

Diversion

Jody lay sprawled, defenceless, waiting for Ligeia to finish her. The evil witch had the sword and there was little doubt about her intent to use it. The fervour burning in her eyes, the blood trickling over her chest and down onto Jody's skin, the triumphant hum in Ligeia's voice, "At last!"

This was it.

Jody took in Ligeia's stiffening hold of the weapon's grip and shut her eyes, awaiting the inevitable.

The jolt that came though, was not from the piercing of her skin, but by the sharp cry of an old woman's voice.

It rang out as song, high and loud, and badly out of pitch. "Regardez cette façon, de mourir!"

It came as such a surprise that Ligeia froze as well, her arms still raised menacingly with the sword only inches from Jody's chest. Jody's heart pounded as the winged vixen fiercely scanned her surroundings.

"Hear my spell, siren! Regardez cette façon, de mourir!"

"Where are you?" Ligeia hissed.

To Jody's total surprise, Gregg's great-grandma lolloped into view at the top of the ridge, awkwardly waving her thick coat.

"Here, you vile enchantress! Regardez cette façon, de mourir!" she sang. It was awful, but it seemed to be having an effect on Ligeia.

Complete confusion on her face, Ligeia stared up at old Iris, her fat lips twitching, and she lowered the sword.

"Another half-breed? Can it be?" A scowl appeared across her brow. With a defiant huff, she pulled her eyes away, giving first Jody a creepy once over, then looking herself up and down.

Taking a brief pause, perhaps to be totally sure, Ligeia appeared convinced. "You're no syrène! What kind of spell was that?"

"A rather impulsive one," Iris admitted. "It's called a diversion."

Understanding dawned on Jody as Ligeia threw the old woman a disapproving frown. She knew what she had to do, and before she could talk herself out of it, she braced herself in the dirt and swiftly kicked Ligeia square between her legs, bellowing, "I am not weak!"

Ligeia's entire body tightened and her normally melodic voice squawked some horribly shrill note. Her eyes almost shot out of her head, but still they were fixed on Jo.

The witch pulled the sword back, wrath gleaming in her eyes, when a blast of lightning struck and wrapped itself around her torso. A swirl of blue light swallowed her up and the sword's blade flashed as Ligeia drove it down at Jody where she lay.

Chapter 78

Loss

The fierce wind swirled around Gregg, deafening him and limiting his vision to mere slits of light. Even so, he scanned frantically for anything that would help him avoid the death-trap that was pulling him in.

There! Jammed under the root of an old tree trunk at the base of the ridge a few feet away, was the branch he had used earlier. He fought his way to it as wailing ghosts flew by.

Dirt and debris blasted his skin, threatening to weaken his resolve. Something hard flew into him and banged his hand. His precarious hold of the book faltered. There was no way, he realized dismally, that he could make it to safety using only one good hand. Whether it remained in his grip or not, the book was going to be lost. He knew it. He had to let it go.

Loosening his hurting, reluctant hand was hard. That crazy book was magical. Who knew what secrets it still held? Maybe there were much needed answers about why mythical creatures really existed, why Jody's back was the way it was and what the hell was a jivita?

It was no use now. He had to save himself.

Gregg let it go and scraped and clawed across the earth to get free of the hole's light. He secured himself on the branch and then watched, bitterly helpless, as *The Book of the Nornir* succumbed to the great pull of the abyss and disappeared into the shining, pulsing blue light.

He wedged his legs between the trunk and a large fern so he could settle his aching arms, but he knew he couldn't do it for long.

"Jody!" he reminded himself. Ligeia was going to kill her. "No!"

He turned his attention farther into the hollow where he'd left Jo with the sword. Light flashed brightly there, wrapped around Ligeia! The lightning was yanking back as Ligeia leaned and lurched with Deleo swaying in her grasp.

Gregg made a mad dash up the ridge and saw Jody on the ground in front of that winged bitch. Gregg watched in horror, still too far away to do anything, as Ligeia pointed the sword's edge toward Jo and drove it down.

"No!"

He tried to focus, barely seeing Ligeia's hands still on Deleo's grip as the lightning kept blazing. "Oh my God. Please, please, please..." he was cracking up, ready to burst into tears. "Damn my fucking eyes!" It was so hard to focus clearly.

He heard a scream. But whose? It sounded too deep to be Jo's.

He scrambled was finally able to make out Ligeia in the midst of the lightning bolt, clinging onto Deleo's hilt. The blade was driven into the ground and she moored onto it to keep from being pulled toward the hole.

Gregg fixed his gaze on the sword. Jody wasn't there. His heart started beating again as he searched and found her hastily crawling away. "Thank you," he breathed to whoever might have been listening. "Oh God, thank you!"

Ligeia's deafening shriek swung his attention back to her. The sword had come free from the ground and now it and the siren were being dragged to the mysterious hole.

Yes! Jo was safe and now Ligeia was about to pay her dues. His feelings changed a second later as he realized she would be taking Deleo with her.

Indecision flooded his mind. *Damn it, I can't lose the sword too!* But throwing himself back into that sucking nightmare, so close to the hole's opening, was suicide.

"Damn it, damn it, damn it!" he swore, evaluating frantically. He yanked the tree branch free and carefully waded back to the light. He struck the lightning bolt and the flashing arm snapped and twitched back, finally dying away and freeing Ligeia.

Gregg jerked Deleo from her hands before she could react and he marvelled at how good it felt to hold the sword again.

But then the hole seemed to implode with rage, sucking everything even more violently.

Gregg was thrust toward it, his feet tripping over Ligeia's smouldering frame. He was so close he could see the arched walls inside it. The floor was cluttered with rocks and bits of trees while the walls were mostly dirt and clay. Farther along everything changed, becoming more fibrous, twisting and winding out of sight like the hollowed centre of a piece of driftwood.

Thinking only of what Ligeia had attempted to do to avoid oblivion earlier, Gregg quickly drove the sword's blade deep into the soft ground beneath him, using it as an anchor. He held on to the hilt for dear life, but there he was destined to stay, for there was no way out. The hole's punishing bite was at his feet, the cave's devouring mouth mere inches away.

Crates and boxes and canvas and poles from Damianos's camp tumbled and flew past Gregg into the abyss, narrowly missing him. With them came Ligeia, screeching and clawing as she slid by.

"I don't want to die!" she screamed, latching on to his legs, digging her claws painfully into his flesh.

His hands slipped and he only barely recovered. Arms and legs on fire, Gregg prayed he could keep holding on and that she would let go.

He looked down, finding it easier to breathe through his nose and avoid being beaten by all the crap flying through the air. Ligeia, he realized, was having a terrible time with her wings getting caught in the gale. They looked awkward. Perhaps she was tired and weak, or maybe her wings were never meant to work like those of a bird in the first place.

He kicked as Ligeia attempted to climb over him, then a torn section of tent canvass whooshed by, straight into her face, and she almost let go.

A great lumbering roar echoed from the hole's depths and more lightning strikes came blasting out. One looped around Ligeia and her face lit up with terror. She screamed and tensed and her hands shot open, letting him go.

The winged siren tumbled out of sight while Gregg strained to avoid a similar fate. But what chance was there for escape?

He thought he heard Ligeia wail from inside the cave and his hold of Deleo slipped. Was there any point in fighting the ceaseless pull?

Damianos and Ligeia were gone, and Jody was going to be okay. Grammy and the Mounties would inevitably come to her rescue and get her out of these *Screaming Woods*, as Gregg now thought of the place.

He felt strangely fulfilled. Perhaps not entirely at peace with the situation, but things being what they were, he supposed everything was going to end all right for Jody. His body shifted, thrown by a twist in the wind, and his hands lost their grip. He felt a burning sting wrap itself around his chest; an electric finger.

Then he heard a cry, loud and urgent, "BESPARRÉ!"

There was a great flash accompanied by a deafening boom... and then everything around him fell deathly silent.

Chapter 79

Relief

Gregg was surrounded by light—warm and inviting—pulling him in. There was a sense of harmony, perfection and well-being within that light and he had a mind to go to it. He would have, if not for that last clinging thread that held him to his memories and desires.

He was aware of the light's purpose, guiding the way home, but what that meant remained a blurred reflection of something he was sure should have been more familiar.

He did not follow.

The light disappeared and he felt heavy, hurt and alone. He lay in the darkness, hearing distant voices as though from deep under water. Time was immeasurable.

Something stirred him, drawing his empty thoughts like a warm hand caressing his heart. Heat beat in him again, though tenuous and with pain. His mind slowly rose to the surface behind his closed eyes and his lungs breathed an infirm breath. He filled his body, sensing a thawing rain melt away the cold from his face.

He sensed a presence next to him, pleasant and toasty, nuzzling closer. His skin became restless, simmering, alive. A hand softly grazed his cheek, wiping at the water that had sprinkled there. It was this gesture that brought him fully to and his eyes flickered open.

He noticed the clear night sky above, stars flickering behind a dappled canopy of trees. The air was fresh and still and the earth was cold at his back. Cuddled beside him was Jody, her body curled up with his. Her incredible eyes were run-over with shimmering tears, her face wrought with grief.

Her tortured gaze drifted over him and stopped, clearly startled. Her confusion was almost as priceless as the indisputable relief that quickly followed.

She trembled, her lips shaking into a smile. It was as if dozens of words were bumping in her throat. She wiped bits of dirt gently from around his nose and lips and finally said simply, thankfully, "Hi."

Gregg blinked.

"You came back." Her happy expression seemed to envelop her.

Although his body ached with every breath, he smiled as brightly as he could. "I told you I would do anything for..."

He broke off, detecting something cold and sharp between them. He glanced down and saw a pocketknife in Jody's other hand.

She let the knife drop out of her grasp, relief written in every line of her moonlit silhouette. She leaned over him, bringing her happy face up close to his, and breathed, "And I told you what I'd do without it."

She kissed his dried lips. Soon, Gregg's eyes closed again and the sweet sound of Jo's soft voice drew him into a restful sleep.

Chapter 80

Renewed

Click "…starting with patches of fog in some low lying areas of the Lower Mainland this morning, but it should clear by lunch time and we'll have sunny skies for the rest of the day with highs of 22 degrees near the water and 27 inland…"

Gregg's arm swung through the air and slapped the top of the clock radio. He lifted his head up from his warm pillow and yawned.

Dave's eyes glared from under his blanket. "What the hell are you doing setting the alarm?"

"I told you I was getting up early. You shouldn't have stayed out so late last night," Gregg answered, quickly leaving his bed and fetching his clothes. "I gotta go."

Dave fumbled with the clock's display with obvious agitation. "Where do you have to go on the first bloody morning of summer holidays? What the…? At 5:30!?!"

"Shh! You'll wake up Mum and Pat. You don't get summer holidays anymore, remember, Mr. Graduate?" Gregg threw an extra pair of briefs at his stepbrother. "Go get a job," he chuckled.

Despite having learned the truth about Laura and his real mother, Samantha, Gregg had decided—with Grammy's restless endorsement—to keep the secret alive. At least at this point in his life, Gregg would rather have the old sex-talk with Laura than try and contend with years of emotional deceit.

Dave carefully inspected the tossed underpants. "Where are you going?"

Gregg couldn't help but smile. "It's a secret. How'd things go with Leah?" He swayed his hips provocatively. Dave and Leah had been practically stuck together like Siamese twins since Mike and Kirk's big shindig in the barn several weeks ago.

Dave flashed a dreamy smile. "Gaw, *awesome*. That woman is everything I've ever fantasized about. And man, she's totally into me. It's great. I feel like I can talk to her about anything, especially when it comes to your flaky-assed life. It doesn't seem to matter how weird the topic, she listens and doesn't freak out. I think I'm in love."

Gregg couldn't remember another time when Dave's smile had been so wide and he was glad his stepbrother had found an outlet for all his pent up anxiety.

"Leah and Mike and Kirk want to go camping in Grammy's field. They want to see ghosts and stuff." Dave didn't look too sure about it. "Watch my life turn into one of those slasher movies. Anyways, they asked if it'd be okay with Grammy and me."

"Yeah, what'd you say?" Like Gregg had to ask.

Dave shrugged, clearly apprehensive, but then he winked coyly and made some obscene movements under his covers. "I haven't asked Grammy yet, but I told Leah it's fine with me, so long as she and I share the same sleeping bag."

Gregg left the horny twit and headed to the bathroom to clean up. He inspected himself in the mirror, even checking his arms and legs.

"Still me." He was relieved. He still couldn't explain why it had taken so long to get his ability to heal back after Ligeia had disappeared into the mystery hole and the entire thing had come crumbling down.

For hours following the cave's total collapse, Gregg had slipped in and out of consciousness, suffering through a lot of pain. He had awoken in the hospital a few times, with Laura and his Grammy leaning over him.

Grammy had been the most upset. "I'm old," she had grumbled, "It's not fair that I should be standing here, while you are lying there." She said she felt guilty for having received Gregg's miraculous rescue, wishing that she could somehow give it back to him.

It wasn't until the night following his and Jody's misadventures that he arose, full of fire and free of injury. The doctor was aghast and wanted to run some tests, but Gregg refused, wanting nothing other than to go home and see Jo.

When he finished brushing his hair just so, Gregg snuck out of the bathroom and down the stairs to the carport. He took in a deep breath of fresh morning air and turned to lock the door.

"You ready?" Jody's sweet voice chimed.

She was on her bike, with an old crate and a folded shovel secured to the tour-rack over her rear wheel. She wore a white tee and blue shorts and her hair was tied neatly in a ponytail. She looked amazing, especially with that wonderful smile of hers.

"Yeah." Gregg spun his bike around, ready to follow her anywhere. He fancied many more early mornings like this, when it seemed so much of the world around them still slumbered. The peace and beauty were for Jody and him alone, tranquilly idyllic moments that calmed his spirit and fed his lovesick heart.

He rode alongside her, skilfully admiring her wonderful curves as she pedalled along, inhaling the fresh smell of cut grass, the sweet scent of blooming flowers, and the spice of tall pines. There was still something burdening her. He could see it in her eyes and it disappointed him.

She didn't need to go on dealing with those nasty scars. Although there wasn't anything he could do about Lois's death, he could certainly have healed Jo's back by now. If only she would let him.

Jody was probably the most stubborn girl on the planet, but he wondered if she knew how patient he could be. Gregg was biding his time.

The day will come, whether she likes it or not.

Chapter 81

Confessions

"You got here fast." Gregg pedalled hard to keep up.

"Not really."

Jody, to Gregg's dismay, had moved with Lloyd to another house a few blocks away. Her adoptive father couldn't stand to be in the home where his wife had been murdered. This was her first morning taking the new route.

Gregg hated the prospect of being so far from her each night. "How'd you sleep?"

"Okay." Her face was hiding something.

"What's that mean?"

She rolled her eyes. "Darn it, Gregg. Grr, why can't I lie to you?"

"Because *I* am a *jivita*!" Gregg announced proudly, almost losing his balance while doing so.

Jody didn't look amused and pedalled ahead, her thoughts clearly elsewhere.

Gregg didn't know what else to say. He rode behind her, curious about the crate because he was sure it was the same one he had pulled out of his Grammy's cellar when the house was on fire. What was inside it remained a mystery. And just what was the shovel for?

He looked up and his eyes were drawn to the abnormal bumps and dips her shirt's back betrayed. A knot tightened in his stomach. He had come home from the hospital completely healed, as if nothing had ever happened, while Jody still suffered flare-ups from her wounds and the mental anguish that always followed.

They went by the gates into the cemetery and stopped at Jody's parents' plaque. Gregg watched respectfully as Jody knelt down, removing a purple flower from her top—the stem of which had been pinched under her bra—and placed it on the memorial. Her gold chain slipped from behind her shirt and drooped under her neck where her precious pendant once rested.

She forced a smile and said, "I'm glad you're here."

Gregg's insides jumped for joy. "Me too," he replied and knelt beside her. He looked down at the bronze plate. "I'm sorry I couldn't save the book."

"It's okay," she shrugged. "You saved me. That's enough . . . this time."

They knelt quietly together, but Gregg found the silence far too much to bear. In the days and weeks that had followed the horror, so much had been left unsaid between them. Most of what he found out had come from Grammy.

He'd known that Grammy had saved the day once the hole had collapsed, but not much else. That wonderful woman may be older than the hills, but she was a blessed rock under pressure.

She had told Gregg that everything went very dark and quiet after the hole gave way. The ghostly apparitions had vanished, yet she could hear their unhappy cries echoing softly amongst the calming woods, until all that was left were those eerie, faint whispers again.

Jody's distraught voice, calling Gregg's name and begging him to wake up, led Grammy to them. Jody was bloodied and topless and Gregg had only his briefs and socks left.

Grammy was sure Gregg had died, but Jody refused to accept it. When Grammy tried to comfort her, Jo swatted her away.

"Don't touch me! Don't you touch me!" She then beat Gregg's chest, screaming, "Damn you, Gregg! Wake up! Don't you dare leave me now! Do you hear me? You promised me! You promised!" Her tears flowed down her worn cheeks and spilled onto Gregg's face and she deflated next to him.

Grammy didn't try to move her again. Instead, she gave Jody space and decided to look for things among all the mangled debris until help arrived. However, when she had heard Jo say, "You better wake up, Gregg, or you won't be able to save me this time," Grammy's curiosity brought her back to see.

Jody had been holding a knife's blade to her own neck with an awful look of despair damning her face. It was then that Gregg had become slowly alert, coming to Jo's rescue without even realizing it.

It was soon after that Gregg remembered hearing a helicopter coming closer and it had been Grammy who quickly set about preparing them both for the inevitable coming of the RCMP.

She had taken off her heavy wool coat for Jo to put on, and had told her not to take it off under any circumstances. The police and paramedics could not force Jody to accept medical aid under the law, and Grammy knew it.

Keeping Jody's secret was most important then, and now, which meant that she had to overcome her injuries alone, without the benefit of X-rays, CT scans, surgery... or any prescription painkillers. Grammy had insisted that Jody travel with Lloyd and be allowed to bathe, sleep and recover as they saw fit.

Perhaps most shrewd of all was when Grammy—knowing full well that he had an under-aged party to prepare for—had bribed Dave into taking the sword through the woods without being seen and hiding it in the barn in exchange for two cases of shiraz she had stacked in her cellar.

All in all, Gregg wasn't sure how things would have gone if it hadn't been for his quick-thinking great-grandma.

As for the forest hollow, things went from mysterious to... even more mysterious.

Once the gloom that night had received the sun's waking light, it seemed to make the inexplicable events it had sheltered lose their clarity in the minds of those that had witnessed them. The accounts of Laura, Patrick, and Dave, and the various emergency crews were at odds with each other and quite confusing. And though the helicopter that arrived had a camera on board, it had suffered a glitch and failed to record anything.

The detectives were baffled and clearly annoyed with all of them.

Police had cordoned off the forest. No one was aloud in or out, except for the RCMP investigators that were combing over the hollow. Helicopters from several TV stations had tried to peer in from above, getting only brief glimpses of strewn debris and upturned earth through the trees' thick canopy.

No one knew exactly what the Mounties found, but on the first night two young officers who had been left guarding the place had vanished. They were still missing weeks later and the forest had been considered a crime scene since.

"Do you think about it much?" Gregg asked Jo. "About what happened...?"

Jody seemed to shrink some. "I try not to. It's all anyone ever wants to talk about and I hate it. I wish I could forget."

"All of it?" He laid his hand on hers and she guardedly peered into his eyes.

"Maybe not all of it." She pursed her lips.

Gregg was trying to be careful not to upset her. She looked so fragile lately. He knew she hadn't slept well since that day and wished like crazy he could put her heart at ease. "Won't you let me heal you?"

She pulled her hand away. "No! I told you a thousand times, no. I don't, I can't..."

"What? What are you afraid of?"

She closed her eyes and made a pained expression.

"Please, Jo. Talk to me." He reached for her, but she jerked back.

"You don't understand anything, Gregg! You still don't get it!" She was angry, Gregg could tell, but that display of rage was governed by something else, perhaps fear, or resentment, or maybe more than that.

He couldn't stop trying. "Let me get it," he told her.

She turned her gaze away, facing her parents ' grave, and showed every sign of an internal struggle. "I know you want to help," she said. "It's amazing what you did for Iris." She peered over her shoulder, to her bike and the things it carried. "What if you healed me, Gregg? How far would it go? Do you just fix those parts of me that are damaged?"

She bit her lip and looked at him, clearly thinking of her back, and Gregg answered, "I want to fix all of you, Jo. I want you to stop hurting."

"All of me?" She got up suddenly and went to her bike to free the crate and shovel. "What does that mean? Like, would you just heal the scars or would you reconstruct what was there in the first place?"

The remark threw him. He hadn't really thought about that. "What?"

Jody's eyes were welling up as she approached him. "You're half-jivita, right? And I'm half-angoros."

"Right."

"Whatever it is you are doesn't seem to have any effect on how you look. Everyone sees you as a typical human boy. But whatever I am, it's different." She put the crate on her lap with a pondering gaze. "I don't want to be different. In all the world, I just want to fit in and not have people staring at me every time I turn around."

"Jo, what's in the box?"

She sighed. "Iris gave it to me. She came over last night, bringing some housewarming gifts, and this. When we were alone, she told me some things about my parents. She said that what's inside this crate will explain exactly what happened to my back, and that my mother wanted me to know about it, while my father was dead-set against it. They fought over this..." She gave it a bump. "Over *me*."

"So, what's in it?" Gregg asked again.

His curiosity was interrupted suddenly by something that made him shudder. He quickly scanned the cemetery, thinking there was a smell that shouldn't be. He breathed in the air another time, but was distracted when Jody spoke.

"I don't know. I didn't open it. But I have this eerie feeling what it might be. When I was tied down in the tent, Damianos cut my back and looked at things. What he said scared the hell out of me. Because of that, I sat awake staring at this old box all night, asking myself if I really wanted to have it all confirmed. And you know what?" She unfolded the shovel. "I don't."

She put the crate to the side and, with obvious misgivings, started digging next to the plaque.

"I don't want any of this. My dad was right. I'm better off not knowing anything about angorosses and jivitas and sirens and stupid Nornirs and an even stupider giant tree and souls and games, and the stupidest dragon of all that wants me so bad!"

"Jo! Please!"

"I just want to be a girl!" she kept digging her hole. "I want to be normal! I want to wear nice clothes. I want to go to the beach! I want people to love me and not be so . . . repelled!"

Gregg yanked the shovel from her hands and cut her ranting short. "I love you!" He wished she would just listen.

He had an urge to take her clenching hand and place it over his heart so that maybe she could somehow sense his attachment to her. If only that stubborn girl understood how strong he felt, that she gave his whole life such purpose. He slowly realized the futility, with his breath getting short and his face getting hot. Hesitantly, he recovered.

"My God, Jo. I will take you to the beach. I'll take you to a beach where no one else will be. I'll take you anywhere you want. Why are you doing this?"

Jody flinched, stared at the plaque and the hole next to it, her breathing shallow and faltering. "Niðhoggr," she said finally.

"Neeth hogger?"

"It's the dragon's name."

Chapter 82

Apprehension

Jody kept trying to smooth her fragmented, blackened thoughts into something more rational. Frustratingly, no amount of effort seemed to work. Nightmarish lumps of memories from that day and her entire life had been knocking about in her head for weeks in an apparent attempt to drive her mad.

What that crate probably contained would only exacerbate things.

She wished with all her heart that it would just go away, that the people she thought were friends, and the pesky reporters she'd never known, and the prying investigators demanding answers would all stop harassing her.

As they stood before her parents' memorial, Jo wanted badly for Gregg to take her into his arms so she could bury her face into his chest. She longed for his safety, the smell of his essence and the warmth of his breath in her hair, yet she could not force the words out to say as much. Instead she freely admired him while he looked back at her with those confused baby blue eyes of his.

She worried that she couldn't fully trust him. Jody didn't know how that whole healing thing worked, only that he had to be touching her in some way. He said she had to accept his offer by answering his declaration, "I wish I could heal you", with something like, "I wish you could too." But she was terrified of what the result might be.

There'd been times since the kidnapping when she couldn't help but seek out physical contact with Gregg, even more than before, because she needed it. She needed him. Yet when flashes of what might happen ignited behind her closed eyes, she always pulled away.

She might have had an ugly, painful back, but at least she looked human. She couldn't bear the thought of becoming a total freak.

"I saw a lot of things," she told Gregg at last. "I wish I'd never had that pendant. I wish I didn't know anything."

"What?"

She looked at Gregg, amazed that he could be so oblivious. He was still cute though, at least to her. "The book..." she started to say.

"But we lost it. And your pendant was attached to it too..."

"Let me finish! It's not the book that's important. And neither is the pendant. Together, they showed me what was important. I saw it, Gregg. I heard all those lost souls in the hollow, and I know why they were there. I saw where they wanted to go . . . inside that book."

"The souls wanted in the book?"

Jody groaned, frustrated, and began explaining what had happened in the tent while Gregg was busy fighting with Ligeia. She remembered being there, on the ground, with the book lying in front of her, glowing. It had hung on her thoughts, smothering her pain and fear. She just looked at it, sensing something...

Chapter 83

Awakening

Jody realized she was crawling toward the book, mesmerized by its strange sheen, and she touched the cover's designs. With reservations and yet an irresistible desire to know, she put her finger into the dragon's mouth.

Its red eyes turned blue as the jaws clamped down, but there was no pain. A moment later, there was an explosion of light from the hollow and the lock shuddered and shook apart, falling away in pieces.

Almost immediately, Jody grasped the cover, eager to see what was inside.

"Get back, mongrel!" Damianos came barging out of nowhere to snatch the book away. He hobbled to the cot and admired the thing—if only for a brief moment—before lifting the cover away.

His face shone at first, then darkened as he flipped the pages one at a time, then many. When he was done, he simply stood there, his dark eyes distant and his hands trembling.

"It's empty. Not a word . . . nothing!"

His eyes scoured the tent as if he was searching for an answer to an impossible question. He picked the book up and shook it, hoping maybe for something useful to fall out. He only got angrier.

"Why? Why is there no writing? What good is a book with no composition, no message, no author?" Becoming all the more enraged, Damianos threw it down right in front of Jody and she heard him sob and stagger out of the tent.

Alone, Jo felt something hum against her chest. She reached for her pendant and it throbbed in her hand as though it had a pulse. She didn't know what to think, only that it made creepy sense to close the book and see its cover again.

Above the artwork of the dragon in the tangled yarn was a small pentagram. She spun her pendant around and looked at its narrow, circular hole. Everything seemed so inconceivable and obvious at the same time. The pentagram on the book had a border around it like the ring that went around the symbols on the other side of her pendant.

At that moment, Jody knew Damianos had been right. Her pendant was the key all along.

Never, so long as she could remember, had she ever been apart from her necklace. To her, it was the last physical connection she had to her mother and father, which made it so very valuable. She never wanted to risk losing it. But in that strange, mind-blowing moment, she made the exception.

Jody placed it into the book's cover and pressed down until she felt a sharp click. She also heard an obvious sigh and her pendant absorbed the book's brightness. For a moment, Jody wondered if it also took in something more.

There was a chill that raked across her skin as a peculiar light flashed from the book's pages. Jody lifted the cover away and was shocked by what she saw. The pages' outermost edges were still intact, but their faces were gone entirely, replaced by water.

She brought her face close to the rippling surface and realized she was looking through it to a bright blue sky, dappled in places by billowing white cloud. It was as if she was looking up from beneath a pool, instead of down into it.

Jody touched the water in disbelief then shot back again, shocked by its coldness.

To make matters even more intriguing, a blurred figure moved behind the water's glazed mask and appeared to be staring straight back at her.

Jody gasped. Her heart raced as a large, muscular arm with a reaching hand stretched up from the water. It stayed there, dripping wet, as if waiting to be touched, or taken.

It was a strong, massive arm, with hair up its length and a broad, impressive hand at its end. There was a ring, a simple gold band on its index finger. The appendage gestured and Jo had an uncontrollable urge to take it.

Jody cautiously reached out. The touch was warm and reassuring, like she imagined her Father's would be. A sense of peace filtered through her skin and she closed her eyes.

Then the hand tightened hard suddenly and Jody gasped. Before she could think, it pulled her toward the book. Jody resisted, falling to her knees. Her right arm touched the water and the icy terror left her breathless. She tried to scream, but the book's magic was freezing, taking her lungs prisoner.

Her right shoulder was next. Then unbelievably, she was twisting her neck to keep her head back. But it was no use. Despite her straining, she could not escape the shock as her ear and face reached the book's splashing page.

Her eyes raced frantically through the tent before the sloshing blinded her and she anchored her left hand to the ground as well as she could. No one was with her to help. She was alone, so nightmarishly alone.

Water covered her mouth, seeping past her lips as she battled on. Finally, horrifically, the frigid water stung her nose. The hand tugged harder and Jody's head slipped all the way through, but her left shoulder got stuck.

Jody held her breath, praying that the end would come mercifully quick. Her mouth spread apart and water rushed to the back of her throat. It's bite hurt and made her want to sharply inhale.

She couldn't stop it. Her lungs demanded air. Intense panic flashed behind her closed eyes. Her windpipe opened and the water gushed noticeably deep into her body.

Please God, she prayed. *Take me now.*

Chapter 84

Reflections

Jody quit the fight, but the hand remained clasped around hers, steady. When her lungs opened up and hungrily inhaled whatever they could to satisfy their urgent want for breath, it took many coughs and hacks before Jody realized that was exactly what they were getting.

Her eyes gaped wide as more cool briny air swept down her throat and soothed her faint body. Immediately beneath her, from one shoulder and neck down, she saw a slow swelling pool at the turn of a long gurgling stream. It meandered from the feet of distant, rocky mountains, underneath a ginormous tree, and across a wide green meadow. Turning the other direction, she saw the water flowing onward to the land's sudden end. Far beyond was a vast expanse of rough, wild sea.

"I've done it! I've done it!" a man's voice burst out happily and Jody swung around again.

A huge, herculean fellow was leaning over her from atop a large boulder at the pool's edge. He was brown-skinned with short dark hair and stunning hazel eyes that shimmered in the light. His beautiful face was clean-shaven, his jaw square and his smile bewitching. And to Jody's complete mortification, this enormous man was completely naked.

She averted her gaze downward, but that only made her queasy. Beneath the water's surface she saw her body contorted through the book's centre and could feel her legs twitch and her other hand push to keep her steady on the tent's dirt floor, bone dry. Her position made no sense and she quickly found herself unsure which way was supposed to be up or down.

"Do you see? Do you see what I have done?" the giant shouted over his shoulder.

Jody looked past him, avoiding eye contact with his nakedness as much as she could under the circumstances, but saw no one behind him.

There was only the huge tree.

It was in fact, the most astonishingly stupendous tree she had ever seen, or imagined for that matter. Aside from tall thick grass, it was the only thing that grew in the meadow and it towered so high above that Jody actually wondered if it challenged the yonder mountain peaks. Its tremendously wide reach stretched almost as far as the valley.

Its boughs were buried under a profusion of oval-shaped leaves that fluttered flamboyantly in the breezes.

The tree seemed strangely magical by its plumage because its leaves were so varied in colour. Most were green, some orange, and still others were gold and red. They fell as if worn by autumn's stresses, while Jody plainly saw new clusters of fresh spring growth already bursting forth.

"So, you found my book," the giant said, appearing quite proud of himself. "And as you are clearly the one to have opened it, I can only presume that you are the Akomadron."

Not sure if she really wanted to know what the hell an Akomadron was, she put her one free hand in her line of sight with the big fella's, well... *really* big fella, and asked. "You did this?"

He nodded very proudly, thumbing the tree. "He didn't think it was going to work. It seems doubt is forever my companion, despite my brilliance."

Jody noticed, with more than a few qualms, the massive tree sort of shake or shudder, to which the giant rolled his eyes and wagged his head. "He thinks he knows everything. Apparently he forgot who made him!"

Jody got the feeling he said that more for the tree's benefit than hers. "And was it you also? That made *him*, I mean."

He looked appalled. "Absolutely not! My sisters' handiwork, that one. I made something much more wicked. That was my job." The tree's limbs creaked and cracked and the giant moved his head left and right again, finally putting his hands over his ears. "I'm not listenin'!"

Jody watched, getting more rattled by the minute. "Are you... *talking* to it?"

"Of course. Would you get him? ...going on with that righteous babble. He'd have you believe that I'm the bad guy. It's not my fault you Fazmatese are thrill-seeking twits. This is what you wanted after all, wasn't it?" Jo didn't think he was asking. "Don't deny it. You've made it abundantly clear what you all crave. And we have given it to you."

"What's a Fazmatese?"

He responded with a bit of a grin. A moment later however, he looked rather confused. Then something must have come to him.

"Oh, that's right. You're still in the game. *Life,* as you call it. You have no idea what you are, do you?"

Jody didn't know how to respond to that.

"And the tree elicits no recognition of any kind, does it?"

She hesitantly gestured no.

The giant laughed and splashed his hand in the water before declaring boastfully, "That was me too! I made it so you wouldn't remember anything..., well, almost anything. No one's perfect I guess, eh? You might call it the living filter, but you'll never find it for sure. I hid it good in you, yes. In all of you. It keeps you in the game, holding you there till the very end so that it all feels so... *real*!"

"I don't understand."

"Of course you don't. You're not supposed to! You blissful lot. You just can't stand being angelic and radiant and pure all the time, can you? No, you need to feel *alive*! And simply moving around and functioning like some beastly tangible brute like me was never the goal. No, that wasn't good enough. You bunch of sensualist whiffs needed drama to go with it. You know, you can only handle so much of that damned imperturbability up there, wherever it is you come from. I never understood this oneness idea... at least, not initially. Love and unity gets a little boring after a while, so I'm told.

"And what do you do about it? You come to Yggdrasil! Latch onto an open spot, ante up your memories, your identity... your *selfness*, and hang on tight because the next thing you know, pop! you're a completely dim-witted infant in a completely bitter and destructive world.

"You want to know what it's like to experience fear, loss, hate, pain and death? Clamp on to the tree of life and let the suffering begin!" He patted Jo on the head, "Tell me, how do you like it so far?"

"I'm not really sure, to be honest."

"Well, keep at it. Let your indulgence in misery facilitate your greater appreciation of eternal paradise. At least, until the next time you need trouble."

Jody took a moment, feeling like reality had just taken a nosedive. "So, where am I?"

"Right, yes. That question makes complete sense, given that you don't remember anything. So, welcome to the Isle of Rahalla Couldéur - population, me and one holier-than-thou tree... and a few unexpected visitors that have only just recently shown up. To what end they will take us, I can't be sure." He paused for a moment, his pondering gaze looking forlornly down at his rippling reflection in the water. "Nor should I be."

He inhaled and his expression showed his strong-willed nature as he pressed his lips tightly shut. He let out that heavy breath and said, "If it suits you, you can count each and every leaf on Yggdrasil as a Fazmatese currently amusing itself in The Width of Stars. That's what we call it, you know. Stars are the important bit, from which we got all of you little offshoots..."

"I still don't think I under..."

"Star dust. That's all anything is down there. Anything that *matters*, if you get me. It wasn't easy, mind you. Creating a reality requires precision work, a full appreciation for causality, and a pretty good grasp of physics." He snorted. "Physics can be such a hang-up though. Boring. You might appreciate that. That's why I like messing things up here and there. I can be mischievous, you know. It's my nature. Just so long as we get the fun we want, I know everything else will just fall into place... eventually. At least, that's what's supposed to happen most of the time. I'm sorry, what was your question?"

Jody pondered things. "Was that your voice that hollered so loudly over the forest?"

The giant looked suddenly flustered. "What?" His bushy brows frisked up his forehead. "What are you talking about?"

"I was almost dead a few moments ago. At least I thought so, until this voice rocked the whole world. It said 'Hear me,' and everything went very quiet. Then it said 'See me,' and I could see clouds of spirits fluttering around the place. Then it said 'Find me,' and that's when my pain went away and the book, *your* book, sort of lit up in front of me and I got it opened. So, was that you too?"

The giant's face looked rather stunned at first and Jody was sure he mumbled something to himself more than once, but she couldn't make out what.

He looked briefly skyward with a nervous grin—perhaps chewing something over in his mind—and said softly, "*He* has taken notice." His hazel eyes slanted down at her. "He will listen to you."

At that moment, a sudden and rough tug on her legs threw Jody totally off balance.

"Oy, what are you doing now?" the giant asked.

Jo spat water from her mouth. "Someone's got me!"

"What do you mean, 'got you'?"

"I don't know!" But she had a pretty good guess. Damianos. "Help me!" It was such a bizarre feeling trying to right herself.

The giant looked curiously stumped. "Are you in trouble? *Proper* trouble? That's not right. We can't let anything happen to you. You need to kill my dragon! You've got something that should do him in right by my reckoning. No telling how far away another chance like this will be, if ever." His eyes turned up again.

"What the hell are you talking about?"

"Look," he said, steadying himself. "My sisters made that tree and the materiality beneath it. That is your world and everything you know. Problem is, it was always missing something and kept falling apart. So I came up with the fixes to make it all work. *Conflict*. You know, light and dark, up and down... all that. It's the gravity that keeps everything from getting carried away and the curtain that keeps the truth from you curious bunch. Turns out, you Fazmatese really liked it... and wanted more. And you fancied something deeper to counter your affectivity altogether. How do you understand love, without knowing fear?

"But to accomplish that, I required a mischief-maker that could operate at the materialistic level, something that could sink to your carnal, temporal standards and adapt to whatever challenges exist there to keep the game as authentically threatened as possible. It's not something that my kind do, you see. I had no interest in playing the villain, only in making one beyond compare.

"I did it. An absolutely nasty sodding serpent named Niðhoggr. Only thing is, I might have made him a bit too skilful and now I've sort of, uhm... lost control of him."

Jody's leg was tugged very hard. "Help!"

"What would you like me to do, tear you in half? You're not supposed to come here that way. I just wanted to see you before it was too late."

"Too late for what?"

The giant averted his eyes, appearing a little gloomy again. "This pool has shown me a lot of things, good and bad. It showed my sisters' deaths, something I thought was impossible. Now, it's showing mine. I don't think I shall be around much longer."

Jo squeaked. Whoever was back in the tent was yanking hard and suddenly had help.

"Please! I don't know what to do. There's a big bad man dressed in black trying to steal the book and kill my friend and torture me! And he's got a sadistic bitch girlfriend that wants to eat me, and I'm not kidding!"

The giant was upset. "Dressed all in black, you say?"

"Yes! He's tall too and..."

The giant gazed over Jody's head. "Is he wearing a tattered-lookin' black coat?"

"Yes!" Jo cried. "Yes! Help me!"

She heard another splash nearby and turned to catch a glimpse. There, bafflingly, standing up to his waist in the ice-cold stream and staring right down at her was Damianos.

Jody's bones suddenly felt rusted and splintered, about to crack and fall to pieces at the sight of that awful man. Damianos grinned, pulled back his coat and threw it to the shore. Jody saw the bloodied hole Gregg's sword had made in the monster's shirt.

Damianos had a wickedly handsome smile on his stupidly good-looking face as he unbuttoned his collared top and showed her his wound underneath—or lack thereof. His skin was perfect. There were no signs of injury anywhere.

Stunned, Jody turned to the giant. "How can he be here? What is this place?"

"Yggdrasil has been reaching for you," the big guy blurted, keeping half an eye on Damianos. "The tree's a master of 'time', you know. My sisters ingrained it in him because, well... we were all a little impatient to get started with things. I mean, do you know how long it takes to set the stage for the most amazing romp ever conceived?"

He shook his head. "Foolish old weed. I've no idea what inspires this kind of behaviour in him and as I said, there's no telling what the outcome will be. He's been trying to bring you to the Island. I've no idea why. Which is for the best. And there's no telling if he meant to pull this lost pith in or not. I told Yggdrasil he shouldn't get involved. You're not ready. None of you are. I can see it plainly. Your living filters cannot fathom it. There are so many things here that you'd be suddenly aware of. It could crush your suppressed mind."

The giant nodded to Damianos. "What's going on in your mind? Do you understand what dangers lay ahead? *Can* you? Fazmatese are not supposed to be burdened with a fleshy, mortal body. Not here anyways."

Damianos stared back, stone-faced.

Another series of wild tugs surprised Jody and she almost slipped through the book's opening. "Oh God, please help me!"

"I cannot!" The giant seemed full of regret. "I can't. You see, He's expecting that from me. It's because I made Him. He thinks like me and because of that, He and I both know that I cannot kill Him, and I mustn't try.

"That's why Yggdrasil is doing what he's doing without my say. I have to leave you all to your own deliverance. We created you, all of you, in our own image, except for the tree of course... and Niðhoggr. And we implanted in your different species qualities that we possess. But not one single race shall hold them all. That would be unacceptable."

The giant leaned down, keeping a wary eye on Damianos, who was edging closer. "But, mix a few genes together? That's the unexpected beauty of our design. My sisters developed the exactness of your reality. It was my job to insert the flaws. By the time I made Niðhoggr though, I had not yet discovered that my sisters had actually overlooked something rather obvious. It's a colossal glitch. *Lust.*

"And I dare say that Niðhoggr doesn't fully understand that its wizardry over all you excitable little procreators may lead to his undoing. So long as I can keep the secret safe..."

Jody's face was almost dragged under the water again, her ears only escaping the stream's rushing flow amidst its rises and falls.

"He's expecting one little hero to rise up, being born with only a few, albeit decent, characteristics of his or her creator. Perhaps the very bit that can destroy Him. What Niðhoggr doesn't know is what happens when the elementary building blocks of one or more species crossbreed with others."

Jody fought to stay, but Damianos had reached her and placed his hand on top of her head. "That's enough chatter. Now, child, I should apologize, but destiny's a bitch." Then he pushed.

Jody sank through the water, her mind caught on the image of the tremendous tree shuddering as the giant said his last words to her before she went under.

"There is a way to shut him out, if you must. It is a word you must say loudly, above all commotion. *Besparré*. He's compelled to obey Nornish commands. Remember, you must say it. Before Yggdrasil drags you in!"

Chapter 85

Consideration

"What in holy hell are you talking about?" Gregg blurted, almost choking. "Damianos is alive? How is that possible?" His legs wobbled, remembering the night in the hollow.

After he and Damianos had pulled Jody out of the book, thinking they were saving her, an arm had risen up from the water. It wasn't large by any stretch, and he could recall seeing no ring on any finger.

"The hand that Damianos grasped. It wasn't the giant's, was it?"

Jody finished digging her hole and grabbed the crate. She looked like she wanted to scream. "It was that asshole's. Damianos was reaching through the book to himself, and there's no telling what happened on the other side. I was hoping it would make him go insane, or that the universe would collapse, *anything* that would have been more helpful!"

"When Damianos got dragged into the hole, he winked at me." Gregg slumped down to the grass. "He knew he wasn't going to die. He told me the dragon will never stop, '...And neither will I!'"

"I think I could have stopped him," Jo complained. "But I just wasn't thinking right. And I couldn't remember that damned word! It was a miracle you weren't dragged in too. I was so scared. I started shouting, spewing out random possibilities until something hopefully sounded right. 'Be smart, eh? Bees fart, eh? Be apart, eh? ...wait. Be-sparr-eh? ...That's it! Besparré! Besparré! BESPARRÉ!'

"And BOOM! It was like someone blew the breaker and everything went pitch black. The hole totally collapsed and the spirits that were left behind cried and howled in the dark. I crawled around to find you. By luck I came across my Dad's knife and, well, the rest is history."

Gregg stared into space. "He's still alive. That prick!" He thought briefly of Ligeia. She too had been lost. *But, is she dead?*

Gregg had his ability to heal back, something Ligeia had refused to return unless Jody was dead. So what happened to the siren?

The breeze turned and he thought he smelled something strange again. His eyes carefully scanned the nearby trees as the hairs on the back of his neck stood on end.

You're just scaring yourself.

He took a deep breath and tried to sound composed, though it was a lie. "So, what now?"

Jody placed the crate in the hole and started refilling it. "They're not coming back, Gregg. They've gone to the place where souls go, and as far as I know, dead people don't come back to life."

Gregg wasn't so sure about that.

"There's nothing we can do," she continued. "The book is gone. The pendant is gone. And now the stupid secrets inside the crate are bloody-well gone."

Jody levelled the dirt and laid the green grass over it as neatly as she could. "No one can touch us." She stroked the grave marker. "Take care of this, Daddy. Don't let it go this time."

Jody leaned over the plaque, kissed her fingers and pressed them down on her father's name. "Sooner or later this whole thing is going to blow over and people will forget. They always do. All it takes is a celebrity with a wardrobe malfunction to get everybody thinking of something else."

She got up, folded her shovel, and tied it back onto her bike.

"Take me home, Greggo." She placed her hands over Gregg's jaw, her touch lighting fireworks in his pants, and slowly drew his lips closer to hers. "Make me forget."

"All of it?" he asked.

She peered at him guardedly. "Maybe not all of it."

Chapter 86

Angoros

She hunched in the bush, keeping herself hidden, cursing the changing winds that threatened to expose her presence.

Keeping her shape was draining, but for this she would bear the hardship. She and her companion had been following, creeping, stalking to find the answer. Now, she was on the verge of validating their suspicions. *Is it true?*

She waited a few more hours until sundown.

With darkness as her cloak, she stepped into the clearing, advancing over graves until she came to the one the young lovers had talked over. Kneeling beside it, she prodded with her hands and peeled back the green turf to reveal the freshly tilled earth.

She dug down and found a wooden crate. *This is it!*

She took it to a spot where the streetlight shone and couldn't help but notice the frantic pace of her heart, thinking of the girl.

She untied the yellowed string and tossed it aside. Then, with great anticipation, she lifted the top and peered in awe at the contents within.

Set upon a black bundle of velvet cloth, amidst dried splashes and crusted pools of blood, were a pair of badly worn, dulled and defiled white feathered wings.

She gasped, excited and disconcerted. These wings were small and their condition ghastly, clearly hacked from a babe. The thought horrified her and she dropped the open crate next to a bush.

She stepped into the darkness, her mind buzzing over the implications as she muttered over and over.

"She is the one."

Acknowledgements

Don't worry. I shan't rattle on as I've already thanked those who deserve it in person. I've done it many times, in fact. So for this, I will make note of only a few particular people that have been exceptionally valuable in making this book what it is today. Which is, if nothing else, done. Thank you, Erin Engstrom, for analyzing, condensing and discarding so much of my writing. You're a good friend who's not afraid of being honest, and I'm sure you and Brian know more synonyms for penis than a common man like me can find using Google. It's funny that we ended up keeping 'penis' in the end. Oops, that sounded naughty.

Thank you, Roxane Christ, for helping me see the good things in the manuscript, where I only found befuddlement.

And thank you to my wifey. My love, without your support, patience, nagging, pushing, shoving, pulling hair, kicking shins and drinking lots of Bacchus wine to help fuzz the memories, I would never have gotten so far on a journey like this.

Ich Liebe dich.

J. Edward Vance

is a guy who sits too much. Once an active, leanly-built fellow living and working in the suburbs of Vancouver, British Columbia, he now pokes excessively at his keyboard and glares at his computer screen praying that something brilliant will appear.

He shares his life happily with his wife and two children... and a cat that shows up now and then.

So, here it is. The first book is done. No sense in turning another page further. It will be quite anti-climactic, I can assure you. I know. I already looked.

Check out therootsofcreation.com for recent blogs and to view, upload and comment on new wonderful images on the Fan Art page.

Thank you everyone, and goodnight!

Made in the USA
Charleston, SC
23 June 2013